Robert Rankin w[...]
in 1949. He attend[...]
Mercury, a fact he[...]
whenever possible.[...]
(West Sussex) with[...]
longer does his ov[...]
'primitive' approach has worn somewhat thin. Neither
is he a sexual athlete nowadays, although he still has
some of his own teeth and hair. He also earns just
enough to pay someone else to mow his lawn while he
writes.

Robert Rankin is the author of *Nostradamus Ate My
Hamster*, *A Dog Called Demolition*, *The Garden of Un-
earthly Delights*, *The Most Amazing Man Who Ever Lived*,
The Greatest Show Off Earth, *Raiders of the Lost Car Park*,
The Book of Ultimate Truths, the *Armageddon* trilogy, and
the *Brentford* quartet which are all published by Corgi
Books. Robert Rankin's latest novel, *The Brentford
Chain Store Massacre*, is now available as a Doubleday
hardback.

What they say about Robert Rankin:

'One of the rare guys who can always make me laugh'
Terry Pratchett

'To the top-selling ranks of humorists such as Douglas
Adams and Terry Pratchett, let us welcome Mr Rankin'
Tom Hutchinson, *The Times*

'A born writer with a taste for the occult. Robert
Rankin is to Brentford what William Faulkner was to
Yoknaptawpha County'
Time Out

'One of the finest living comic writers . . . a sort of
drinking man's H.G. Wells'
Midweek

Also by Robert Rankin

ARMAGEDDON: THE MUSICAL

THEY CAME AND ATE US:
ARMAGEDDON II THE B MOVIE

THE SUBURBAN BOOK OF THE DEAD:
ARMAGEDDON III THE REMAKE

THE ANTIPOPE

THE BRENTFORD TRIANGLE

EAST OF EALING

THE SPROUTS OF WRATH

THE BOOK OF ULTIMATE TRUTHS

RAIDERS OF THE LOST CAR PARK

THE GREATEST SHOW OFF EARTH

THE MOST AMAZING MAN WHO EVER LIVED

THE GARDEN OF UNEARTHLY DELIGHTS

A DOG CALLED DEMOLITION

NOSTRADAMUS ATE MY HAMSTER

and published by Corgi Books

SPROUT MASK REPLICA

Robert Rankin

CORGI BOOKS

SPROUT MASK REPLICA
A CORGI BOOK : 0 552 14356 1

Originally published in Great Britain by Doubleday,
a division of Transworld Publishers Ltd

PRINTING HISTORY
Doubleday edition published 1997
Corgi edition published 1997

Copyright © Robert Rankin 1997

The right of Robert Rankin to be identified
as the author of this work has been asserted in accordance
with sections 77 and 78 of the Copyright Designs and
Patents Act 1988

All the characters in this book are fictitious,
and any resemblance to actual persons, living or dead,
is purely coincidental.

Condition of Sale
This book is sold subject to the condition that it shall not,
by way of trade or otherwise, be lent, re-sold, hired out or
otherwise circulated in any form of binding or cover other
than that in which it is published and without a similar
condition including this condition being imposed on the
subsequent purchaser.

Set in 11/12½pt Monotype Bembo by
Kestrel Data, Exeter, Devon.

Corgi Books are published by Transworld Publishers Ltd,
61–63 Uxbridge Road, London W5 5SA,
in Australia by Transworld Publishers (Australia) Pty Ltd,
15–25 Helles Avenue, Moorebank, NSW 2170,
and in New Zealand by Transworld Publishers (NZ) Ltd,
3 William Pickering Drive, Albany, Auckland.

Reproduced, printed and bound in Great Britain by
Cox & Wyman Ltd, Reading, Berks.

For Jo Goldsworthy
who creates order from
my chaos on a regular
basis.
Thank you very much
indeed.

BURNING ROPE

My father smoked a pipe that smelt like burning
   rope,
But he had met the crowned heads of Europe,
And he'd walked across the desert, when all had
   said, no hope.
And he used to keep a monkey on a string.
And he once saw a sheep that had six legs.
And he passed a copper penny through a giant's
   signet ring.
And he beat a man of letters playing pegs.
And he saw the star of David in the West.
And he touched the spray-lined Goddess on her
   saline wooden breast.
And he smelt the salt of seven different seas.
And could tell the age of women by their knees.
And he sang the songs the sparrows teach their
   young.
And he felt the actual rope that Crippen hung.
And he knew the way from here to Kingdom
   Come.
And we wondered why he ever married Mum.
My father smoked a pipe that smelt like burning
   rope.
But he *had* met the crowned heads of Europe.

1

THE PARABLE OF THE CHAIR AND THE SPORRAN OF THE DEVIL

My father was a devout man and so the bedtime stories he told us often came in the form of parables. He was also a carpenter and so most of these parables concerned wood and furniture.

It had always puzzled my father that, if the Good Lord had been a carpenter, how come none of *His* parables ever concerned wood and furniture. They were always about sowing seeds or fishing or things of that nature. All right, so He *did* tell the one about the foolish man who built his house upon the sand, but that was really all about a stonemason, as the carpenters would never have had a chance to get in and do the second fixings before the house got washed away.

My father, therefore, sought to make up the deficit in the Good Lord's woodwork parable account. And although, for the most part, the actual meaning of the parables was totally lost upon us, we being young and foolish and all, they were never without interest.

I recall, in particular, the parable of the chair, because it, in turn, recalls to me the tale of my great great great grandaddy's sporran.

So I shall narrate both here.

Oh, I should just mention that when my father used to tell us these parables, he would do so in his 'Laurence Olivier, Richard-the-Third, now-is-the-winter-of-our-discontent' voice.

THE PARABLE OF THE CHAIR
A moral tale in seven parts

1
The chair was old
Which is to say that the chair had age upon its side, not as antagonist, but as companion.

Like wine, good wine, the chair had improved, grown mellow, matured with age.

Not that age is any friend of chairs! Nay! Age has no respect for furniture. No cabriole leg, no varnished surface, no lacquered frame is inviolate to its sinister attentions.

Age is no lover of chairs.

2
The chair was brown
Which is to say that the chair had been newly painted.

Not by some professional with no love for his work, but by an amateur, who did it because it needed doing and he wanted to be the one who did it.

10

Not that a professional could not have done a better job.

He could.

But for all the drips and runs and missed bits, the paint which had been put upon that chair had been put there with concern.

And concern is ever the friend of good furniture.

3
The chair had three legs

Which is not to say that it had not once possessed four.

It had.

But now, alas, there were but three.

Fine and well-turned fellows they, but for all their brown gloss glory, most sadly did they miss their wayward brother.

Whither he?

Perhaps now timber-toe to some pirate captain sailing on the Spanish Main?

Perhaps in some celestial chair-leg kingdom yet unknown to man?

Or, mayhap now a leg upon the throne of a cannibal chief?

Or mayhap not!

But sorely did those three remaining legs pine★ for the fourth.

For upon those three, though loyal legs, that brown chair could not stand.

And being unable so to do, fell over.

And being of no further use, Sid burned it!

★Pine legs! Ha ha ha . . .

11

Regarding Sid

When Sid had burned the chair, he laughed.

'That', laughed Sid, 'is a chair well burned.'

For of that once proud brown chair very little remained, save for a pile of smouldering ashes and a few charred nails.

'That chair is no more,' laughed Sid.

And Sid turned away from his fireplace and sought a place to sit.

But none there was, for he had burned his only chair.

'Damn!' cried Sid, not laughing. 'I have burned my only chair.'

'But', he continued, 'it had just the three legs and was no use for sitting on anyway.'

And *happily* this was the case. Or, *unhappily*, depending on your point of view.

As Sid turned away from the fireplace, he tripped upon a length of wood which lay upon the rug and, falling backwards, struck his head on the mantelpiece and fell into the fire, dying instantly.

And was not that length of wood on which he had tripped a chair leg?

I'll say it was!

The quietness of Sid

Sid, now being dead, said nothing more.

And when, at last, he too had all burned away, a gentle breeze, coming through the open window, turned his ashes amongst those of the brown three-legged chair, until one was indistinguishable from the other.

There was something almost poetic about it.

And it didn't go unnoticed.

'There is something almost poetic about that,' said Sid's brother Norman, who stood watching from a corner.

'I agree with you there,' said Jack (Sid's other brother) who stood nearby.

'Our Sid has never been quieter,' said Tony (brother to Norman, Jack and the late Sid).

And no-one chose to disagree with that.

6

A question of laying-to-rest

Norman's thoughtful expression prompted Jack to ask, 'What is on your mind, Norman?'

Norman scratched at his nose. 'There is the question of laying-to-rest,' he said.

'That is a question requiring careful consideration,' replied Jack.

Tony asked why.

Jack said he didn't know.

'Because', Norman scratched at his nose once more, 'the ashes of Sid and the ashes of the brown three-legged chair are now thoroughly mixed. I, for one, would not care an attempt at separating them.'

'Nor me,' said Jack.

And Tony shook his head.

'So', Norman continued, 'if we were to gather up *all* the ashes and pass them to a cleric for a laying-to-rest with a Christian service, we might

well be committing heresy or blasphemy or something similar.'

Jack asked how so.

Tony shook his head once more.

'Because', Norman explained, 'I have never
heard of a chair being given a Christian burial. It
does not seem proper to dignify a three-legged
chair with a service essentially reserved for man.'

Tony observed that it wasn't the chair's fault that
it only had three legs. In fact, if Norman would
care to remember, it was he, Norman, who had
broken off the fourth leg earlier in the day.

Norman coughed nervously. 'Well,' said he,
'that is my opinion. Although I might well be
micturating windward.'

Tony turned to Jack. 'He has a point,' Tony
said. 'After all, we don't even know if the chair
was a Christian.'

'Come to think about it,' Jack replied, 'we don't
even know if Sid was a Christian.'

'We do,' said Norman. 'He wasn't.'

7

The four winds have it

'If we were to scatter *all* the ashes to the four
winds,' said Norman, 'then we could feel
reasonably assured that Sid, even if mixed with a
lot of three-legged chair, would get some sort of
decent send-off. And *we* would not incur the wrath
of God or the Church.'

'I worry for the chair,' said Tony.

'I worry about that fourth leg,' said Jack.

'Oh, I worry *a lot* about *that*,' said Tony. 'But

with Sid all burned away and everything, I don't think we should complicate the issue.'

'Do you think my four-winds suggestion a worthy one?' asked Norman.

Jack now scratched *his* nose.

Tony looked doubtful.

'Only I think we should hurry, because if we don't sweep Sid up quite soon, the breeze coming in through the open window is likely to blow him all away.'

'I think the four winds have it then,' said Jack.

'I think the breeze has done its work,' said Tony, pointing to the spot where Sid's ashes had so recently lain.

'I think you're right,' said Norman.

And through the open window, and borne upon the breeze that had now blown Sid all away, there came the cry of a tradesman plying for hire.

'Old chairs to mend,' he called. 'Old chairs to mend.'

THE SPORRAN OF THE DEVIL

It seems strange now to think that as children we didn't understand the meaning of that parable. Still, we *were* young and foolish and all, which probably accounts for it.

And so bearing the meaning in mind, let us now consider the tale of my great great great grandaddy's sporran. This piece of prose perfectly parallels the parable.

Oh yes.

The great[3] grandaddy died at The Battle of the Little Bighorn. He wasn't with Custer though. He was holding a sprout-bake and tent meeting in the field next door and went over to complain about the noise.

With regard to the question of *his* laying-to-rest, it was decided that what remained of his mortal remains should be shipped back home for a Christian burial. The family being 'careful with money' and considering that the great[3] grandaddy was probably not in too much of a hurry, the actual shipping home was done in dribs and drabs over a number of months. Great[3] grandaddy eventually turned up at Tilbury aboard a whaling vessel mastered by the infamous Captain Leonard 'Legless' Lemon (of whom more later).

After further weeks of travel, the coffin finally arrived in Brentford, carried on the back of a coalman's cart, but still, remarkably, in the company of the great[3] grandaddy's tartan portmanteau. This gaily coloured chest contained the old boy's personal effects: his sprout catalogues, grower's manuals, bell cloches, dibbers, hoes and the like, along with his Highland Regiment full ceremonial uniform.*

The family had moved south many years before to escape the Great Haggis Famine, which explains why they lived in Brentford rather than Scotland, in case anyone was wondering.

*The one he had worn whilst winning medals at The Battle of Maiwand, where he was struck on the shoulder by a Jezail bullet.

The family sold off the horticultural bits and bobs and raised enough money to employ the local undertaker to take care of the necessaries. This fellow upped the coffin lid and very hastily dressed the great[3] grandaddy in the full Highland Regimental finery (for as you can imagine, the great[3] grandaddy was pretty niffy by now). But the undertaker couldn't get the coffin lid back on, due to the size of the great[3] grandaddy's sporran, it being one of those magnificent hairy affairs with lots of silver twiddly bits and tassels and Celtic knick-knackery and so forth.

So the undertaker did the most logical thing. He removed the sporran, nailed down the coffin lid and arranged the sporran on the top, where it looked very imposing and pretty damn proud and most splendid.

Or so *he* thought.

The trouble began as the coffin was being borne through the streets of Brentford. At this time, 1877, Brentford was but a small farming community and superstitious with it.

None of the locals had ever seen a sporran before, and in particular they had never seen one so large and magnificent as that of the great[3] grandaddy.

As the coffin passed upon its final journey, the peasants looked on and took to muttering and the crossing of themselves.

'Surely', they whispered, one unto another, 'that is nothing other than a devil's familiar that rides upon the Rankin's coffin.' And the old ones made protective finger-signs and spat into the wind and wiped down their lowly smocks and hustled their children into their rude huts.

The undertaker, being also a local, but of relatively sound mind, endeavoured to explain that they had nothing to fear, that the thing was but an article of dress called a sporran. This did nothing to ease the situation, for word now passed from rustic mouth to rustic ear that the Rankin was being buried in a dress and the thing on top of the coffin was (and here local accent came into its own) a '*spawn*'.

Spawn of the Devil!

Naturally.

The officiating vicar, the infamous Victor 'Vaseline' Vez (of whom more later), was also a local man, but one of unsound mind, and he refused point-blanket to bury the sporran.

He would bury the remains in the coffin, but would not incur the wrath of God or the Church by giving a Christian burial to the 'foul issue of Satan's botty-parts'. And he too crossed himself, then folded his arms in a huff.

The great[3] grandmummy, who had more soundness of mind than the lot of them put together, agreed to the vicar's demands, took the sporran home after the service, but returned late that night to lay it on the grave.

And there it lay. No-one dared to venture close to it, not even the Reverend Vez. The years passed, grass grew up around it, ivy entwined about it. A robin built a nest in it.

But that was all a *very* long time ago.

You see, the graveyard is no longer there. The

18

council pulled it down, or rather up, and built a gymnasium on the spot. The Sir John Doveston* Memorial Gymnasium, or Johnny Gym as it was locally known.

And it was to this very gym that, upon a bright spring morning in the year of 1977, the hopeful, agile, fighting-fit form of eighteen-year-old plater's mate Billy 'The Whirlwind' Bennet came jogging, *Adidas* sports bag in one hand and borrowed training gloves in the other.

The gym had never proved a success. Some claimed that the ghost of a sporran haunted its midnight corridors. But others, who were more accurately informed, put the gym's failure down to the ineptitude and almost permanent drunkenness of its resident caretaker/manager/trainer, Mr Ernest Potts, who had lived there for almost thirty years as a virtual recluse.

Potts was an ex-pugilist of the cauliflower-ear persuasion, given to such lines as 'I could have been a contender, Charlie,' and 'I'll moider da bum.' And on the bright spring morning in question, he was draped over the corner stool of the barely used ring, reliving former glories.

'And it was in with the left. Then in with the right. Then slam slam slam slam.' Ernie took another slug from the corner bottle and there was more than just a hint of gin-stink evident in that early morning air. 'Up and across and slam slam

*Sir John Doveston being the famous local brewer, knighted by the late King George for his services to brewing.

slam. And then,' he gestured to the canvas, 'eight, nine, ten, OUT!'

Ernie sighed and squared his sagging shoulders. 'I remember that night as if it were only yesterday. They had to scrape me off the floor. Took two of them to carry me back to the dressing-room. Old Fudger Marteene, my manager, and Dave 'Boy' Botticelli. I wonder whatever happened to them.'

The could-have-been-a-contender of yesteryear wiped a ragged shirtcuff across his chin and squinted down in some surprise at the boyish figure who had appeared, as if through magic, at the ringside.

For a terrorsome moment Ernie thought, perhaps, that this was some mental manifestation caused by the gin, or even the phantom sporran itself. But no, it was but a ruddy-faced lad.

'What do you want here, boy?' The voice of Ernie echoed round the hall.

'Is this the Sir John Doveston Memorial Gymnasium? And are you Mr Ernest Potts, its trainer in residence, sir?' asked a small clear voice.

'Mr Ernest Potts?' Ernie raked at the stubble on his chin. '*Sir?*' He made an attempt to square his shoulders once more, but twice in a single day was pushing it a bit and he collapsed in a fit of coughing.

'You were a fighter, sir, weren't you?' asked Billy 'The Whirlwind' Bennet. 'My father said he saw you spar at The Thomas à Becket.'

Ernie leaned heavily upon the top rope and stared hard at the lad. 'That was a long time ago,' he managed, between what had now become wheezings. 'What did your daddy say of me?'

'He said you were a stiff, sir,' answered Billy.

'Then your daddy knows his stuff,' said Ernie, much to the surprise of young Bill, who had calculated that this remark would get the old bloke's rag up. 'What do *you* do, sonny?'

'I box a bit,' said Billy. 'I was hoping I might join your gym.'

'Box a bit?' Ernie chuckled, then coughed, then chuckled again. 'I used to box *a bit*. But I used to get knocked down, *a lot*!' He beckoned to the young intruder. 'Come up here and let's have a look at you.'

Billy jogged up the steps, set down his bag and gloves and, with a jaunty skip, vaulted clean over the top rope.

We've a live one here, thought Ernie. 'Go on then,' he said. 'Do your stuff.'

Billy 'The Whirlwind' Bennet stripped down to his singlet and shorts, put on his training gloves and began to shadow-box about the ring. Ernie slouched upon the corner stool and viewed this with a professional, if somewhat bloodshot, eye.

Billy thundered around the mat, making with the dazzling footwork. Twisting and dipping and weaving, he brought into play astonishing combinations of punches. 'Fish!' he went as he hammered his imaginary opponent from eye to solar plexus. 'Fish! Fish! Fish!'

'Why do you keep going *fish*?' enquired Ernie, as he lit up a Woodbine.

'I hate fish,' snarled Billy. 'Hate 'em.'

Ernie nodded and sucked upon his fag. 'I used to know a fighter called Sam 'Sprout-hater' Slingsby. He used to imagine his opponent was a giant sprout.'

'Was he any good?' asked Billy, as he made sushi out of his shadow-spar.

'A complete stiff,' came the not-unexpected reply. 'Never had the sense to think that, unlike a sprout, a man might kick the shit out of him.'

'That's why I chose fish,' said Billy, bobbing and feinting and blasting away. 'Fish are slippery and fast and sly. Like boxers, I think.'

Ernie nodded. This boy is not the fool I have yet to give him the credit for being, he thought. 'Have you had any experience?' he asked, as he rang the bell and examined the lad who stood before him, as fit and full of breath as if he had yet to throw a punch.

'None,' said Billy. 'That's why I came here. My father said that although he thought you were a stiff, he considered you one of the dirtiest fighters he'd ever seen and could think of no-one better to give me the benefit of your years of experience.'

Ernie was most impressed by this. 'You have *some* potential,' sniffed the old blighter, who had, to his own mind, just witnessed possibly the most stunning display of pugilistic skill ever seen in his entire life and who, for all his drunkenness and dead-lossery, knew genius when he saw it.

And who knew that he must own this lad or die.

'I'll train you, if you want,' he said in an off-hand tone.

22

Billy 'The Whirlwind' Bennet grinned a toothy grin. 'I would be honoured, sir,' he lied.

There was to be deception and chicanery on both sides of this partnership. And although Ernie's motives were blatant and obvious, exactly what Billy was up to was anyone's guess.

The Whirlwind's training began the next day. There were five-mile runs, which Ernie supervised from the gym, by means of a two-way radio; press-ups and chin-ups and plenty of work-outs on the speedball and heavy bag.

'We must find you a partner to spar with,' said Ernie. 'One who can give you a real taste of ring action.'

'Fish! Fish!' went Billy, as he beat the speedball to shreds.

Lightweight Jimmy Netley arrived at the gym that very evening in response to Ernie's telephone call. For a man of twenty-three years, Jimmy wasn't wearing well. His eyes bespoke him a late-nighter and his sallow complexion gave added eloquence to this bespeaking. Jimmy's hands toyed nervously with his copy of *The Boxing News* and these hands were never very far from the glass handle of a pint pot.

He *had* been a promising youngster, but had become too susceptible to the pleasures of the pump room. Jimmy dug about in Ernie's ring-corner ashtray in search of a serviceable dog-end, as the manager of Billy The Whirlwind (the inverted commas had now been dropped) Bennet swaggered in, wearing a very dapper lime-green suit.

'Good evening to you, Jimmy me bucko,' called Ernie, affecting an Irish brogue to go with his attire.

'Good evening to *you*,' called Jimmy, who favoured an Italian sling-back himself, but only when home alone with the blinds drawn. 'Would you have a spare fag about your person?'

'No ciggies for you, you're in training.'

'I'm bloody well not.'

'You bloody well are.'

And bloody well he was.

One week turned into another and this one into a further one still. Jimmy and The Whirlwind sparred and jogged and did the inevitable work-outs on the speedball and heavy bag.

Ernie watched the young men train. He watched The Whirlwind pour forward with a gathering storm of punches, rain down upon Jimmy with a gale force of blows. Everything about this boy was meteorological. Except for the fish.

He watched as Jimmy 'I'd-rather-be-home-with-my-footwear-collection' Netley stumbled about the ring, catching every punch and making heavy weather of it all.

'This will give *our* boy the confidence he needs,' Ernie whispered to the storm-damaged Jimmy, whom he had cut in for 1 per cent of the action.

'Gawd bless you, boss,' mumbled Jimmy from the canvas.

★　　★　　★

Friday night was fight night. Billy would have his first professional bout. Even for a loser like Ernie Potts certain things could be achieved through discreet phonecalls to the right people and veiled threats regarding doubtful decisions, mysterious fixtures and vanishing purses . . . and the cutting in of powerful gangland figures for 33 per cent of the action.

Billy The Whirlwind Bennet had even gone to the trouble of fly-posting the entire borough with broadsheets, printed at his own expense, announcing the event. He would be boxing AT WEMBLEY! three fights up from the bottom of the card on a bill topped by the British Heavy-weight Championship.

Some showcase.

For *some* fighter.

This *had* to be seen.

Now, the atmosphere at fight night is really like no other. Electric it is and it crackles. The crowd is composed of the very rich and the very poor and all in between, drawn together as one through their love and appreciation of the noble art.

There are captains of industry,
Men of the cloth,
Sailors at home from the sea.
There are three jolly butchers
And two bally bakers
And Eric and Derek and me.

There's a gutter of fish
And a breeder of snails

And a chap who takes whippets for walks.
There's a bloke from the zoo
And he walks whippets too,
But he's also a monkey that talks.

There are doctors and dentists
And Seventh Adventists
And pop stars and patrons of arts.
There's that guy off the telly
Who isn't George Melly,
The one who wrote Naming of Parts.★

There are chaps with cigars
Who have bloody great cars
And bracelets as gold as can be.
They've got wives who wear diamonds
And coats made of mink
And they don't give a toss for PC.

There's a coach-load from Lewes
Of girls with tattoos
Who've all got pierced . . .

Well, you get the picture. They come from all
walks of life, but they all share that love and
appreciation of the noble art, of a classic sport
that dates back thousands of years; to watch highly
trained athletes, their bodies honed to physical
perfection, exhibit their skills. The bravery, the
competition, the artistry. The poetry.

★The poet Henry Read, except he couldn't be there because
he's dead.

The blood.

Electric it is and it crackles.

Minutes before the first fight, the house lights go down and the ring illuminates. The crowd dip and hover, form tight knots about the doorways and bars, wave programmes and cheer wildly. Many pounds change hands and many loyalties also.

Then a ring of the bell. The man in the tuxedo. The announcements of benefit nights and early retirements (as with disgraced politicians, broken boxers leave the arena to spend more time with their families).

There are bows from visiting ex-champs and then the game is afoot.

Billy The Whirlwind Bennet sat in his changing-room, his hands, neatly bandaged, resting in his black satin lap and his legs dangling down from the bench. Ernie, almost sober, was administering the last-minute advice.

'Now this *won't* be the doddle I was hoping it would be,' said he. 'The fellow I had lined up for you got walloped last night in a disco; they've substituted a rather hard case. But you'll take him. If you just box clever, you'll take him.'

'I certainly will,' agreed Bill. 'Fish fish fish.'

There was a rapity-rap-rap at the door and a voice called, 'Bennet.'

It was time to go.

The walk from the changing-room to the ring has been compared to that from the condemned cell to the electric chair. And there are *some* similarities, from that scrubbed and clinical room, along that darkened corridor and then out into the bright bright lights.

'Roar!' and 'Cheer!' went the crowd.

'Fish fish fish,' went Billy, as he jogged towards the ring, punching holes in the air.

As he neared the squared circle he spied out his opponent being uncaged and led forward on a chain.

'Oh dear, oh dear,' mumbled Ernie. 'Just box clever,' he told young Bill.

Billy The Whirlwind Bennet cartwheeled over the top rope and did the old soft-shoe shuffle in the sand tray.

'Will you be wearing any gloves?' asked the referee, who had been following the story closely and had noted the omission.

The two fearless facilitators of fisticuffs faced each other. (Forcefully.)

Kevin 'Mad Dog' Smith, tattooed terror from Tottenham, glared down at Billy Bennet. 'You're dead,' was all *he* had to say.

Billy just winked and spoke a single word.

And that single word was 'fish'.

'Seconds out. Round one.' The bell went ding and Billy went to work.

He rushed across the ring like a human tornado. He battered Smith with a blizzard of body-blows. He tormented him with a tempest of trouncings.

'Fish,' went Billy. 'Fish fish fish.'

Stormy weather though it was, Smith fought bravely back, but he couldn't lay a glove on Billy.

The boy was a blur. A thunderstorm. A buster. A tornado. A typhoon. A cyclone. A simoom.

28

The fight lasted just the two rounds. The broken bloodstained ruin that had once been Kevin Smith was stretchered away to hospital and the fight scribes at the ringside abandoned the rest of their evening of boxing to rush to their offices and file reports on this sensational discovery.

The crowd rose as the one it was and the applause reached ninety-eight on the clapometer.

Billy The Whirlwind Bennet had found his way into the people's hearts. He was borne, shoulder-high, to the changing-room.

He would never box again.

The plot was an old one and owed much to Sir Arthur Conan Doyle who had used it twice in his Sherlock Holmes stories. The object of the exercise had *not* been to create a boxing legend. It had been to keep Ernie Potts away from his gym for one full evening, Potts, as has been stated, being a virtual recluse.

The full evening in question being this very one. 16 August 1977. Because this very one was the hundredth anniversary of the burial of my great[3] grandaddy.

For while Billy fought bravely and scored great points in the annals of boxing, his brother Nigel packed thirty pounds of dynamite into the basement of the Sir John Doveston Memorial Gymnasium and blew the whole caboodle to oblivion.

This act of vandalism would normally have raised a few eyebrows and caused a bit of a to-do. But not tonight. Tonight the locality was deserted.

29

Tonight all the folk for a half-mile radius of the gym were packing Wembley, hoping to see a local boy make good.

It was a brilliantly conceived plan.

Nigel Bennet now stood in the tumbled ruins of the gym, an ancient map in his hands.

'Twenty paces north and four west,' he said, pacing appropriately and studying his compass. And then 'aha,' and he kicked amongst the fallen bricks. 'This must be the spot.'

Nigel Bennet had come in search of my great[3] grandaddy's sporran which local legend (for local legend is a funny old fellow and tales grow with the telling) now foretold, would, upon the one-hundredth anniversary of its laying-to-rest, pass on magical powers to whoever should unearth it.

Exactly what these powers might be, no-one seemed absolutely sure, but that they would be pretty awesome was the general opinion.

Oh what fools we mortals be. And such like.

Nigel stumbled around in the moonlit ruination. 'Come on,' he shouted. 'I'm here. I've released you from your tomb. Pass on your powers to me.'

It wasn't all that likely, was it?

Nigel kicked about. 'Come on,' he growled, 'come on. I paid good money for that dynamite. I can't hang around here all night.'

A sudden rustling at his feet caused him to jump backwards and he fell heavily, tearing the arse out of his trousers.

A rat scuttled by.

'Bugger,' swore Nigel. 'Oh bugger me to Hell.'

Another rustling, this time beneath his bum, caused him to leap once more to his feet.

Something stirred.

Nigel stared down. Something seemed to be burrowing up through the dirt.

'A bloody mole.' Nigel raised a boot to stamp the beastie down. But it wasn't a mole. Nigel's foot hovered in the air. Something large heaved itself up from the earth, something large and hairy.

'A beaver?'

Not a beaver! This was large and it was hairy. But it was also bright and silvery about the bright and silvery parts. And these bright and silvery parts were all engraved in a Celtic manner.

The sporran rose slowly into view.

'Great Caesar's ghost,' whispered Nigel, who favoured an archaic comic book ejaculation during periods when he wasn't swearing. 'It isn't, is it?'

But it was.

Now fully emerged from its hundred-year hibernation, the mighty sporran lay a-gleaming (about the silvery bits) by the light of the full moon. And as Nigel leaned forward, hands upon his knees, it creaked open (at the opening bit) to reveal what looked for all this wild and whacky world of ours to be nothing more nor less than emeralds of vast dimension.

'Emeralds,' Nigel's lips went all a quiver. 'Emeralds the size of tennis balls.'

Nigel dug in deep, plucked out an emerald and held it to a greedy eye. 'This ain't an emerald, it's a bleeding sprou—'

But he never had time to finish the word. There

was a ghastly gasp, a sickly snap and the sporran of the Devil swallowed Nigel in a single gulp.

The crowd at Wembley and the folk later packing the pubs of Brentford knew nothing of this. Billy, unaware of his brother's hideous fate, but sure that a share of something awesome would soon be heading his way, drank champagne, posed for photographs with local publicans and made certain that Ernie was in no fit state to get back to the gym before morning.

And when morning finally came and Ernie staggered back to find his gym gone and Billy became aware that his brother had gone with it, rumour spread across the borough like a social disease.

'Smith's manager did it,' claimed someone.

'More like the council,' claimed someone else.

And someone else again spoke of a natural disaster. 'Look at that hole,' this someone said. 'Surely a meteor hit this place.'

Nigel Bennet was never seen again. Billy, who now considered that his brother had absconded, taking with him whatever awesome powers the magic sporran had seen fit to dish him out, joined Jimmy at the bar and took to drink.

Whether he would ever have made a champion, who can say, but Ernie still dines out on tales of his greatness.

And there is talk of the council building another gym.

Not on the site of the old graveyard though.

CAMPING OUT

My Uncle Brian, whom Mum never cared for,
Would come up to see us, each once in a while,
And we'd sit and listen for hours as he told us
Of things that he'd done long ago, when a child.

Like camping out, for instance.

You'll need a good penknife and three yards of
    string.
Some pegs and some canvas, a tent is the thing.
A sturdy tin-opener, never forget
You can't light a fire if your matches are wet.
Keep socks on at night and you'll never catch flu.
Don't camp near an ant hill whatever you do.
Take plenty of water and plenty of beans,
You can always scrounge milk by all manner of
    means.
Elastoplast dressings, you'll need quite a lot,
And your trunks and a lilo in case it gets hot.
Never leave litter all lying about
And you'll do the job proper when you're
    camping out.

I began to understand why Mum never cared for
    Uncle Brian.

2

THE LAWS OF POSSIBILITY
THE LAWS OF SCIENCE
AND THE LAWS OF NATURE
And how the man who is
foolish enough to tamper with
any of these will inevitably
come to grief

The word lunatic, or so my father told me, comes
from the conjoining of two separate words: luna,
meaning moon, and attic, meaning upper storey.

Hence, lunatic means 'having the moon in your
upper storey'.

My Uncle Brian certainly had the moon in his
upper storey, but it hadn't always been so. Sanity's
sun once shone brightly through Uncle Brian's
skylight, but a dark cloud had crossed its face. A
cloud in the shape of a motorbike.

And I shall tell you how this came about and
how this concerned one of

The laws of possibility
According to one of the above mentioned laws,
and to quote the great Jack Vance, 'In a situation

of infinity, every possibility, no matter how remote, must find physical expression.' And given
this, it follows that there must be one man who
has eaten, is about to eat, or will eventually eat an
entire motorbike.

It stands to reason, if you think about it. Everything conceivable is bound to happen *eventually*,
and not just once, but many times. It's an old story,
and one, if this particular law is to be believed, that
has probably been told before.

Perhaps on several occasions.

Whether, on the dreadful day that the moon
chose to enter Uncle's attic, Uncle Brian knew
anything about the laws of possibility, I am not
qualified to say. But as far as can be ascertained,
and to set the scene as it were, the uncle was
standing in his garden at the time, the time being
a little after ten of the morning clock, a packet of
premier sprout seeds in one hand and a fretful
frown on his face.

You see, there was he and there were his seeds,
yet there, over there, in the corner of the garden,
in the very place where his new sprout bed was
intended to be, *it* stood.

Rusty old
Crusty old
Big, beefy, well dug in.
Left by the folk
Who moved out
Before he moved in.
Hideous eye-scar
Complete with a side car.

35

One Heck of a
Wreck of a
Motorbike.

Uncle Brian glared at the abomination.

'To paraphrase Oscar Wilde,' he said, 'that bloody bike must go, or *I* must.'

The bike didn't look too keen. And why should it have? It *was* well dug in, entrenched, ensconced. Had been for some thirty-seven years. The folk who'd moved out had made a feature of the thing. They had painted it buttercup yellow.

Uncle Brian telephoned the council.

'Would you please send over some of your big strong boys with a lorry to collect an old motorbike that is standing untenanted on what is to be my sprout patch?' he asked.

The chap at the council who had taken the call thanked my uncle for making it. He was most polite and there was grief in his voice as he spoke of cut-backs and slashed subsidies and how things had never been like this in his father's day and how the council owed a duty to ratepayers and how it made him sick to his very soul that hitherto-considered-essential services were being axed all around him.

'Then you'll send over some of your big strong boys?' asked my uncle.

'No,' said the chap and rang off.

My uncle telephoned the police.

The constable who took the call thanked my uncle for making it.

Regrettably, he said, the police had sworn off going near private back gardens, 'things being what they were', and could only suggest calling the council.

'Oh you have,' the constable continued, 'well, there's not much we can do.' As an afterthought he added, 'Has this motorbike of yours got a current road fund licence?'

Uncle hurriedly put down the phone.

Two rag-and-bone men refused the motorbike, saying that a thing like that would lower the tone of their barrows. A scout troop canvassing for jumble said, thank you no. And a vicar with a collecting-tin declined it on religious grounds, stating that he feared to incur the wrath of God and the Church.

'You could always just eat it, you know,' said Norman,★ Uncle Brian's best chum. 'People do,' he said, in a most convincing tone.

'What people?' asked my uncle. 'And what parts could you eat? You couldn't eat all of it, could you?'

'Of course you could.' And Norman went on to tell my uncle about how his family, the Suffolk-shire Crombies, had been veritable gourmets of almost every conceivable type of wheeled conveyance.

'In 1865,' said Norman, 'my great grandfather, Sir John Crombie (of India), ate an entire hansom cab, horses and all. His son, the late Earl Mortimer of Crombie, munched his way through an entire

★Brother of Sid from the parable.

37

Pullman car in Paddington Station, the stunt taking nearly three years.* Many of the aristocracy came to witness the spectacle, some bringing hampers from Fortnum and Mason and others shooting-sticks to sit on, while they watched the more dramatic moments. It was said that Queen Victoria herself stopped off on her way to Windsor and spent a pleasant hour watching Earl Mortimer devour a number of velvet cushions and a coupling.† My uncle had his doubts. 'You can't digest metal,' he said.

'Of course you can.' Norman kicked about in the dirt, turned up a couple of nuts and bolts and thrust these into his mouth. 'You can eat anything.' He munched a moment, hesitated and then, with a somewhat pained expression on his face, spat the nuts and bolts onto the ground. 'I'm not hungry right now,' he said. 'But you no doubt get my drift.'

Uncle Brian nodded. 'You mean you can really eat anything?'

Norman nodded back; his eyes were beginning to roll.

'And a motorbike isn't poisonous?'

Norman shook his head and clutched his jaw.

'It's very big. And it does have a side-car.'

'Smash it up with a sledgehammer . . . ooh . . . ouch.' And with that suggestion made, Norman

---

*Well, no-one said anything about it being fast.
†History does not disclose how the late Earl met his end, but the fact that totters broke into his tomb and stole his body, lends a certain credibility to all the foregoing.

mumbled out a fond farewell and sped away to his dentist.

'Smash it up and eat it,' said my uncle. 'Now why didn't *I* think of that?'

By three of the afternoon clock, on a day that was none but the same, Uncle Brian was to be found standing on the dusty plot that was to be his sprout patch, sledgehammer in hand and look of determination on his face. Three of his fingers now sported elastoplast dressings of the kind he had once recommended as an essential adjunct to camping out. The thumb of his left hand was sorely missing its nail.

'Take that, you *bastard*!' His fine clear voice boomed towards the house, bounced off the kitchen wall and travelled back over his head to vanish in a neighbour's garden. The sound of the sledgehammer smiting the motorbike followed it swiftly.

Another swing. An inner wrench. And what is known in medical circles as an *aneurysmic diverticulum*. Or Hernia.

Uncle Brian sank to the ground clutching those parts that a gentleman does not even allude to, let alone clutch.

'Oh my God!' screamed the uncle. 'My God, oh my God.'

As bad as the smashing up of the bike was proving to be, it was a huge success when compared to the eating part. Uncle Brian, whose smile had once dazzled the ladies with its dental glare, now wore the blackened stumps of the social outcast. He was ragged and stained with oil. His toupee had slipped from his head and become buried in the dust. All seemed lost.

All, in fact, was lost.

Quite suddenly, *very* suddenly – well, *just* suddenly, because *suddenly* is enough – there came the sound of a siren going 'Waaaah-ooooh, waaaah-ooooh'; the way sirens used to do, a screeching of brakes and a regular pounding of police feet.

All this hullabaloo caused Uncle Brian to un-clutch his privy parts and take stock of the situation.

Hands gripped him firmly by the shoulders and he was drawn to his feet. Then he was shaken all about.

'Come quietly, my lad,' advised a young constable, kneeing my uncle in his oh-so-tenders. 'Did you see that, Sarge? He went for me.'

'Employ your truncheon, Constable.'

'Right, sir, yes.'

The young constable took to striking Uncle Brian about the head.

'Stop!' wailed my uncle. 'Stop. Why are you doing this?'

'Don't come the innocent with me,' advised the police sergeant, bringing out his regulation note-book (which is always a bad sign). 'It's a fair cop and you know it. This garden is the property of a Mr Brian Rankin. One of Mr Rankin's neighbours telephoned a few minutes ago to say that they had just arrived home to discover a tramp in Mr Rankin's garden smashing up his motorbike. Oh my God!'

40

'Oh my God?' queried the young constable.

The police sergeant stooped down and picked up a small enamelled badge that lay in the dirt. 'Oh my God, say it's not true.'

'It's not true,' said the constable, stamping on my uncle's foot.

'Ouch,' said my uncle, in ready response.

'But it *is*.' The police sergeant fell to his knees and began to beat his fists in the dirt and foam somewhat at the mouth.

'Now look what you've done,' the constable told my uncle. 'Take that, you villain.'

'Ouch,' went my uncle again.

The police sergeant drew himself slowly to his feet and did what he could to recover his dignity. 'You,' he mumbled, waggling a shaky finger in my uncle's face. 'You iconoclast. Do you realize what you've done?'

Uncle Brian shook his head feebly.

'A 1935 Vincent Alostrael. You've smashed up a 1935 Vincent Alostrael.'

'Is that bad?' asked the constable.

'Bad?' The sergeant snatched the truncheon from the young man's fist. '*Bad?* There were only six ever made. Even if this one had been rusted to buggeration and painted buttercup yellow it would still have been worth a fortune.'

He raised the truncheon high and brought it down with considerable force.

My uncle was dragged unconscious to the Black Maria and heaved there-into. The police sergeant rolled up his sleeves and joined him in the back.

Now it has to be said that according to the laws

of possibility, to which this little episode is dedicated, it is more than likely that this very same incident has occurred before.

Possibly even as many as *five times* before.

But given the growing rarity of the 1935 Vincent Alostrael, the likelihood of it ever occurring again is pretty remote, really. Fascinating, isn't it?

The laws of science

Uncle Brian spent quite some time in the hospital. The doctors marvelled at the X-rays of his stomach. These revealed a regular scrapyard of nuts and bolts and piston rings. Copious quantities of cod liver oil were administered in the hope of easing these through his system and their exit was made clearer by the surgical removal of a police truncheon.

A specialist diagnosed my uncle's condition as a rare psychopathic eating disorder known as *Crombie's Syndrome* and recommended a long stay in a soft room, with plenty of experimental medication.

It was all a bit much for my uncle.

When the doctors finally lost interest in him, he was dispatched home for a bit of care in the community. He was never the same man again.

My Uncle Brian had found *science*.

Now there is nothing altogether strange about a Rankin finding *religion*. Religion is in the genes with us. And I have set about the writing of this work with the intention to explain, through a brief history of my lineage, how it was I came to the discovery that *I* am the long awaited *Chosen One*.

But more, much more, of *that* later.

For now, be it known that Uncle Brian had found *science*.

He found also, upon returning home, that the remains of the motorbike had mysteriously vanished from his back garden. And it was no coincidence that a certain truncheon-happy police sergeant had taken early retirement and vanished with them.

Uncle Brian sighed and nodded and took to the pacing up and down of his back garden, muttering to himself and occasionally stopping to strike the fist of one hand into the palm of the other and cry aloud such things as, 'Yes, I have it now!' and, 'All becomes clear!'

'What *all* is that?' asked best friend Norman, leaning over the garden gate.

Uncle Brian sucked upon his new false teeth. 'Science,' said he. 'Now bugger off, I've lots to do.'

So Norman buggered off.

Pressing family business kept Norman buggered off for almost a month. A television company researching a documentary about the sinking of the *Titanic* had turned up the name of Norman's grandad, Sir Rupert Crombie, on the passenger list. The documentary makers were eager to interview Norman about an eye-witness report that Sir Rupert had been seen on the night of the disaster in the vicinity of one of the watertight bulkheads which later inexplicably collapsed, causing the ship to sink.

This eye-witness report stated that Sir Rupert was 'eyeing the rivets, hungrily'.

When Norman next chanced by at my uncle's back gate he was surprised to notice that certain changes of an environmental nature had taken place thereabouts.

The little white wicket fence had gone, to be replaced by a huge stockade of ten-foot telephone poles closely bound with rope. A door of similar stuff took the place of the gate. On this door was a notice.

Norman knocked on the door, then pushed and entered. Entered all-but darkness.

'Back, back!' A fearsome figure sprang up before him, a pointed stick clutched in a filthy mitt. 'Read the notice, then come in again.'

Norman beat a retreat and the door slammed upon him. He now perused the notice.

D.M.Z.
DE-METALLIZED ZONE
IT IS STRICTLY FORBIDDEN TO
ENTER THIS GARDEN WHILE IN
POSSESSION OF
ANY METAL ITEMS.
To wit, watch, money, fountain or
ball-point pens, rings, or other jewellery,
hair slides, combs, belts (metal buckles),
braces (likewise), shoes (metal eyelets &
Blakeys) etc. REMOVE ALL and place
in the box provided.
Then shout 'ALL CLEAR'.

Norman pursed his lips and gave his head a scratch. Now what was all *this* about? Well, there was only one way to find out. Norman hastily divested himself of metal objects, belt and braces, shoes and all and popped them into the box provided.

'All clear,' shouted Norman.

A weighty-looking length of wood eased out through a slot in the barricade and secured the lid of the box provided. A voice called, 'Enter, friend.'

Norman entered, holding up his trousers.

It was pretty dark in there, because the out-there which had lately been Uncle Brian's back garden, was now definitely *in-there*. The fences had been raised to either side and even against the back of the house. Telegraph poles, in regimental rows, all bound one to the next. The whole was roofed over with lesser timbers and thatch. The effect was that of being inside an old log cabin, whilst also being inside the roof of a thatched cottage. It was probably a bit like one of those bronze-age long-houses that you used to make models of in the history lesson at school.

It was a curious effect.

It was also very dark and gloomy. There weren't any windows.

'Whatever have you done to the garden?' Norman asked. 'I mean that is *you* there, isn't it, Brian? I mean where are you anyway?'

'I'm here.' Uncle Brian loomed from the gloom.

'Cor,' said Norman. 'You don't half pong.'

Uncle Brian sniffed at himself. 'I can't smell anything. But what do you think, Norman? Is this something, or what?'

'Or what?' Norman strained his eyes. Light fell in narrow shafts between the raised timbers. Some of it fell upon Uncle Brian. 'And what *have* you got on?'

'It's a sort of smock,' Uncle Brian explained. 'I knitted it myself with two sticks. It's made out of dry grass.'

'It looks very uncomfortable.'

'Oh, it is. *Very*.'

'Then why are you wearing it?'

Uncle Brian tapped at his nose. The finger that did the tapping was a very dirty finger. It quite matched the nose. 'I will tell you if you'll stay awhile.'

'Well, I can't stay long. I have to see my solicitor, my family is being sued by The White Star Line. I'd rather not go into it, if you don't mind.'

'Not in the least. Now take a seat.'

'Where?'

'Anywhere you like, there's only the ground.'

Norman took a seat on the ground. Uncle Brian took another.

'Would you mind taking your seat just a little further away?' Norman asked. 'No offence meant.'

'None taken.' Uncle re-seated himself and crossed his legs.

'Straw shoes,' observed Norman.

'I knitted them myself. Now are you sitting comfortably?'

'Not really, no, but begin anyway.'

'So I shall.' And Uncle Brian began. 'It was all to do with the motorbike.'

Norman groaned. 'I think I must be off,' said he.

'No, listen. I was in the hospital, in one of the soft rooms, and I was wearing a long-sleeved-shirt affair that did up at the back.'

'A strait-jacket?' Norman suggested.

'Yes, all right, it was a strait-jacket. And I was lying on the soft floor and looking up at this single barred window, and all became suddenly clear – the science of things and where the world has gone wrong.'

'Indeed?' said Norman, shifting uneasily.

'Iron. The bars were iron and the bars put me in mind of the motorbike. Bars. *Handle* bars. And I thought how much ill luck that motorbike had brought me and all became suddenly clear.'

'Go on,' said Norman.

'It is my belief,' said Uncle Brian, 'well, it is *more* than just a belief, it is my *utter conviction* that everything has a resonance, or frequency, *everything*. That's matter and thought and good and evil and good luck and bad luck and everything. And my utter conviction is that metal is capable of absorbing good luck or bad luck, absorbing it and then discharging it.'

'Like batteries,' said Norman.

'A bit like batteries,' said Uncle Brian.

'But good luck and bad luck? I don't see how.'

'Then allow me to explain. Think about what metal is used for. There're a lot of good things, but there're a lot of bad things, bullets and missiles, bayonets and bombs. Go back in history. Imagine, say, one thousand years ago. Some iron ore is mined and a blacksmith forges it into a sword. At this time the metal is quite healthy.'

47

'Healthy?' asked Norman.

'Let's say uncontaminated.'

'All right,' said Norman. 'Let's say that.'

'It's uncontaminated.'

'Well said,' said Norman.

'Be quiet,' said my uncle.

'I'm sorry.'

'There is this iron sword. And a soldier gets hold of it and he goes into battle and it's hack hack, stab, thrust, slice, stab, disembowel, decapitate, chop, mutilate, gouge—'

'Steady on,' said Norman. 'I get the picture.'

'Right, so now the iron of the sword is contaminated, it has absorbed this horror, this ill luck. It now resonates with it. It oozes with it.'

Norman shrugged. 'It's possible, I suppose, but unlikely.'

Uncle Brian scowled through the gloom. 'The iron has absorbed the unpleasantness. It is contaminated. Now, let's say the sword is later broken. It's melted down again, becomes a bit of a farmer's plough.'

'And they shall beat their swords into ploughshares,' said Norman, almost quoting scripture.

'So the farmer gets the plough, but what has he got? I'll tell you what he's got, he's got an unlucky plough. He ploughs his fields and his crops fail. His crops fail, so he goes bust and he sells his plough.'

'And the blacksmith makes another sword out of it.'

'Wrong,' said Uncle Brian.

'Wrong?' asked Norman.

'Wrong. This time he makes an axe.'

'Are you just making this up as you go along, Brian?'

Uncle Brian shook his head, releasing a cloud of dust that whirled as golden motes within a shaft of light. 'I've given this much thought. Our lump of contaminated metal travels on through history. Spearhead, cannonball, bit of a gun barrel, and when it's not these it's something else, passing on its badness to poor, unsuspecting folk. The frying-pan that catches fire, that nail you stepped on that went right through your foot, that hammer you smashed your thumb with.'

'That was *your* hammer,' said Norman. 'I've been meaning to give it back.'

'What about the Second World War?' asked Uncle Brian. 'All those lovely cast-iron railings, melted down and made into tanks. And after the war, what industry uses more recycled metal than any other?'

'The motor industry?' said Norman.

'The motor industry. And what have we got now?'

Norman shrugged. 'Motor cars?'

'*Road rage!*' cried my uncle, with triumph in his voice. 'Cars smashing into each other and people going off their nuts. The metal's to blame. The contaminated metal. I'll bet that if you traced back the history of any single car, at some time a bit of it was part of a weapon. Or something similar. And why is it that your watch only runs slow when you've got an important appointment?'

'Because I forgot to wind it, I think.'

'You think, but you don't know. When I said

that the metal became *contaminated*, that is *exactly* what I meant. I am convinced that bad luck is a virus. You can catch it.'

'I thought you said it was frequencies and resonances.'

'I was just warming you up. It's a virus, that's what it is.'

'And you catch it off metal?'

'Off contaminated metal, yes. Let's take gold, for instance. Not much gold has ever been used for making weapons. It's mostly been used for jewellery. And jewellery makes people happy. Gold is associated with prosperity and good luck.'

'It's certainly considered good luck to own lots of gold.'

'There you are then.'

Norman made a thoughtful, if poorly illuminated face. 'So what *exactly* are you doing, cowering in the dark here, Brian?'

'I'm *not* cowering. I am conducting a scientific experiment. And when I have conducted it and proved it conclusively, I have no doubt that I will be awarded the Nobel prize, for my services to mankind.'

'I see,' said Norman, who didn't.

'You don't,' said my uncle, who did.

'All right, I don't.'

'Consider this', Uncle Brian gestured all-encompassingly, though Norman didn't see him, 'as an isolation ward, or a convalescence room. I am ridding myself of the bad luck virus by avoiding *all* contact with metal. Here in my DMZ I wear nothing that has ever come into contact with metal and I eat only hand-picked vegetables from my allotment which I eat raw.'

'Why only vegetables?'

'Because cattle and chickens are slaughtered with metal instruments, you can imagine the intense contamination of those.'

'Yeah,' said Norman. 'I *can*. But why *raw* veggies?'

'Well, I could hardly cook them in a metal saucepan, could I?'

'I suppose not.'

'And anyway I couldn't spare the rain water.'

'Rain water?'

'That's all that I drink or wash with. Tap water comes out of metal pipes.'

'And metal taps.'

'And metal taps, right. I've fashioned a crude wooden bowl that catches rain water. But it hasn't rained much lately, so I'm a bit thirsty.'

'And smelly,' said Norman. 'No offence meant, once again.'

'None taken, once again. But it will all be worth it. I am crossing new frontiers of science. Imagine the human potential of a man who acts under his own volition, utterly unaffected by either good luck or bad.'

'But surely such a man would have no luck at all, which would be the same as having only bad luck.'

'To the unscientific mind all things are un-scientific,' said my uncle. 'Now bugger off, Norman, I've much that needs doing.'

And Norman buggered off once more.

The laws of nature

Norman pondered greatly over what my uncle had said. Certainly the digestion of metal had never brought much luck to the Crombie clan. Norman wondered whether he should give up his own hobby, that of sword swallowing, or at least restrict himself to bicycle pumps for a while. But it was all a load of old totters, wasn't it? Brian clearly had a screw loose somewhere.

'A screw loose!' Norman tittered foolishly. But there might be *some* truth to it. 'No,' Norman shook his head. The whole thing was ludicrous. Luck wasn't a virus. Accidents simply happen because accidents simply happen. Why only yesterday he'd read in the paper about a newly retired police sergeant who was restoring some rare motorbike he'd found. This chap had the thing upon blocks and was underneath tinkering, when the bike rolled off and squashed his head. Accident, pure and simple.

Norman cut himself a slice of bread, then went in search of an Elastoplast to dress the thumb he'd nearly severed.

Accident, pure and simple.

And painful.

Another month went by before Norman returned to my uncle's DMZ. Norman would have liked to have returned sooner, but he was kept rather busy issuing high court injunctions against the publication of two books in the disaster series *The Truth Behind . . .* These books, *The Truth Behind the R101 Disaster* and *The Truth Behind the Destruction of Crystal Palace*, mentioned the names of certain past members of the Crombie family, in connection with the consumption of fire extinguishers.

It was a somewhat penniless Norman who eventually found himself once again knocking at the stockade door.

All seemed rather quiet within, and answer came there none.

'Hello.' Norman knocked again. 'It's me, Norman. Are you in there, Brian?' Norman put his ear to the door. Nothing. Or? Norman's ear pressed closer. What was that? It sounded a bit like a distant choir singing. It sounded *exactly* like a distant choir singing.

Norman drew his ear from the door and cocked his head on one side. Perhaps someone had a wireless on near by. He pushed upon the stockade door, which creaked open a few inches and then jammed. Norman put his shoulder to it and pushed again.

'Go back, go back,' called a voice. 'You're rucking up the carpet.'

The door went slam and Norman went, 'What?'

There were scuffling sounds and then the door opened a crack and a wary eye peeped out. It was one of a pair of such eyes and both belonged to Uncle Brian. They blinked and then they stared a bit and then they sort of crossed.

'What order of being are *you*?' asked their owner.

'Don't lark about, Brian. It's me, Norman.'

'I dimly recall the name.'

He's lost it completely, thought Norman, I wonder if I should call an ambulance.

'No, don't do that.'

'Do what?'

'Call an ambulance.'

'How did you—'

'I just do. Are you *all clear*?'

'Actually I am,' said Norman. 'I have absolutely no metal about my person whatsoever. I'm right off metal at the moment.'

'Then you can come in. But first you'll have to promise.'

'Go on.'

'Promise that you won't speak a word of anything I show you to anyone. Promise?'

'Cross my heart and hope to die.' Norman made the appropriate motions with a bespittled finger.

'Then enter, friend.'

Uncle Brian swung open the heavy door. A light welled from within. It was of that order we know as 'ethereal'. A smell welled with it.

'Lavender,' said Norman, taking a sniff.

'It might well be. Now hurry before something sees you.'

'Some *thing*?'

'Just hurry.'

And so Norman hurried.

Uncle Brian slammed shut the door and turned to grin at his bestest friend. His bestest friend had no grin to return, his face wore a foolish expression. The one called a gawp.

'God's gaiters,' whispered Norman. 'Whatever is it all?'

'Isn't it just the business?' Uncle Brian rubbed his hands together. They were very clean hands, the nails were nicely manicured.

'It's—' Norman turned to view his host. 'Whoa!' he continued. 'What happened to *you*?'

Uncle Brian did a little twirl. The transformation was somewhat dramatic. Gone the matted hair, greasy aspect, ghastly dried-grass smock and unmentionable whiskers. He was now as clean as a baby's post-bath bum and perky as a fan dancer's nipple. On his head he wore a monstrous bejewelled turban, of a type once favoured by Eastern potentates as they rode upon magic carpets. And gathered about him, by a silken cummerbund, great robes of similar stuff. That stuff being decorative brocade and a good deal of it.

'Dig the slippers.' Uncle Brian raised the hem of his garment to expose a pair of those curly-toed numbers that the potentate lads always favoured. 'Hip to trip and hot to trot, what say you?'

'I'm somewhat stuck to say anything as it happens, this place it's—'

'Bloody marvellous,' said Uncle Brian. 'It's an exact re-creation of the harem of the Sultan Suleiman the Magnificent, who ruled the Ottoman Empire from 1520 to 1566.'

'Yes, of course,' mumbled Norman. 'Well I recognized it straightaway, naturally. But where did you get it from? I mean, Shiva's sheep, Brian, you didn't nick it, did you?'

'Certainly not.' Uncle Brian swept over to a low carved satinwood couch and flung himself onto an abundance of cushions. 'It's all a present.'

'A *present*? From who, or is it from *whom*, I can never remember.'

'It's from *whom*, I think. And that whom is . . .' Uncle Brian paused for effect. 'The fairies,' he said.

Oh dear, thought Norman, he's a basket case.

'I never am. I did it, Norman, I did it. Cured myself of the good luck-bad luck virus, freed myself from the influence of iron. And lo and behold.'

'Curiously I don't understand,' said Norman, who curiously didn't.

'Iron, dear boy. Don't you know your folklore? It all makes sense to me now.'

'It's still got me baffled.' Norman shuffled his feet on the deep-pile carpet that smothered the ground and tapped his toe on a Persian pouffe.

'Iron repels fairies,' said Uncle Brian. 'Surely everyone knows that. In the old days it was regular to hang a pair of scissors over the cradle of a new-born infant to protect it from being carried away by the fairies. There was a dual protection in that because open scissors form a cross.'

'But what has that got to do with all this?'

Uncle Brian shrugged up from his cushions. 'Get a grip, Norman. I freed myself from the influence of iron. The reason fairies are no longer to be seen is because there's too much iron. It's everywhere. And it's bad for their health. So they've retreated. But my DMZ, the old Demetallized Zone, attracted them, like,' Uncle Brian gave a foolish titter, 'like, dare I say, a magnet.'

'Preposterous,' said Norman. 'Ludicrous, in fact.'

'If you say so.' My uncle plumped himself up

and down on his cushions. 'You'd know best, I suppose. Shall I bring on the dancing girls?'

'*What?*'

'Well, it is a harem after all.'

'You've got *dancing girls*? You're kidding, surely?'

Uncle Brian rose to clap his hands.

'No no,' Norman raised his and then slumped down onto the Persian pouffe. 'This can't be true,' he said. 'It just can't.'

'I knew I wasn't wrong about the iron,' said Uncle Brian, re-seating himself in a sumptuous manner. 'Although I'll admit that I wasn't expecting all this. Things have worked out rather well really. How's it all going for you, by the way?'

'Oh, swimmingly,' said Norman. 'I'm virtually bankrupt. It seems that my ancestors have been responsible for almost every major disaster in the last one hundred years and thanks to this wonderful world of information technology and stuff that we're presently living in, all their dirty deeds are now being brought to light and I'm knee-deep in doggy doo.'

'I hope you didn't bring any in on your shoes, that's a very expensive carpet.'

'Cheers,' said Norman.

'Still,' said my uncle, 'chin up, old friend, you're here now and it would be uncharitable of me not to share some of my largesse with you. What would you say to a helping of untold worth?'

'I'd say thank you very much indeed.'

'Well, there's treasure chests all over the place, why not fill your pockets?'

57

'Can I?' Norman's mouth dropped open and his eyes grew rather wide.

'Least I can do for you, old man. After all, if you'd never suggested that I eat my motorbike, I would never have formulated my theory about iron, been visited by the fairyfolk and come to gain all this.'

'No, you're right,' said Norman. 'You're absolutely right. Where are the treasure chests?'

'Well, there's a big pouch of jewels over there,' said my uncle, pointing. 'The fairies only delivered it today, I haven't got around to opening it yet. Help yourself, dig in.'

Now there are some among you, and you know who you are, who just *know* what's coming next. And churlish of me it would be to deny you your triumph. I could simply leave a space at the bottom of the page for you to write it in yourself, but then that would be to deny the others, who hadn't seen it coming a mile off, and who might cry, 'Cop out ending!'

So here it comes.

'This pouch here?' asked Norman, spying out a large furry-looking purse-like thing with silver attachments.

'Yes, that's the one.'

And of course it was.

Norman opened up the opening bit and peered inside.

'Emeralds,' he cried. 'Emeralds the size of tennis balls.'

And in he delved, most greedily.

And then he said, 'Hey, these aren't emeralds, these are sprou—'

And snap went the sporran of the Devil, gobbling him up with a single gulp and concluding with a huge highland hogmanay of a belch.

'Baaaaaaeeeeeuuuuugh!' by the sound of it.

Uncle Brian reclined upon his couch, blew upon his fingernails and buffed them on his robe. 'That will teach you, you bastard,' said he. 'Revenge is sweet, oh yes indeed. Are my dancing girls there?' And he clapped his hands.

Clap-clap.

And he brought on the dancing girls.

This is not, of course, the end of the story, but it's all there is for now.

MURDER IN DISTANT LANDS

A captive tribesman told to me
How many ships that went to sea
Wound up on ancient coral reefs,
Their crews devoured by wild beasts.
I used to lie awake and wonder
If what he said was true.

A captive tribesman said he saw
A twenty-masted man-of-war
Sail out from fair Atlantis Isle.
He said he stood and waved a while.
I used to sit for hours and wonder
If what he said was true.

A captive tribesman told me when
He and his fellows lived on men
They found washed up upon the shore.
He said he'd eaten five or more.
I used to gasp, my mouth wide open,
If what he said was true.

My father said the man was mad
And though I really trusted Dad
I thought about those pointed teeth
And how those sailors came to grief
And I am still inclined to think
That what he said was true.

3

THE ALPHA MAN

'Caricature is the tribute that
mediocrity pays genius.'
OSCAR WILDE

When you are young and foolish you believe the
things you are told. And why should you not? You
have yet to learn the terrible truth that most adults
lie most of the time.

Whether the captive tribesman who lived in our
shed told all of the truth, I do not know. Certainly
the tinker I sold him to, in exchange for five magic
beans, was not being altogether honest with me.

I recall my dad saying that the tribesman was
easily worth *six*.

My Uncle Felix told all of the truth. And it got
him in trouble. He wasn't my real uncle, because
his surname was Lemon.* And ours wasn't (or
isn't). But we called him Uncle, because those
were the days when children called adults Mr or

*He claimed direct descendance from the infamous Captain
Leonard 'Legless' Lemon (of whom more later).

Mrs or Uncle or Aunty, and would no more have thought of using their Christian names than telling a lie.

Uncle Felix, or just plain Felix, was a much-copied man.

'Look at that,' he would cry, as he stared through the window of some fashionable boutique. 'Ripped off again.'*

The troubled passer-by to whom this cry was directed would turn to Felix and reply, 'How so?' or 'What do you mean?'

Felix would then point to some article of clothing on display and ask, 'Now who do you think originally designed that then?'

And the passer-by, with the words 'Better humour this one' flashing up on the old mental warning-board, would then say, 'Your good self, might it be?'

And Felix would nod and answer, 'Just so.'

Exactly why it was that Felix only managed to reveal that he was the progenitor of such an item shortly after it had become the current fashion was a mystery not only to others, but also to himself.

The phrases, 'I thought of that first' and 'another of my ideas', were never very far from his lips.

The story I am about to relate begins shortly after the Second World War† (an event which Felix had foreseen, but kept to himself for fear of spreading panic). Felix was at that time occupied as a clerk in a government building, Gaumont

---

*So this was probably the nineteen-sixties.
†So I must have been wrong about the nineteen-sixties!

House on the Uxbridge Road. It was ten of the morning clock, the time when plugs are pulled from government switchboards up and down the land and her majesty's servants ease their stiffened collars and put their spats up for a well-earned ten minutes of tea and bourbon biscuits.

Felix was thoughtfully stirring his Earl Grey and running his eye across the front page of the *Daily Sketch*.

The news was bleak, but then the news was *always* bleak, always had been bleak and always would be. It is a recognized fact that the paper with the bleakest news has the largest circulation and in those days every household in the Empire subscribed to the *Daily Sketch*. Except for those that didn't.

Once, and I mention this only in passing, there was a newspaper in America that called itself *The Good News* and printed nothing other. It ran to three editions before closing.

'I see that the Prime Minister has finally taken my advice over this Spanish thing,' said Felix, dunking his biscuit.

Norman Crombie (for indeed it was he) looked up from his copy of *Tit Bits*. 'What advice was that, Felix?' he asked.

'Withdrawal, my boy, withdrawal.'

Norman, whose tastes in literature at that time were limited to 'the sensational novel' and 'naturists' publications', knew only one meaning for the word 'withdrawal'.

'Good Lord, Felix. You told him *that*?'

'I had been meaning to,' said Felix.

63

The door opened and Mrs Molloy entered the office.

Mrs Molloy was short and stout and smelt of Parma violets. One day (and this was a fact known only to Felix Lemon), she would give birth to a son. He would be christened Ernest and grow up to be a serial killer of unparalleled ferocity.

'There's a letter for you, Mr Lemon,' said Mrs Molloy, adding in a tone of undisguised glee, 'It's an OHMS.'

Felix accepted the brown, windowed envelope and held it up to the light. 'I've been expecting this,' he said.

Norman, who greatly feared all things official and only worked at Gaumont House because of the luncheon vouchers and his unrequited love for a switchboard girl called Joyce, took to the crossing of himself. 'I would much prefer it if you opened that elsewhere,' he told Felix.

Felix Lemon thrust the envelope into a pocket of his pin-striped suit. 'I will read it later,' he said, promptly forgetting its existence.

The day followed its regular format. A memo came down from the higher-ups regarding a new filing system which Felix assured Norman had been on his mind for quite some time. Lunch-hour found Felix pleasantly surprised that the snack bar opposite had taken the advice he'd been meaning to give and had its windows cleaned. And the afternoon turned up three more incidents where Felix's uncanny powers of second (hind?) sight proved once more infallible.

That night Norman returned home praying that a bus, which Felix had foreseen but failed to mention, might mount the pavement and flatten Mr Lemon for good and all.

'That Felix is becoming utterly unbearable,' Norman told his small wife, who sadly (for had Felix chosen to mention it, the accident need never have happened) would later trip upon the torn piece of lino in the hall and break her leg.

'Never mind, Norman,' said the ill-fated Mrs Crombie. 'We both know that when it comes to having ideas stolen by ungrateful ne'er-do-wells, you are top of the list.'

Norman nodded thoughtfully at this ambiguous statement. 'I think she knows what I'm on about,' he said.

Norman's wife went out to the kitchen, tripped on a piece of torn lino in the hall and broke her leg.

On Saturday morning Felix took his pin-striped suit to The Blue Bird Cleaners. This was not a company that specialized in avian hygiene, but an early form of dry-cleaners. At that time a *wet*-cleaners.

Felix placed his suit upon the counter. Had he remembered to mention it, he would have told the cleaner not to over-iron the trousers. But he did not and the suit would later return with a ventilated rear end.

'Anything in the pockets, guv?' asked the careful cleaner, recalling how Felix always remembered afterwards that he'd left a five-pound note in his pocket, caused a stink and got his dry-cleaning done for nothing.*

A thorough search turned up a brown, windowed envelope.

'Oh and oh,' said Felix. And then regaining his composure. 'I will take this envelope with me, rather than leave it here, thank you.'

The cleaner nodded politely, gave Felix a little blue slip (with a bird logo on it), and went off to perform his heinous work on Felix's doomed trousers.

Felix took the envelope and himself off to a secluded bench in Walpole Park. Here he opened the envelope at arm's length.

The words MINISTRY OF SERENDIPITY caught his eye.

'Aha,' said Felix, as he read through the text, 'exactly as I would have predicted. I wonder what *serendipity* means,' he wondered.

The missive was short to the point of abruptness.

As you will know (it ran),
Your name has been put before us
regarding your special gift. Please report
at once to the address below:
    Department 23
    Ministry of Serendipity
    Mornington Crescent
    (take train from South Ealing Station)

---

*Even the most sinned against are sometimes to be caught sinning.

Felix scratched at his head, which now had the dandruff he'd been expecting, and rose to the dizzying height of five feet eight and a half. He opened his mouth to speak, but as there was no-one present to listen, he closed it again. And he took himself off to the station.

Felix stood shuffling his feet for quite some time before he could buck up enough courage to purchase the ticket. Some inner something advised caution, but just what this was Felix couldn't quite say.

'A return to Mornington Crescent,' he said at last.

The ticket office clerk eyed Felix up and down. 'Are you quite sure about that?' he asked.

'Quite,' said Felix.

'Five pounds,' said the ticket office clerk.

'*Five pounds?*' Felix took a step backwards. 'But I can get a Red Rover that will take me anywhere in London, train *and* bus, for five shillings.'

'That's nothing,' said the ticket office clerk. 'In communist Russia you can ride on any train for nothing. You could get on the Trans-Siberian Express at, say, Grymsk, which is in the province of Scrovenia, and travel more than one thousand miles across the Russian steppes to Kroskow in Morovia, which is near to the Black Sea and it wouldn't cost you a penny, or in their case a rouble.'

'Is that really true?' Felix asked.

'No,' said the ticket office clerk, 'I made it all up.'

'Why?' Felix asked.

The ticket office clerk shrugged. 'I don't know. I suppose I'm a bit of an anarchist really. You know how it is, square peg in a round hole, free spirit trapped in a ticket office. I'm thinking of chucking it all in and taking the hippie trail to Kathmandu.'

Felix flipped back a couple of pages. 'I think this story is set in the late nineteen-forties,' he said. 'Hippies don't come along until the Sixties.'

'I wouldn't know about that,' said the ticket office clerk. 'You see I was just lying again.'

'Oh,' said Felix. 'Well, can I have a ticket to Mornington Crescent, please?'

'No you can't. Sorry.'

'Why can't I?'

'Because there's no such station.'

'Of course there is.'

'There isn't.'

'Is.'

'Is not.' The ticket office clerk pointed a long slim finger, the shape of an asparagus tip, towards the Underground map on the wall. 'See for yourself.'

Felix saw for himself. 'It's been crossed out,' he said.

'It's always been crossed out. No-one has ever been to Mornington Crescent.'*

'But I *have* to get there. I've got an appointment at the Ministry of Serendipity.'

'Ooh!' said the ticket office clerk. 'Well, that's

*This is absolutely true. Check any map of the London Underground, if you don't believe me.

another matter entirely.' He dug about in some cubby hole beneath his little window and drew out a strip of aluminium foil embossed with runic symbols, odd ciphers and the like. 'Here you go then, there's no charge.'

'No charge?'

'Well, call it five pounds.'

'Fair enough.' And Felix paid up.

He wandered down to the platform to await the train. Normally on a Saturday morning such as this, the platform would be a carnival of colour, Exotic Ealingites, togged up in their finery, setting off 'up West'. But today, not a soul. The platform was deserted but for Felix, which meant it wasn't *really* deserted at all, but it *almost* was. As near as makes no odds.

'I wonder where everyone is,' Felix wondered.

And then the train came in.

It was a very odd train, of a design quite new to Felix, although one he *had* considered drawing up and sending off to London Transport. It was sleek and black and there didn't seem to be any windows. A door hissed open and Felix peered in. The carriage was empty.

Felix sighed. 'This might appear strange to someone who wasn't in the know,' he told himself.

'*Please enter the carriage, Mr Lemon,*' came a mechanized voice. Mr Lemon entered the carriage, with some degree of uncertainty. The door hissed shut and the train sped off.

Felix sat down on the only seat. It was spot-lit. It was very comfortable, but there was nothing much to look at. There not being any windows, or anything.

Presently the train drew to a halt and the door hissed open. *'Kindly disembark, Mr Lemon,'* said the voice. So Felix did so.

He now stood upon the platform of Mornington Crescent. And a very smart platform it was too, all litter free and no graffiti. There were posters advertising seaside resorts such as Skegness and Scarborough. These were printed in those soft pastel colours that say 1930s to anyone who cares to listen.

'Up the stairs please, Mr Lemon.'

Felix found the stairs and trudged up them. At the top a door blocked further progress, so Felix knocked upon it with his knuckle. The door went hiss and slid back. Felix poked his head through the opening and then followed it with his body. The door hissed shut again.

Felix now stood in one of *those* rooms. You know the ones. The ones with the leather chesterfields and the Victorian busts and the picture of Her Majesty on the wall and the tall window that looks out on to Big Ben and the great big desk with the leather desk-set and brass trough lamp and the man from the ministry who sits behind it with his back to the window. We've been here before, we know this room.

'Glad you could make it, Mr Lemon,' said the man behind the desk. It was the ticket office clerk from South Ealing Station.

'How did you do that?' asked Felix.

'I just opened my mouth', said the man, 'and the words came out.'

'No,' said Felix. 'I mean how did you get here before me?'

'I was driving the train.'

'Oh I see.' Felix didn't.

'Well, come and sit down, we have much to discuss.'

'We do? I mean, yes, *we do*.'

'Exactly.'

Felix seated himself on one of the leather chesterfields.

'Now,' said the man, 'as you are no doubt aware, we at the Ministry of Serendipity have had our eye on you for quite some time.'

'I thought as much,' said Felix. 'Although of course I never said anything, because I realized that it's all very hush-hush.' He tapped at his nose in the approved manner.

'Quite,' said the man, tapping his. 'So, as you must also know, we have a very good reason for having our eye upon you.'

'Of course,' said Felix, stroking his chin. 'Indeed, but would you care to refresh my memory?'

'Most amusing,' said the man. 'But why not. It is no doubt clear to you, Mr Lemon, that you are not as other men.'

Felix nodded vigorously.

'You are different,' said the man. 'You are special. You see, all fads and fashions, inventions, innovations, thoughts and theories have their origins somewhere. People take a hint from others who have previously taken a hint from others still, but somewhere at the back of it all there is an originator. What we have come to recognize as the Alpha Man. He is the last, or rather the first, in the line. The average man-in-the-street doesn't really have any ideas of his own. He merely reflects upon ideas that are given to him, through books, through the media. Ideas which come from *the few*. The few control the many, thus it was ever so.'

'Thus it was ever so *what*?' asked Felix.

'Most amusing,' said the man once more. 'The Alpha Man is the first in the line of idea-to-creation-of-form. And our researches tell us that for the most part the Alpha Man is unaware of what he is. He is constantly plagued by seeing his original ideas being exploited by others.'

'Quite true,' said Felix. 'I was just going to say the very same thing. Said it plenty of times before, also.'

'Quite. Well our researches lead us to believe that you are such an Alpha Man. We have so far found only one other.'

'Yes,' said Felix, adding, for good measure, 'I know.'

'You *do* know. Splendid, splendid.' The man leaned back in his chair and twiddled his thumbs. 'What a relief that is. We have made the occasional slip up, as you can imagine.'

'Indeed I can.'

'Poor Larry.'

'Larry?'

'Our first Alpha Man. But let us not speak of such horrors, let us concentrate on your good self.'

'Are you offering me a job?' Felix asked.

'*The* job,' said the man. '*The* job.'

'Larry's job?'

'Got it in one.'

'And what exactly would this job entail?'

'Just sitting mostly. Sitting and thinking.'

'Thinking about what?'

'All manner of things. It's *your thoughts* we want. Just *yours* and *nobody else's*. You love your country, don't you?'

'Of course,' said Felix. 'But what has that got to do with it?'

'It has *everything* to do with it. It is the whole point of it. To be very brief, those who run our country do not always run it well. The public's view, the view of the-man-in-the-street, is that politicians are all careerists, out for what they can get at the expense of the general population. But this is *not* the case. Politicians are, for the most part, sincere individuals. It's just that when they get into power they realize that they're not actually any good at running the country. All they were ever any good at was being politicians. And it's not quite the same thing.'

'You want me to be Prime Minister,' said Felix, warming to the idea.

'Not exactly. We want you to be more "the power behind the throne".'

'Does the Prime Minister have a throne?'

'Most amusing. Your job will be to apply your special gift to affairs of state. Problems that baffle the average cabinet minister will be as nothing to you. With an Alpha Man at the helm, the Empire will flourish. Jobs for all, prosperity for all. An end

73

to sorrow and deprivation, the dawn of a new tomorrow. Why, we'll have an Englishman on the moon by nineteen-sixty and a queen who'll rule the whole wide world. Will you do it, Felix? Will you do it?'

'Oh yes,' said Felix. 'I will.'

And so he did. And the rest, as they say, is history.

THE END

Oh no.

Sorry.

There were two pages stuck together. And some crossings out.

That is *not* the end of the story.

'Oh yes,' said Felix, 'I will.' He didn't mean to say it, but it just came out. The truth of the matter was that Felix was becoming very very uncomfortable. It now occurred to him that he was getting in well over his head on this one. But old habits do die very hard, so Felix went on to say, 'I just knew you were going to say that.'

'Of course you did.' The chap behind the desk's head bobbed up and down in the manner of a nodding dog in a Cortina rear window (whatever happened to them?).

'So you will therefore have realized that what we must do, must be done.'

'Er,' said Felix. 'Mm, yes.'

'Good. Good. We have, of course, prepared the isolation chamber. It is constructed entirely of wood so that no interference will reach you. A special bath of sterile solution has been constructed to contain your brain, it will float upon this, wired up to an electrical contrivance that will channel its brainwaves through—'

And so on and so forth and Felix listened, somewhat slack-jawed and all agape.

'And with your naked unfettered brain, world domination should be a piece of pork pie, as it were,' the chap concluded.

And his words hung in the air like drying laundry.

'A piece of pork pie.' Felix's slackened jaw became all wibbly-wobbly. He was indeed in this thing well over his head. In fact, this thing was going to cost him his head.

This man, this *we*; because it was definitely a *we* rather than a *me*, was going to do for him good and proper and Felix now knew for absolutely good and proper and certain that there was about as much chance of he himself really being one of these so called Alpha Men as there was of him piloting the aforementioned English moonship.

'Well,' said the truly rattled Felix, 'this has really been most interesting, but I think I must be off about my business now. Things to do, people to see, you know how it is.'

'Things to think,' said the chap. 'People to mould.'

'That's not exactly what I said, nor what I meant.'

'We know *exactly* what you mean.'

'I don't think you do. Honestly I don't.'

'Let's get you down to pre-med,' said the chap.

'Oh no, let's don't!'

And then there was some unpleasantness. Felix rose to take his leave. The chap rose to stop him, there was some pushing and shoving and then there was some punching and running. The latter all the work of Felix.

★   ★   ★

Monday morning and ten of that clock found a most worried Felix sipping his tea and declining his Bourbon biscuit.

'Did you have a nice weekend, Felix?' Norman's voice was that of the condemned prisoner who asks the captain of the firing squad what tomorrow's weather forecast is.

But instead of the usual, 'Well, on Saturday I'm off down the boozer and what do I see but someone wearing the very shoes I've had in my mind to put on the market for months now,' there came a dismal groan and a sad little voice that said, 'Bad news, Norman. Bad news.'

'I suppose you know my wife broke her leg?'

'No.'

Norman slumped back in his utility office chair. '*No*, Felix? What do you mean, no?'

Felix shook his head. 'Well, how would I know? No-one told *me*.' And then Felix went on to tell Norman all about the Ministry of Serendipity and his escape and his running along railway tunnels and falling down and taking the knee out of his trousers and having to go back to the dry-cleaners to discover that a steam iron had been left on his best ones and burned the bum out and how he was a doomed man and everything. Everything.

When Norman went to visit his wife in hospital that evening he told her all about everything. Everything that Felix had told to him.

'Well, I knew that was bound to happen,' said Norman's wife. 'But, of course, no-one ever listens to me.'

Norman raised a quizzical eyebrow to this and then shook his head. 'Nah,' he told himself, 'not a chance.'

As for the Ministry of Serendipity. Well, who can say? You certainly can't get a train to Mornington Crescent and that must prove something. Felix is still up and about and occasionally, *very* occasionally, phrases such as 'I suppose you know who they nicked that idea from' can be heard coming from his direction. But these are accompanied by much nervous over-the-shoulder looking and rarely go any further.

It's a bit of a shame really, as he's a harmless enough fellow. Of course, *I* knew it was all going to happen. But then no-one ever listens to me.

But they *will*.

Oh *yes* they *will*.

Because finally, in case you were wondering where all this has been leading, it's now that my story truly begins.

ROPED INTO SOCCER

Roped into soccer on Thursdays.
Pair of old boots on my shoulder.
Pads made of bone
To protect precious shin,
Big brother's shorts
Secured by a pin.
I shan't do this stuff when I'm older.

Roped into soccer? Not me, sir!
Roped into games, Friday morning.
Plimsolls that smell in the summer.
Horses to vault
When you haven't a note.
Mats made of rush
And you can't wear your coat.
Burns upon hands that might play the piano.
Roped into games? No, not me, sir!

Roped into dull social studies
By teachers with beards and bad jackets.
Learning of Lenin
And Stalin and Marx,
Tolpuddle Martyrs,
Sedition and sparks,
Crass revolutions in God-awful places.
Roped into that lot? Not me, sir!

Roped into prizes on Prize Day.
Projects that no-one approved of.
Always some boff
From the fourth form or third

Who writes some great thesis
On 'Flight of the bird'
And wins every prize and becomes the school
  captain.
Roped into prizes. NO THANK YOU!

I was always a loner really.

4

Now there are revelations.

And there are *REVELATIONS*.

The preceding chapters were laid before you not without good reason. The matter of my great[3] grandaddy's sporran, my Uncle Brian's discoveries regarding the hidden properties of metal, Felix Lemon's encounter with the Ministry of Serendipity, all these play a part in revelations yet to come.

But of the *REVELATIONS*, these begin right here.

My discovery that I was the Chosen One came quite without warning. Although I had always considered myself a bit of a loner, I had no idea just how much of a loner I really was. The sudden revelation came as quite a shock and unleashed a chain of events that I could never have foreseen.

But I am getting ahead of myself here. Let me begin at the beginning, or as near to the beginning as is necessary. To begin . . .

Let me tell you about my brother.

Being four years my senior, he held for me the status of a demi-god. While Mother shooed away my questions with talk of pressing housework, and

Father replied to my askings with parables, brother Andy was always there to provide an answer when one was required.

How well I recall the occasion of my eighth birthday, when he taught me all about the workings of our record player. It being my birthday, I was allowed, as a very special treat, to sit alone beneath the kitchen table and lick the varnish on the legs. Ah, such childhood bliss. My brother was playing the gramophone record he had bought me as a present. It was by Captain Beefheart and his Magic Band and although it made little sense to me at the time, I was pleased that at least my brother seemed to be enjoying it.

I remember sitting there in the damp and darkness, a fine veneer of rosy varnish crusting my tongue, watching the god-like being as he sat yonder on the area of linoleum that caught the afternoon sun, tapping his bare toes to the beat and picking the scabs from his knees.

And eating them.

A question had entered my head, most probably through the bald patch on the top where the ring worm nested, and I was eager to pass the question on to my brother.

I waited patiently for the opportunity and this came shortly after the sixth playing of the record's A side, when brother Andy got up to fetch some rose hip syrup to wash down the last of his scabs.

'Brother Andy,' I called from the damp and darkness, 'tell me, pray, how that thing works.'

'How what thing works, young Dog's Breath?'

he replied, for this was his affectionate 'pet name' for me.

'The stereo system, O Great One.' For this was the name he had chosen for himself.

'It has an electrical motor,' he said informatively.

'No. I understand *that*.' I didn't. 'I mean the music. The music comes off the record and goes out of the speakers, doesn't it?'

'It certainly does.'

'So how come there's any music left on the record to play a second time? Wouldn't it all have come off and gone out of the speakers?'

'Good point, DB,' said the Great One. And then he went on to explain. 'You see, in the old days that's exactly what happened. At the music factory where the record was made they put the music on in layers, like paint. But old-fashioned gramophones just had this needle connected to a horn for the music to come out of and the needle scratched the music off layer by layer until none was left. If you play an old seventy-eight on a modern record player, all you'll hear is crackles, because most of the music has been scraped off.'

Impressed so far? *I* certainly was, and there was more to come.

'Now,' said he, beckoning me from the damp and darkness of my birthday treat, 'you will notice that great progress has been made since those bad old days. Behold, if you will, this cable that runs from the record deck here, to the left speaker, there.'

I beheld this.

'Behold that it is a *double* cable. There are two separate wires inside.'

I beheld this also.

'The reason there are *two* is as follows. The music travels from the gramophone needle, along *one* of these wires and comes out of the speaker for us to hear. *But* and this is a big *but*, there is the second wire. Attached to the end of this second wire and inside the speaker itself there is a microphone. This picks up the music coming out of the speaker and carries it back to the stylus (which is the modern name for the needle) and right back onto the record again. It's clever, isn't it?'

And I had to admit that it was.

I would later discover that brother Andy had not been altogether honest with me in regard to this matter and so when it became necessary for me to kill and eat him, I did so without hesitation or regret.*

If there was ever proof needed for the existence of the Alpha Man, then that proof came in the shape of my brother. He was certainly an innovative inventor, but time and again his innovative inventions were callously poached away and perverted to the profit of other lesser men.

I will offer just two examples of this, although the list is endless.†

My brother's favourite number was 300. Because if you turn 300 on its side it looks a bit like a bum pooing. Hence every innovative invention he came

---

*I didn't really. But there were times when I wished I had.
†Of course the list isn't really endless. This is just a figure of speech.

up with was inevitably one in the *300 Series*. One of his earliest, and to my mind still one of his finest, was the

RANKIN 300 SERIES PATENT SMOKE-EEZEE PERSONAL LEISURE FACILITY

Allow me to explain, by asking you this: how many times have you been doing something tricky, where a cigarette would really help with the concentration, but smoking the cigarette only makes the job more difficult?

My brother came up with the smoke-eezee. It was a metal harness that hung about the neck with a clip on the front at mouth level to hold your cigarette, and a small bowl slung beneath to catch the falling ash. Thus you could puff away to your heart's content, whilst having both hands free for the work in hand. So to speak.

The obvious applications were, well, obvious.

Certain things in life require the smoking of a cigarette if they are to be done with any degree of conviction. Things such as typing up a novel about an American private detective, or playing blues piano in a nightclub, or even everyday things, like working a lathe or digging a hole or driving a car or having sex.

The list is endless.*

My brother made several modifications to the smoke-eezee, in order to cater to all tastes. He

---

*Actually, in this case, the list *is* endless.

added extra attachments, to hold a pipe, a cigar, a cigarette in a holder, a joint. He even constructed a plastic flask that could be filled with alcohol and strapped to the top of the head. A straw depended from this and led to a sucking arrangement positioned next to the cigarette. Thus you could smoke *and* drink without having to use your hands.

Brilliant!

But!

But, do you ever see people walking around nowadays wearing the smoke-eezee cigarette harness, with or without the optional head flask? When was the last time you saw a blues pianist or a rock guitarist wearing one? When was the last time you made love to someone wearing one?

Never! That's when.

And I'll tell you for why. The idea was stolen and perverted, and by its perversion it became a thing of ridicule and contempt.

And it was all the fault of Woody Guthrie.

He got hold of one of my brother's cigarette harnesses, made an adaptation of his own and slotted in a harmonica.

And the rest is music history.

And far from bloody tuneful it is too.

Not that I think folk music is something that should be tossed aside lightly. On the contrary, I think it should be hurled with great force.

And whilst on the subject of music, did you know that it was my brother who invented the discothèque? Well it was. Sort of. There was once a time *before* the discothèque and this was the time when my brother came up with another of his innovative inventions. The one that would lead to my *REVELATION*, but one which was once again cruelly lifted and perverted.

My brother invented the travelling discothèque. Which is *not* to be confused with its subsequent rip-off, the *mobile* discothèque, although it was mobile, for that was the point.

Allow me to explain.

My brother liked going to nightclubs. We had just the one in Ealing, the imaginatively named Ealing Club. Many bands, later to find fame, played their early gigs there; Manfred Mann, The Who, The Rolling Stones, but we never got to see any of them. Although we did get to *hear* them.

The reason for this was that the Ealing Club was a bus ride away and once you had paid your bus fare there was no money left for the entrance fee. So we just had to stand outside and listen.

My brother set himself to the solving of this conundrum and this led to the innovative invention in question.

And it came about in this fashion.

An uncle of ours, I forget his name, Uncle Charles it was, had a big old box van. One of those ones with plenty of headroom in the back and room for thirty or forty people standing up. My brother's idea was to start his own nightclub in the back of this van and cash in on all those folk who only had money enough for bus fares.

He would pick up club members at their own front doors, drive them about, taking in a scenic spot or two for romance and use of a toilet, then drop them home again at the end of the evening.

Blinder!

In the big box back of the van there would be a little bar in one corner, a pianist with cigarette harness in another, a few chairs, a table or two nailed to the floor and room for people to dance. A bit of moody lighting and away you'd go. He put adverts in the local paper.

CLUB 300
The most exclusive nightclub in town.
You don't have to go to it.
It will come to you.
Ring this number for further details.
etc.

He got some bookings but it wasn't a success. There simply wasn't enough room in the back of the van. And once he'd paid the pianist and the barman, there was no profit left.

So my brother, being an innovator, sacked the barman, a Mr Stringfellow, and the pianist, a Mr Charles, tore out the piano, bar, tables and chairs and turned the entire back of the van into a single dance floor.

On the ceiling he arranged a small mirror globe that turned by a clockwork motor and he would sit in the cab, shining a torch onto it through the little hatch behind the seats. To make things really special he got one of those torches that will shine three different colours.

Music was provided by the van's radio turned up full blast.

Blinder!

It was a *big* success. And my brother was able, by studying the *Radio Times* in order to see what was on the radio each night, to organize 'theme evenings'. Country-and-western, reggae, psychedelic, etc. Forty people at least could be crammed in on a good night, each picked up from home and dropped back at the end of the evening.

Blinder! Blinder!

Looking into the future my brother foresaw an entire fleet of such disco vans, three hundred at the very least, covering the entire length and breadth of the country, supplying the night-life of the big city to outlying rural communities.

Blinder! Blinder! Blinder!

But it was not to be.

There were some unfortunate accidents. My brother lost his first van-load on an unmanned level crossing just outside Orton Goldhay. There was a party of old folk on board. Local Darby and Joan Club. My brother had discovered a radio station that played nineteen-thirties dance-band music, and old people can't get out much to go to dances, can they?

The van was just crossing the railway line when the old folk took it upon themselves to go into the hokey-cokey. They put their left leg in and their left leg out and shook them all about with such enthusiasm that they turned the van on its side.

In the path of an oncoming train.

My brother and the uncle whose name I can't remember, Uncle Charles (who was driving), managed to scramble free of the cab, but the rear door of the van had been padlocked on the outside to prevent the old folk falling out at roundabouts. And the key to the padlock was on the keyring with the ignition key. And the ignition key was still in the ignition. And the train was coming.

My brother didn't get paid that night.

The tragedy didn't put him off though.

He just made sure that from then on he always got paid in advance.

I asked him later how he felt about all those people getting snuffed out like that. He said, with a rationality unclouded by emotion, that although it was sad, particularly about the money and everything, it didn't really matter about the old people, because old people didn't serve much of a purpose in the community anyway.

I mentioned this to a doctor friend of mine who deals a lot with old people. My doctor friend said that he thought my brother's remark was cynical and uninformed. And he went on to tell me (in confidence, of course) that old people serve a real purpose in medical terms. 'Without old people,' he said, 'who could we let medical students practise and experiment on?'

And I was stuck for an answer.

My brother lost his replacement van a scant three weeks later. He had fitted an extra-large aerial to this in order to pick up pirate radio, which was very popular at the time. On the evening of the disaster, John Peel was playing the psychedelic good stuff and there was 'A Happening' taking place in the back of the van.

More than fifty proto-hippies were squeezed in and, unknown to my brother, every time the van stopped at traffic lights a few more climbed aboard to join the event and enjoy the good vibrations.

The last thing my brother recalls, prior to awakening in a hospital bed, was Peely playing 'Eight Miles High' by the Byrds.

Apparently what happened was this: the number of proto-hippies crammed into the back eventually became so great that it reached critical mass. There was then a mighty implosion which sucked the van's sides into the shape of the great pyramid and resulted in the creation of one single super-dense proto-hippy, who was left sitting cross-legged on the floor.

And this cosmic event spelt the end for Club 300.

The end was as mundane as could be imagined. While my brother regained his senses in hospital, the uncle whose name I never can remember, returned to his old profession of light removals. And the very first job he took was to transport some record decks and lighting equipment from a private house to the local church hall. My uncle recognized his employer at once (although he couldn't recall his name) as a Club 300 regular.

This fellow had come up with an idea based upon my brother's, but one that could be turned to even greater profit. Forget about holding your disco in a van, hold it in a hall where you can get more people in. Use the van to transport your own sound equipment.

And such was the birth of the mobile disco-thèque.

And the death of its travelling progenitor.

*　　*　　*

But it must have been fate. For if it had not happened then I would never have met the super-dense proto-hippy and received my great *REVELATION*.

It came about in this fashion. The year was 1966. England had just pulled off the double by winning the World Cup and putting the first man on the moon. Sonic Energy Authority were celebrating their tenth number-one hit single and the summer of love had arrived a year early.

The truth that I was partially responsible for all this had yet to dawn.

Allow me now to set the scene and explain how it all came about.

The Ealing Club had changed hands and was now called Fangio's Bar. Getting there on the bus was no longer a problem as, since the October Revolution of the previous year, all public transport was now free.

Things have changed a lot since then.

But that's the way I like it.

With jobs for all and any job you fancy, I had become a private eye. And, with the national drinking age lowered to fifteen, a semi-alcoholic. On the evening of the great REVELATION I was sitting in Fangio's Bar, sipping from a bottle of Bud and chewing the fat with the fat boy.

The fat boy's name was Fangio but I hadn't decided yet upon mine.

In those days I had a lot of time for Fangio, although thinking back I can't recall why.

Certainly the guy was fair, he never spoke well of anyone. And when it came to clothes, he had the most impeccable bad taste I've ever encountered. He suffered from delusions of adequacy and his conversation was enlivened by the occasional brilliant flash of silence.

Once seen, never remembered, that was Fangio. Many put this down to his shortness of stature, for as Noel Coward observed, 'Never trust a man with short legs, brain's too near their bottoms.'

But he did have obesity on his side. And on his back. And on his front and Fangio was ever a great man when it came to the Zen Question. The one he posed for me upon this fateful evening was the ever popular, '*Why is cheese?*' Of course I knew the answer to this, every good private eye did, but I wasn't going to let on.

The way I saw it, if you've got a small green ball in each hand, you may not win the snooker, but you'll have the undivided attention of a leprechaun.

Fangio pushed a plate across the bar top. 'More fat?' he asked.

'No thanks, I'm still chewing this piece.'

'Might I ask you a personal question?'

'I'm easy.'

'That wasn't the one I was going to ask.'

We laughed together, what was friendship for after all?

'It's a dress code thing,' said the fat boy.

'Go on then.'

Fangio fingered his goitre. The guy had more chins than a Chinese telephone directory. 'You cut a dashing figure,' said he. 'And I speak as I find, as you know.'

'I do know that,' I said, and I did.

'I'm thinking of buying a hat,' said Fangio. 'But the question is, brim or no brim?'

'No brim,' said I. 'Peak at a pinch, but no brim.'

'So, a fez, you think?'

'Fez, pill box, brimless fedora, beret if you're travelling the continent, balaclava for mountain wear, cloche for cross-dressing parties—'

'But a cloche has a brim.'

'But nothing to write home about.'

'Ah, I get your point.' And I saw that he did.

'Busby, turban, puggaree, tarboosh, tam-o'-shanter, coonskin Davy Crocket—'

'You sure know your hats,' said Fangio.

'You have to in my business,' I told him. 'In my business wearing the right hat for the job can mean the difference between cocking the snook or kicking the can, if you catch my drift, and I'm sure that you do.'

'So tell me,' said the fat boy, 'how come you always go hatless?'

'Why is cheese?' I replied.

We chewed some more upon the fat and I saw that gleam come into Fangio's good eye. I've seen that gleam before, plenty of times in plenty of places. And here it was again, right here.

'Why the gleam?' I enquired and we both laughed again.

'To be serious,' said Fangio, when at last we had done with the mirth, 'there's something else I've been meaning to ask.'

'Ask away.'

The barman sucked air up his nostrils, causing ears to pop about the bar, and blew it out of his mouth. 'I was just wondering why it is that you have five matchsticks sellotaped across your forehead.'

I stiffened inwardly but maintained my composure. In my business maintaining your composure can mean the difference between laughing like a drain or howling up a gum tree. As for stiffening inwardly, I just don't know. 'I have to use the lavvy,' I said and made away from the bar.

I crossed the dance floor at the trot. It was a fox trot but I was in no mood to tango. This was the week of The Brentford Bee Festival and most of the dancers wore insect costumes. I felt for those guys, if only they'd known that the posters were supposed to read BEER instead of BEE.

Such is life.

I felt odd as I moved between the dancers, curiously out of place. A stranger in my own back passage, you might say. I entered the Gents and found my way to the wash-hand basin. Above it the mirror. I peered into the mirror.

I *did* have five matchsticks sellotaped to my forehead.

And that wasn't all.

My left eyebrow had been dyed lime green and I had two paperclips attached to the lobe of my right ear. Looking down I spied for the first time the blue nail varnish on my left thumbnail and the purple on my right. About my neck I wore two school ties. A number of watch springs had been sewn to the lapels of my riding jacket. My shoes were odd and I wasn't wearing any socks.

A dress code thing? What had happened to me? Was I hallucinating or just seeing things? Had I passed out at a party and fallen prey to merry pranksters? That seemed the most probable.

Embarrassment! Oh, the shame.

I rooted about in my pockets for a hankie to wipe off the eyebrow dye, but turned up an assortment of incongruous objects instead. Chicken bones, glass marbles, bottle tops, several biros bound together with pink ribbon. A half-pack of playing cards. A dead mouse.

Someone was definitely having a pop.

'Who did this to me?' I asked the mirror.

The mirror had nothing to say.

'Come on, speak up!' I told it.

'You did it to yourself.'

I all but soiled my underlinen. But the voice came not from the looking-glass, but a chap at the cubicle door.

He just stood there looking, and very well he did it too. He was tall and lean and frocked out in kaftan and sandals. It was hard to say just how, but he exuded charisma as others might aftershave. One of those people who can strut while still sitting down. As I didn't want to waste time later, I hated him at once.

'Did you do this to me?' I asked, reaching for the gun that I might have carried if I did carry one. Which I didn't.

'No. Not me.' He shook a head-load of golden hair and flashed me a pair of ice-blue eyes. He had the kind of voice that could talk the knickers off a nun, but I wasn't buying the baby oil.

'Who are you?' I asked, just to keep things pally.

'My name is Colon,' he said, 'the super-dense proto-hippy.' If there was a gag in that it passed me by. 'You stuck the matchsticks on yourself. If you'd care to step outside, I'll explain everything to you.'

I wasn't keen, I can tell you. But there was something so compelling about this fellow, I thought I might give it a try. I reached up to tear the Sellotape from my forehead.

'No. Don't do that.'

'Why not?'

'You put it there for a purpose.'

'What purpose?'

'I'm not entirely sure.'

'Well, if I put it there for one purpose, I'm taking it off for another. In order not to look absurd.'

I ripped off the Sellotape.

Somewhere over the Andes a pilot lost control and his aeroplane fell towards a mountainside.

I shook my head. 'Something just happened,' I said. 'Something bad.'

'Did you cause it?'

'No, I don't think I did.'

'Let's go outside.'

And outside we went.

We stood together in the alleyway. It was a *real* alleyway, one of those with the trash cans and the fire escape with the retractable bottom section. From an open window somewhere near came the sound of a lonely saxophone, beneath our feet was terra firma, high over all the sky.

'What do you see up there?' he asked.

'Only stars,' I said.

'*Only* stars?'

'That's all.'

'That's far from all, my friend.'

'If this is to be an esoteric conversation, is it OK if I smoke?'

'I really couldn't say.'

The night was nippy, hands-in-pockets weather. I slotted a Woodbine into my cigarette harness.

'You're smoking Woodbine tonight,' he said. 'Is that significant?'

'An earthquake in Honduras.'

'What did you say?'

'I didn't say anything.' But I was sure that I had, I couldn't remember just what it was.

'You don't know you're doing it,' he said. 'You have no idea at all. Perhaps it would be better if I didn't tell you.'

I lit my cigarette, took two extra matchsticks from the box and placed one behind each ear.

'Why two?' he asked.

'Bulb sales are down again in Holland.'

'Ah yes, I see.'

'What do you see?' Something was happening here. Something that made me feel uncomfortable.

'Tell me about the stars,' he said. 'What *do* they mean?'

'The stars are the simplest of all,' I explained. 'But also the most difficult. When you look up at the night sky, you see stars, white dots on black.

All you have to do is join the dots and see what they spell out. The answer's up there, but everyone knows that.'

'No-one but you knows that.'

'Knows *what*?'

'About the stars.'

He smiled, it was the kind of smile that could make a lighthouse out of a dead man's willy and a sailor come home from sea. 'I'm sorry,' he said. 'I've broken your train of thought. Forget I said anything. Go on about the stars.'

'The truth is really out there,' I said. 'The message is written in the heavens. The problem is in knowing *how* to join up the dots. Which star is dot number one and which is dot number two and so on. It all depends on where you're standing on the planet and how good your eyesight is.'

'So there's a different message for each of us.'

'What are you talking about?' I tapped cigarette ash into the palm of my hand, divided it into three small piles, discarded two and devoured the third.

'Why only eat one?'

'Red is this year's colour, everyone's wearing it.'

'Yes,' said he, 'it all adds up.'

'Listen, Mr Colon,' said I, 'there's something funny happening around here and you're at the back of it. Spill the beans pronto or I'll never forgive myself for the hiding I'm going to give you.'

'How long have you been a private detective?'

'About twenty minutes. Why do you ask?'

'What did you do before that?'

'Nothing much. Dossed about. Tried to get into art school. Thought about joining the space programme. Fancied being a rock star for a while, and a gardener. Thought about combining the two, couldn't quite make them gel together though.'

'You've always been a bit of a loner.'

'One bit in particular.'

'And do private eyes get the girls?'

'The ones I read about do. Hey, what is all this? I'm supposed to be asking the questions. What are we doing out here anyway?'

'Remember the matchsticks and the Sellotape?'

'The *what*? No.'

'Why were they stuck to your forehead?'

'An aircraft over the Andes. It *had* to crash, I couldn't compensate for *that*. If the guns had got through to the rebels, the government would have been overthrown. The matches were a mistake so they had to come off, I had no control over the situation. I never do.'

'Interesting.'

'What is interesting?'

'Go on about having no control over the situation.'

'You know all the stuff that's been written about chaos theory and this holistic overview of the ecology. That everything is interlinked. Everything. A butterfly flutters its wings in the Amazon basin and ultimately the price of beef goes up in New Zealand. Well, it's partially true, but not quite. You see there never can be an imbalance in nature, because nature is not static. Nature is always moving forward, always evolving, developing, never still. It's harmonious. Except sometimes it's not completely harmonious. And that's where I come in. I compensate for partial imbalance, partial lack of harmony. It's a reverse of the butterfly. I balance the big events. The other way round, you see. I compensate for this year's red fashions by swallowing cigarette ash. Don't ask me how it works and why I'm the one who has to do it. I don't know.'

'That was quite a speech.'

'What was?'

'Go on with what you were saying.'

'I'm not the first and I won't be the last. There's others like me, loners who can't fit in. You might see them in rags sleeping in doorways, muttering to themselves. They're compensators too, maintaining the balance of equipoise, helping things along. It might be in how they mumble, or the way they let their hair grow, or the number of holes in their shoes. The world wouldn't function without them, but the world doesn't even know the debt it owes them.'

'*I* know,' said Colon. 'At the moment of my implosion, I saw it all.'

'Saw *what* all?'

'You can only answer every second question, I see that. But weren't you ever aware of what you were doing?'

'It's something I've done all my life. It came naturally. I've never given it any thought at all.'

'But what—' He paused.

'What?'

'What if it worked the other way round? What if you could reverse the process? Be the mythical butterfly? Put two fountain pens in your top pocket and make next year's fashion green?'

'A man who could do that', I said, 'would have the world to play with. Such a man would be as God.'

'God, or something else.'

'What did you say?'

'It doesn't matter. I have said enough. Continue with your good work. But lay off the Sellotape. Keep it low profile. Do it in the comfort of your own bedroom. Will you do that for me?'

'Yes I will.'

'And *what* will you do for me?'

I scratched my head. 'I don't know. What are you talking about?'

He smiled that smile again. 'Absolutely nothing. I'm sorry that I bothered you. Enjoy your evening. Goodbye.'

'Goodbye.'

I stood there in the alleyway and watched him walk away. Something very odd had just occurred and I meant to find out just what it was.

I reached into the inner pocket of my jacket, oblivious to the fact that it contained three fir cones painted silver and a cork which had compensated for the new train timetables and fished out my private eye tape recorder.

I'd set it recording back in the Gents and was eager to hear just what was *really* on it.

In my business, tape-recording your conversations can sometimes mean the difference between a revelation and a *REVELATION*.

This was one of those sometimes.

HOTEL JERICHO

The last time I saw Sparrow
He was leaning on his barrow
Where he sold the spud and marrow
And the sprout of ill repute.
He was tall and tanned and well advised,
His ego too was over-sized,
And I looked on in wonder
At the brightness of his suit.

For he would swagger to and fro
En route to Hotel Jericho.

The last time I saw Norman
He was working as a storeman
And a part-time western lawman
Of the Wyatt Earp brigade.
He was dressed in rags and tatters,
Versed in all the legal matters,
And the natives came to watch him
As he strolled the esplanade.

For thus he strolled, both thus and so
En route to Hotel Jericho.

The last time I saw Wheeler
He was training as a Peeler
And making quite a mealer (meal of)
Doing press-ups for the boys.
They were standing round in motley knots,
Like leopards who were changing spots,

You couldn't see or hear or think because of
  all the noise.

The blighters come, the blighters go
En route to Hotel Jericho.

The last time I, well, never mind
I'm leaving all those lads behind
They really are the common kind
And quite below my style.
I'm selling up my stocks and shares,
The dogs I've trained for baiting bears,
My bingo halls and wax museums on the
  Golden Mile.

It's hi de hi and ho de ho
I'm buying Hotel Jericho.

5

In Hotel Jericho the beds are never changed, the windows never opened. Flies circle the naked light bulbs, static crackles on the broken TV screens. The taps all drip and the plugs all leak and the people all smell bad.

Someone's crying in the basement, someone's lying in the hall. No-one notices as I glide by, nobody at all.

I speak to no-one now. I dare not speak. Words have power and power corrupts. I spend all the time I can in my room. I only shop at night and I'm very careful what I buy. I have to keep the balance right. Too much salt and there might be another war. Too little sugar and who knows what might happen? I know, so I always take three in my coffee. No milk though, that might be dangerous.

I write only on lined paper in red exercise books. Thirty lines to the page, twenty pages to the book. I count the number of words on each page very carefully. The number of misspellings. The number of letters to each word, where to put the punctuation marks. If I'm wrong by a comma the results could be catastrophic.

I work *very* slowly. Very is in italics. I have to be *very* careful about italics.

I'm remembering back again now. Back to how it started. Back to when I became aware. The *REVELATION*.

So long ago.

I walked home from Fangio's Bar that night. I didn't take the free bus. It was a long walk home, but it seemed the thing to do at the time. I walked on the pavement cracks to compensate for the new trees they'd planted in the park and went part of the way barefoot because Sonic Energy Authority were at number one for the third consecutive week.

Of course I didn't know I was doing it.

Not then.

But later. Later I would. Oh my word, yes.

I entered our house through the unlocked front door. No-one ever locked their doors in those days, not in our neighbourhood. It wasn't that people were more honest back then, it's just that no-one had anything worth nicking.

Muffled screams issued from the kitchen. Mum was ironing Dad's shirt again. Since Dad had pawned the ironing-board, clothes had to be ironed while still on the body. It was a messy business, but wasn't everything?

I wandered into the front parlour. Brother Andy sat in the armchair with a strained expression on his face. He was trying very hard to grow a moustache.

'How's it coming, Great One?' I asked.

'I had half a Zappata an hour ago, but it's gone back in again.'

I seated myself on the Persian pouffe, a present from Uncle Brian. 'Tell me,' I said, 'do I look strange to you?'

'No, I recognized you at once.'

'Nothing odd about me, you would say?'

'Have you grown a moustache?'

I felt my upper-lip area. 'No,' I said.

'Well, don't interrupt me when I'm trying to.'

I left him to his concentration and went up to my room.

I occupied the loft at this time. Once I had a bedroom of my own, next to my brother's. But I came home from school one day to find all my things in the loft and his room knocked through into mine.

After several months I plucked up enough courage to ask him why I had been moved into the loft.

'Why have I been moved into the loft, Great One?' I asked him.

'To keep the tigers away.'

'But there are no tigers round here.'

'There. So it works, doesn't it?'

And that was that.

My brother had converted the loft. To Islam. It had been a simple ceremony, but moving. At the end of it he charged me a pound and informed me that I now had the power to issue fatwas, but only small ones and only against domestic animals. I looked up the word *fatwa* in the dictionary. It wasn't there. The nearest to it was *fatuous*, which meant complacently or inanely stupid.

This bothered me.

Up in the loft I lit a candle and sat down upon my Lilo. I took out the tape recorder from my pocket and gave it a thoughtful looking-over. There was something important on the tape, I just knew it. But it bothered me. Something deep inside was saying, 'Don't play it, don't play it.' Something even deeper was saying, 'Go on, you have to.' And something even deeper made a rude noise come out of my bottom.

I watched the candle flame turn green. An omen? It had to be. I rewound the tape and pressed the play button.

And nothing whatever came out.

So that was that.

Oh no it wasn't. I had the pause button on.

I pressed upon the pause button and listened in awe to the conversation I'd had with Mr Colon in the alleyway.

The whole bit.

It was crazy stuff. The craziest. The message written in the stars. The butterfly's wings. The compensating. And finally the line that sent shivers down my spine. 'A man who could do that', I had said, 'would have the world to play with. Such a man would be as God.'

I rewound the tape and played it again. And again and again and again until the batteries ran out. Then I pulled off the full spool and hid it away behind the water-tank. A chapter of my life was over.

A very short one, as it happened.

But there were further chapters yet to come and these, I felt certain, would be gloriously long.

CAPTAIN OF THE HEAD

I've a way with the old Rosie Lee
That keeps all the sailors amused,
When they come home on leave
I've some tricks up my sleeve
To impress all the salts when they're used.

I do speeches from most of the classics
And readings from Judges and Kings,
A sprinkling of farce
In a champagne glass
And a remake of *Lord of the Rings*.

I pull bunnies out of my topper
And invoke ancient runes on a scroll.
I call up the shit
From the bottomless pit
And finish by swallowing coal.

The sailors throw pennies and halfpennies
And promise me trips round the bay.
I just bow to them all,
Take a quick curtain call
And then I am off on my way.

I'm in constant demand for bar mitzvahs
And weddings and stag nights to boot.
I charge very good rates

And supply my own plates (Pyrex of course)
And an ample selection of fruit.*

There's no business like show business, is there,
eh?

*For my Carmen Miranda impersonations.

6

A NIGHT TO REMEMBER

It was sprouts for breakfast. But then it was always sprouts for breakfast. I arranged those on my plate into a V formation to balance the eight o'clock news on the wireless set. Wars and rumours of wars, three sprouts to the left and two to the right. A mail train had been held up and many pounds stolen; I angled my fork towards the north to compensate for that. Sonic Energy Authority were still at number one. I might have to wear a blue shirt this morning.

Although I had played the tape many times I still did not fully understand its implications. I would have to find out more about this chaos theory business, find out how it really worked, *if* it really worked. It all seemed very unlikely, something tiny happening somewhere, causing something huge to happen somewhere else. That defied Newtonian Laws, didn't it? And the idea that I was doing the reverse, how could any of that really be? I had to know more. I knew just who I should ask about it.

And it wasn't my brother.

It was my Uncle Brian.

I would go round and see him after breakfast, play him the tape, ask his advice, decide what to do next.

Of course I did have *some* ideas of my own about *that*, based in part on a certain event I had recently witnessed in a local drinking house called The Flying Swan.

Although still only a lad of fifteen, I looked far older than I actually was, a gift that I still possess today, and I had been a regular drinker at The Swan for at least five years.

It was there that I met Jim Pooley and John Omally, who would later find fame in several world-wide best-selling novels and numerous Hollywood musicals.

I usually went to The Flying Swan on Thursday night, which was talent night.

The certain event occurred on one of these.

You really should have been there.

It began in this fashion.

'Anyone else? Come up and give us a song?'

Thursday night at The Flying Swan.

'Come on now, don't be shy.'

Talent night. Live music. Come and try.

Hector would get up and do 'Green Green Grass of Home' and 'I Did It My Way'.

John Omally would do a recitation, rumoured to be the same one every week, but notable for its infinitely variable and often controversial last line.

Pooley would sing 'Orange Claw Hammer' when pushed, with particular emphasis on the cherry phosphate line.

And then there was Small Dave.

Small Dave was the local postman and he was also a dwarf. And Small Dave hated Thursday nights.

He never missed one though, because, as he said, it was his right as a regular to use the facilities of the saloon bar on Thursday nights if he wanted to. Young aspiring talents were sometimes brought sobbing to their knees, vowing to abandon the bright lights for ever after falling prey to his manic stare and blistering comments.

Small Dave considered himself something of an authority on show business, having once unsuccessfully auditioned for *The Time Bandits*, and was always ready to voice his opinion, welcome or not.

For the most part, *not*.

Certainly, what he lacked in inches he made up for in belligerence and outspokenness. He was indeed what P. P. Penrose, author of the ever popular Lazlo Woodbine novels, would have referred to as 'a vindictive grudge-bearing wee bastard'.

I rather liked him though.

One night it became known to us that Small Dave had fallen under the spell of the aforementioned bright lights. How or why, no-one could say for sure. It was a bizarre transformation and by no means a welcome one.

'Why are you wearing a tricorn, Small Dave?' someone asked.

'Silver. Long John.' He raised one leg and rolled his eyes about.

'And the dancing pumps?'

'A bit of the old Fred and Gingers.' Small Dave did a kind of a skip.

'The white gloves? No, don't tell me.'

'Jolson.' Down on one knee, arms spread wide.

'And the pillow stuffed up the back of your shirt?'

'Laughton. The now legendary Charles in the role he made his own.' Small Dave began to lurch about the bar, muttering such phrases as 'the bells, the bells,' and 'father, I'm ugly,' and *Sanctuary! Sanctuary!* This accompanied by a beating upon the door of the Gents. A frightened patron within made his escape through the window.

'A bit of an all-rounder then?' said Omally, affecting what is known as 'The Po Face'.

Small Dave grinned and nodded.

Glances were passed about the bar, thoughts exchanged. Small Dave was a bad man to cross.

'You just wait until Thursday,' he said.

But none of us was keen.

'This is quite a change that's come over you,' said Jim Pooley. 'I mean, wishing to participate, rather than . . .' Jim chose his words carefully, 'er, offer constructive criticism. For which, I may say, you are greatly admired.'

'*Greatly*,' chorused the rest of us.

'Greatly,' said Jim. 'Greatly indeed.'

Talking to Small Dave could be a perilous affair as strangers to The Flying Swan sometimes discovered.

A sample conversation might go as follows.

116

Stranger to Small Dave:	Nice weather.
Small Dave:	For *what*?
Stranger:	For the time of year, I suppose.
Small Dave:	And what's wrong with the weather the rest of the year, do you *suppose*?
Stranger (becoming apprehensive):	Nothing. I suppose.
Small Dave:	You do a lot of *supposing*, don't you, mate?
Stranger (the now traditional):	But I—
Small Dave:	I think you'd better push off, don't you, mate?
Stranger (picking up hat):	I suppose so. (Makes for door)
Small Dave:	Bloody *suppose*! (Drinks stranger's beer)

'Care for another?' asks Neville, the part-time barman.

'Suppose so,' says Small Dave.

Small Dave smiled the sort of smile that helped make Chris Eubank so very popular. 'I feel I have it in me to make my name famous,' he plagiarized loosely.

Pooley bought Small Dave a drink and we all stood about trying to look enthusiastic, as the wee postman ran through his repertoire.

'You have to imagine it with the music,' he said.

'Music?' we said.

'String section,' he said.

Small Dave took to dancing, he waved a toy umbrella about and flicked beer over himself. 'Gene Kelly,' he said, breathlessly. '*Singing in the Rain.*'

We all nodded gravely. Next Thursday evening had suddenly lost its appeal.

Pooley put a gentle hand upon the great entertainer's small shoulder. 'Dave,' he said, 'might I have a minute of your time?'

'What is it, Pooley?'

Eyes were averted all about the bar. 'Rhubarb, rhubarb, rhubarb,' went the conversation.

'If you wouldn't mind stepping outside, I'd like to speak to you in private.'

Small Dave followed Pooley outside.

We drew deep breaths and listened. We heard muttered words and then Small Dave's voice.

'*NOT QUITE READY?*' it went.

Then there was a hideous crunching whack of a sound and shortly after Pooley limped into the saloon bar holding his right knee.

Neville drew him a large free Scotch. 'That was a very brave thing to do,' he told the damaged hero. 'But has it done the trick?'

Pooley shrugged and accepted his golden prize.

Omally watched the following swallowing, and wondered whether Jim had, perchance, planned the whole thing in the noble cause of a free drink.

He hadn't.

Having none of the sorceric powers of Nostradamus, the patrons of The Swan watched Thursday night approach as a dark and mysterious being wearing a cloak of danger.

'Although I doubt that the word "sorceric" actually exists,' said Jim Pooley, 'the point is well made and the night in question will soon be upon us.' He crossed himself and stroked his amulet.

'Don't do that in here,' said Neville, hoping for a cheap laugh.

Wednesday followed Tuesday, then Thursday came along.

It was raining. In fact it was pouring. There was thunder, there was lightning. It was not a fit night out for man nor beast. If ever an excuse were needed for spending the night in, catching up on the telly, then here was one falling in bucket loads. But Small Dave *was* a bad man to cross. So to not attend an event which promised, according to rumours in circulation, to be nothing short of a Busby Berkeley Musical Extravaganza, might incur a certain social stigma and ensure that the absentee never again saw the Queen's mail coming through his or her letter box.

'I don't know what we're all getting ourselves in such a state about,' said Omally. 'After all, this is just a local talent competition with a bottle of Scotch for a prize.' Then shaking his head at what he had said, he vanished away to the Gents muttering a strangely familiar recitation.

Neville was looking horribly pale. 'Suppose he doesn't win,' he murmured to Pooley.

'Who? Omally? He never wins.'

'Small Dave,' said Neville, and those with a mind

to crossed themselves. And Jim gave a squeeze to his amulet.

At seven-thirty, 'Laughing' Jack Vermont, the self-styled Eric Morley of the small pub talent competition circuit, stuck his toothy grin through the saloon bar door and doffed his sou'wester and cycling cape. Within no time at all, or an interminable duration if you're nervous, he had set up his crumbling PA system, seated himself at The Swan's elderly piano, blown into his microphone, said 'one-two, one-two', and distributed a sheath of entry forms.

'Just fill them in and pop them into the magic box,' he called, indicating the tin-foil-covered biscuit tin on the piano lid.

Pooley watched the hopefuls as they took to their form-filling. There were not quite so many as usual. And those that there were, were strangers.

'I've a very very bad feeling about this,' Jim told Omally.

'How *do* you spell recitation?' the other replied.

'If I were you I wouldn't even try.' Jim drew John's attention to his still bruised kneecap.

Omally bit his lip. 'Yes, you're right. No point in handing in a badly spelt form.' He crumpled up the paper and tossed it aside.

The minute hand on the Guinness clock moved towards eight-thirty. Laughing Jack sprung up from the piano, blew once more into the mic' and said, 'Well, well, well, it's Howdy Doody Time. And tonight it gives me enormous pleasure . . .' He paused and peered about the crowded bar wearing what he considered to be a wickedly mischievous grin. 'But then it always does.'

Jack considered himself to be a master of comic timing. Most of his audience considered him to be a prize prat, but a possible means by which to gain a free bottle of Scotch.

'All joking aside,' Jack continued, 'tonight we have a *big* line-up. And a mystery guest star. That's right. Oh yes.' He tapped his nose and winked a knowing eye.

'That man is a prize prat,' said Omally. 'And would you look at that jacket of his.'

That jacket was Laughing Jack's pride and joy.

He had explained it once to Omally.

'Some people', Jack named Liberace, 'have teeth.'

'Others,' he let slip Maurice Chevalier, 'straw boaters.'

'But I', he made an expansive gesture, 'have my Laughing Jack Jacket.'

Omally had drawn the laughing one's attention to the fact that Liberace was not a man known for his conservatism when it came to the matter of jackets.

'A mere sham,' said Laughing Jack, turning to reveal the sequinned wonder of it all and the words LARFING JOCK VERMOUTH embroidered in rhinestones by his inebriated mother.

'A mystery guest star,' said Jim. 'I'll bet we can all guess who that's going to be.'

Omally cast his eye over the night's contestants who were now milling around Jack, few in number as they were and looking nervous with it.

'I wonder where the fat boy who sings 'Danny Boy' has got to tonight,' wondered Pooley.

'And what of Old Pete and his performing dog?' asked Omally.

'And the rabbi ventriloquist who won twice last month.'

First up on the tiny stage was a grey-bearded Scot in antique highland dress, who juggled sprouts, whilst regaling the audience with humorous anecdotes concerning Custer's Last Stand.

The only one I can remember went as follows.

It seems that a sculptor was commissioned to create a suitable monument to the general's final encounter with the red Indians. And when this was unveiled before the crowds of attending dignitaries, casual onlookers and members of the press it was revealed to be a monolith of the *2001* persuasion.

On the top half of this were carved a number of fish with haloes above their heads; on the lower portion, Red Indians enthusiastically making love.

The fellow who had commissioned the sculpture took its creator to one side and demanded an explanation.

'It represents the last words Custer ever spoke,' explained the sculptor. 'These were, *Holy Mackerel, look at all those fucking Indians!*'

Well, it made me laugh at the time. But then *I* hadn't heard it before.

Few in the audience clapped and the two members of the local council, who claimed to be the twin reincarnation of Geronimo, walked out in disgust.

Next up was a poet called Johnny. I have never had a lot of truck with poetry myself, but on this occasion I must say that I was truly moved.

I trust that you will also be. For I include his poem here.

UNCLE FUGGER CLAUDE ROE
(AT HOME)

Taking a suck at his old cherry wood
(His Briars numbered three in the rack),
The crackling fire as it danced in the grate,
The frost-bitten dane at his back.

Old Uncle Claude Roe, please tell us a tale,
Asked Arthur and Willy and Moon.
Tell us conundrums and rose carborundems,
And shanties to sing out of tune.

Tell us of airmen who ride in the clouds
And pirates who see through one eye.
But Uncle Claude Roe did not want to know,
He sat there and played with his tie.

Tell us of Lizst and Marcova
And how Einstein learned counting off you.
But old Uncle Claude looked thoroughly
   bored,
He had fallen asleep in his shoe.

And while Fugger slept like a baby
The children went outside to play.

And his cherry wood Briar set the whole house
    on fire
And nobody cares to this day.

I wept real tears at the end of that one, I can tell
you. But disguised them as a touch of hay fever
for fear of looking like a big Jessie.

A very large woman called Jessie was next up on
the stage. She stripped down to her liberty bodice
and camiknickers to display an ample selection of
Magic Eye 3D tattoos. Again, I was favourably
impressed, particularly with the Red Indian display, but not so the rest of the audience, who
hadn't clapped once as yet.

I will pass on the one-legged seafarer who sang
about a recent whaling voyage.

'Sounds a little too much like "Orange Claw
Hammer",' Pooley observed.

I must also pass on Norman the sword swallower,
who did not receive a standing ovation.

'Any more?' asked Laughing Jack, but the biscuit
tin was empty and the crowd wore vacant stares.

And then it happened. And it happened in a big
way and one not easily forgotten. The saloon bar
door burst open.

There was a mighty drum roll and then in
marched the world famous Brentford Secondary
School drum majorettes.

They didn't march far due to the density of the
crowd, but they forced their way in bravely. Tassels
twirling, batons whirling, young knees high and
painted smiles.

In came the drummers, thrashing away upon snares and tom-toms, halting to march upon the spot.

Then part.

Then in *He* came.

A diminutive figure in a gold lamé mask and matching jump-suit. He cartwheeled into the bar, did an impossible triple flip over cowering heads and landed on his feet upon the stage.

Mouths fell open, breath became a thing to hold.

The tiny figure bowed and then began.

He knelt, threw wide his arms, sang Jolson.

And he *was* Jolson.

He impersonated Laughton.

And he *was* Laughton.

He lifted a leg and Robert Newton was reborn to play his finest role.

The superstitious crossed themselves.

Omally whispered, 'Witchcraft.'

It was a spectacle unlike any other that The Swan had witnessed during its long and colourful history. Strong men wept into their beer and mothers covered the eyes of their teenage daughters.

To gasps and then wild applause, the tiny gold-clad figure concluded with a fire-eating, unicycling, beer-bottle-juggling, reworking of 'Singing in the Rain' that would have had Sam Goldwyn reaching for his cheque-book.

Laughing Jack came forward with the bottle of Scotch.

'Sir,' was all he could manage to say.

As suddenly as he had appeared the tiny man

was gone, cartwheeling, somersaulting, spinning through the saloon bar door. The drummers and majorettes followed, along with the Scotsman who told the General Custer yarns, who had taken up his pipes to play 'Amazing Grace'.

And then The Swan fell into silence.

And might well still be doing it to this day if Neville hadn't managed to speak.

'Never in my long years as a barman,' he said in a quavery voice, 'have I seen *anything* to rival that.'

'It is truly the wonder of the age,' said Jim Pooley.

'There are more things in Heaven and Earth and so on,' agreed John Omally.

'It leaves my 'Green, Green, Grass of Home' with egg on its face,' said Hector, who hadn't had a mention for quite some time.

'I must say that I rather enjoyed that myself,' said Small Dave, who had been standing unnoticed by the ladies' toilet.

All heads present turned in his direction, all mouths that were not already open now opened. Wide.

'My appearance in this book has been nothing more than a cameo,' said Neville the part-time barman, 'but given the evidence of the previous chapters, *that* is the kind of cop-out ending I would have expected.'

'I'm sorry,' said Small Dave, 'but my bottle went and I just couldn't go through with it. Damn fine show though. Who *was* that masked man?'

SONG WITH NO WORDS

He'd been out on a busy Friday,
Singing that song with no words.
But the going had been as tough as could be,
He'd fallen twice and ricked his knee
And he was glad to get home at all,
Singing that song with no words.

He'd fallen in love with a check-out girl,
Singing that song with no words.
Though she had spots of a generous size
And something strange about one of her eyes,
He'd offered his heart and she'd punched out
  his lights,
Singing that song with no words.

He'd got in a fight with a hot dog man,
Singing that song with no words.
He'd only said to the fellow in fun
That he thought his hot dogs smelt like dun(g)
And just for that he'd been soundly thrashed,
Singing that song with no words.

He'd been for a boat trip round the bay,
Singing that song with no words.
He'd exposed himself to a party of Czechs
Who were making charts of sunken wrecks
So they'd tossed him off* and he'd gone down,†
Singing that song with no words.

*The boat of course.
†Still the boat.

He'd finally fallen foul of the law,
Singing that song with no words.
He'd shouted abuse at a copper on point
Said he was a fairy and smoking a joint

So he'd been dragged away to the Nick and given a right good truncheoning by several irate constables who'd had a proper day of it chasing up reports of some limping loon who'd been bothering check-out girls, getting into fights with hot dog men and flashing his willy at foreigners.

And enough was enough!

Singing that song with no words.

Amen.

7

UNCLE BRIAN EXPLAINS EVERYTHING (ALMOST)

I arrived at Uncle Brian's house a little after ten.

The walk took longer than usual as it looked like rain. I had to write the word 'sun' on the palm of my left hand to balance that out, then walk part of the way backwards for peace in our time. When Uncle Brian didn't answer the doorbell I had to arrange five pieces of chalk on his window-sill.

It's better to be safe than sorry.

He arrived home at sixteen minutes to eleven, which was also 10.44, which was all right by me as my shirt cuffs were unbuttoned. Uncle Brian looked somewhat the worse for wear. A police car dropped him off, well, flung him out. It didn't stop. Uncle Brian limped up the garden path singing that song with no words. It didn't look to me as if he wanted anything mentioned. So I didn't mention anything.

'What's red and stands in the corner?' I asked Uncle Brian.

He shrugged.

'A naughty bus,' I told him, as humour sometimes helps to break the ice at parties.

'You'd better come inside,' said Uncle Brian. 'You clearly need a cup of hot sweet tea.'

I couldn't have argued with that if I'd wanted to.

'Not your mates, though,' said Uncle Brian, half turning as he turned the key. 'They'll have to stay in the garden.'

'Sorry, lads,' I said, dismissing the Kalahari bushmen who so often accompanied me upon my ventures to the interior. 'Go and play in the park, I'll see you later!' But I never did.

Uncle Brian made tea and served it. Then he settled himself on the box ottoman in the front room and sucked life into his briar. 'So, son,' he said, through pale-blue plumes of smoke, 'what is it you would like to know?'

'Speak to me of chaos theory,' I suggested.

'What, all that stuff about a butterfly flapping its wings in the Indus Valley causing a sweet shop in Huddersfield to catch fire?'

'That's the kiddie,' I told him.

'Don't believe a word of it. It's a sophism.'

'And what is that?'

'An argument that is deliberately invalid, specious or misleading. As opposed to a paralogism, which is an argument that is *unintentionally* invalid, specious or misleading.'

'Why?' I asked.

'Conspiracy,' he said in a hushed whisper.

'Ah,' I said. 'One of those lads, eh?'

'Would you care for me to explain?'

'Very much indeed.'

'You're all right for tea?'

'Fine, thank you.'

'And biscuits?'

'You didn't offer me any biscuits.'

'Because I have no biscuits.'

'Please explain,' I said. 'About the conspiracy.'

'All right,' said he. 'In a nutshell, nothing measurable can ever be proven absolutely.'

'Why not?'

'Because, well, let me think of a simple example. Something obvious. Ah yes. Suppose you wanted to know the precise temperature of this room, what would you do?'

'Look at a thermometer?' I suggested.

'On the face of it that would seem to be the solution.'

'But it's not?'

'No,' said Uncle Brian. 'Because you could not be certain how accurate your thermometer was. In order to find this out you would require a more subtle and sensitive instrument to test the thermometer's accuracy.'

'Then you'd know for certain,' I said.

'No, you wouldn't.'

'Why not?'

'Because you would require an even more sensitive piece of apparatus to test the accuracy of the instrument that tested the accuracy of the thermometer.'

'You'd be certain then,' I said.

Uncle Brian shook his head. 'Not until you'd tested the accuracy of that instrument with another, and that one with yet another and so on and so forth until infinity. And you really can't measure infinity, can you?'

I shook my head. 'So what *is* the temperature of this room?'

'Ultimately nobody knows for certain.'

'Blimey,' said I.

'Ultimately,' said Uncle Brian, 'nobody knows anything.'

'*Some* people must know *some* things,' I said.

'Who?'

'Well, people at the top. The Prime Minister, for example.'

Uncle Brian laughed. 'Not a bit of it,' he said. 'The man at the top of the chain of command is constantly being misled by his subordinates. They lie to him all the time, to flatter him, to avoid punishment for their misdeeds, to further their own ends, to curry favour with him. The man at the top has the most distorted view of the world imaginable.'

'That sounds somewhat cynical,' I suggested.

'Never confuse cynicism with scepticism. The two are mutually incompatible. Let us return to the principle of the thermometer. Let us say that the prime minister is *not* being lied to, he is simply being advised by advisers.'

I shrugged. 'Let's say that.'

'So who advises the advisers and who advises the advisers of the advisers and who advises—'

'I get the picture.'

'It's like the police force. Someone has to police the police force and so someone has to police the police that police the police force.'

'But they don't, there's no such someones.'

'No, my point exactly. Therefore the Prime Minister receives incorrect advice from his advisers, because there is no ultimate adviser to pass the advice down the infinite chain of advisers to him.'

'So we all ultimately know nothing.'

'I would like to say, precisely. But ultimately I don't know.'

'But when I originally asked about chaos theory, you said that it was a sophism rather than a paralogism, that we were being *deliberately* mislead. If ultimately nothing is ultimately knowable, then how can you know *that*?'

'You're catching on,' said Uncle Brian. 'I know *that* because I'm the man who invented chaos theory in the first place.'

My thoughts turned to my non-uncle Felix, the Alpha Man theory and the Ministry of Serendipity. '*You* thought up chaos theory?' I said.

'It was a joke. I thought it up for a laugh and sent it off as a thesis under an assumed name to an American scientific journal. I didn't expect them to take it seriously. Although thinking about it, I should have. After all the art world took Picasso seriously and he was only pulling their legs.'

'So chaos theory is just a wind-up?'

'Not as good as the ones Einstein came up with, but not a bad one, I think you'll agree.'

'So none of it's true? In fact *nothing* is true.'

'There are no ultimate truths.'

'But what about *me*?'

'What *about* you?'

'I have this gift, or curse, or something. I

compensate, all the time, I'm the butterfly in reverse, big events reflect upon me, I balance them with small events. I'm doing it now.'

And I was. To compensate for the angle of the sunlight coming in through the front-room window I had placed my saucer over my tea cup and orientated my armchair three degrees towards the north.

'Ah,' said my uncle. 'Well, you're different. You're as different as it's possible to be.'

'But what does it *really* mean? Why do I do it?'

'We all do it to a certain extent. We all try to impose order upon chaos. In universal terms, order out of chaos may be nothing more than a passing fad, but in human terms, we all prefer order to its dire alternative. For the most part people don't take risks, risks incur the possibility of chaos. For the most part people are unambitious, ambition leads to all manner of chaos. For the most part people do not question what they are told, be it by their "superiors" at work, or by the media, or by politicians or by priests. To question orthodoxy is to risk chaos. The *status quo* exists to maintain order, those who create chaos within it are dealt with severely.'

'And who determines this *status quo*, who decides what order should be and what should be defined as chaos?'

'That, my boy, is the big conspiracy. Is it a *who*? Is it a *what*? Maybe it's God.'

'I don't think it's God,' I said.

'Nor do I. After all, God is the divine creator, but which divine creator created that divine creator, and who is the divine creator who created the creator of the divine creator and—'

'All right then, it's *not* God. But I'm as baffled now as when I came in here. Possibly more so. You still haven't explained to me why I do the things I do.'

'You do them because you're different. That's it. That's the reason. Each person is more than just the sum of their inherited genes. Each person is an individual, unique. Except possibly for identical twins. All right, so some people get a bad deal. They're the bottom feeders in the gene pool, but others, my oh my, others have enormous potential. Potential to change the *status quo*, possibly even to come up with a minor truth or two. Possibly you do the things you do because you are one of these. Or possibly you do it out of nothing more than a personal need to impose order upon chaos. You don't actually compensate, or reflect, or balance, you just think that you do.'

'So which is it?' I asked.

'Probably the latter,' said my uncle. 'You always were a bit of a weirdo.'

'You haven't actually been the slightest help to me at all,' I said, rising to take my leave.

'Only winding you up,' said Uncle Brian, gesturing me back into my chair. 'You *are* different and you have enormous potential. You could do great things, wonderful things. You *do* have a gift, but it is chaotic, it's all over the place. You're at least two degrees out on the orientation of the armchair and this *is* a Friday, so why aren't you wearing a red hat?'

'Thursday is a red hat, Friday is one black sock.'

'Just testing,' said Uncle Brian. 'You seem to know your stuff.'

'So you *do* understand why I do these things?'

'I have explained that we all do them to a certain extent in an attempt to impose order on chaos. You do them to a *major* extent and *actually* impose order on chaos. It's cause and effect. The cause filters down to you and you produce the effect. The buck stops with you. Without you to stop it, it might go on and on and we would have *chaos*.'

'You might have explained this earlier,' I suggested. 'To save time.'

'What, and had you miss out on all that esoteric wisdom?'

'Well, it was certainly esoteric, as I'm the only one here.'

'You have thought about trying to reverse the process, of course?'

'It has been mooted. I only became aware of this last night.'

'Well, it's not beyond the realms of possibility. We might experiment. If you were to put yourself totally in my hands, let me personally manage your career, as it were, there's no telling what might be achieved. The potential is there, have you considered just what you might do with it?'

I shrugged in a casual manner. 'Aid mankind, end wars, feed the hungry, that kind of thing.'

'Hm,' went my uncle, thoughtfully. He looked unconvinced.

'Is that not a happening thing?'

My uncle shrugged, even more casually than I

had. 'Perhaps a tad ambitious,' he said, 'something you could work up to.'

'My thoughts entirely.'

'Ah,' said my uncle. 'Go on.'

'Show business,' I said. 'I've always fancied show business.'

'Yes,' said my uncle. 'Show business, right.'

'That's why I *really* came to you.'

'*What?*' went my uncle. 'Not for all the esoteric wisdom?'

'Nah,' I said. 'I recognized you in The Flying Swan, you were the mystery contestant on talent night. I want you to teach me how to do those back flips.'

SWAN SONG

Out of his case came General Tom
Onto the knee of Dicky.
Out for his final curtain-call
Doing the dashed and tricky.

Drinking the pint without getting wet
While you're saying the alphabet.
All dolled up in your moth-balled schmutter.
Saying 'gread', and saying 'gutter'.

Getting the laugh with the well-timed pun.
Saying, 'Who's a son of a gun?'
Saying, 'Give us a song then, son,'
Saying, 'Isn't he the one?'
Saying, 'Everyone having fun?'

Then back in your box and put away,
Till the Christmas matinée.
What a bloody cock-eyed existence it is,
Being a bleeding dummy.

8

SHOW BUSINESS?

All right, I know what you're thinking. You're thinking, Show business? He wants to get into *show business*? What's all *that* about? He might have the power to do literally *anything*, but he wants to get into *show business*!

But you have to understand, I didn't know anything for certain. Not then. It had yet to be proven whether the process *could* be reversed. Whether I *could* actually make things happen.

And you learn things in show business: self-confidence, how to project, timing, stagecraft, how to put yourself across to people.

And it's a good bird-puller too.

And let's face it, this is *my* life story and I haven't got my leg over once yet. In fact, apart from my mum, who only got the briefest of mentions, there hasn't been a single woman in this at all.

And that's not healthy.

I was fifteen, my loins were stirring.

'This is Julie,' said my Uncle Brian. 'She'll show you the ropes.'

They were nice ropes. And between sessions,

when she taught me tap and ballet, Julie let me tie her up with them.

Things were looking up already.

Julie taught me escapology.

Things weren't really looking up.

'You haven't been in for a while,' said Fangio as I entered Fangio's Bar. 'Word is you've turned in your trenchcoat and taken to treading the boards.'

'Watch this trick,' I told him. 'Now you see it, now you don't.'

'I've seen that one before,' he replied. 'But all right, I give up, what did you do with the Statue of Liberty?'

'It's right here.'

'Very clever.'

And it was.

'Care for some chewing fat?'

'Don't mind if I do.'

Fangio passed me over the plate, then that look came into his eye once more. I'd seen that look before. I'd seen it the last time he'd given it to me.

'What *does* that look mean?' I asked him.

'It means there's been some guy in here asking for you,' he said, tipping me the wink.

'A promoter?' I tipped the wink back at him. Word was probably already out on the street regarding the talents I was daily acquiring. I could already juggle six sprouts, mime being trapped inside a phone booth and sing 'Orange Claw Hammer' with a spectacular emphasis on the cherry phosphate line.

'Looked more like a Fed to me,' said Fangio. 'He left his card.'

He passed me the item in question. It was a questionable item. I questioned it. 'Is this the item?' (I questioned.)

'You've lost me,' said Fangio.

I examined the card.

> Mr J Smith
> Department 23
> Ministry of Serendipity
> Mornington Crescent

It rang a bell somewhere.

'Is that last orders?' somebody asked.

'Not *that* bell,' said Fangio.

I further examined the card. This card felt bad. Well, not the card as such, but something about it. Something felt bad. Something smelt bad. Smelt very bad. Smelt very very bad. Smelt—

'Get a grip,' said Fangio. 'It's only a piece of card.'

'Something about this smells bad,' I told him.

'I dropped it in the slops pail. Give me a break.'

'You know,' I told Fangio, 'although I'm dead keen on show business, what with it being a potential fanny-magnet and everything, I like being a private detective best. You get to stand about in bars and talk a load of old toot. That's what *I* call having a good time.'*

'You might one day have to solve a case.'

---

*And trust me, friends, my opinion has never altered on this.

'Yeah, that could be hairy.'

'A hairy case? Surely that would be a sporran.'

The bar went silent. I looked up at the clock. It was twenty to nine. Have you ever noticed that when the conversation suddenly stops, it's always either twenty to something or twenty past something?

No?

Well, it must be me then.

'The Ministry of Serendipity,' I said. 'I wonder what that's all about.'

'Possibly some weird parapsychological unit,' said Fangio, tipping me yet another wink. 'And Department 23. 23 is an illuminati number.'

'In the TV series, Tony Hancock lived at number 23 Railway Cuttings,' I said (knowledgeably).

'And Mornington Crescent *is* a railway station,' said Fangio (perceptively).

'Ooooooooooo-weeeeeee-oooooooo,' chorused the patrons about the bar (tunelessly).

'So did this J. Smith guy say anything?' I asked (enquiringly).

'He said he wanted to book you for the Christmas staff party,' said Fangio (cop-out-endingly).

'We'll take that booking,' said my Uncle Brian, who had entered the bar (surreptitiously). 'And why all the adjectives in brackets?'

'It's a private eye thing,' I told him (genre-istically).

'Yes, well, we have to go. You're on in eighteen minutes.'

'Got a gig?' asked Fangio.

'Why do you think I'm wearing the gold lamé catsuit?'

Fangio made the face that says, Listen, just because I've never seen you with a girlfriend, doesn't mean to say I think you're a pou—

'How dare you!' I said, striking that face with my fist.

'My face never said that,' complained the fat boy from the floor.

But I didn't hear him, because Uncle Brian and I were off to the gig.

We didn't take the free bus. We took the limo. Well, you have to, first impressions are everything. Come on like a superstar and they'll treat you like a superstar. After all, as Uncle Brian had explained, nobody really knows anything. So they'll believe what they think they see.

Small Dave drove the limo. As he was too short to see over the dashboard, Uncle Brian gave directions. I sat in the back chewing my fingernails and repeating the cherry phosphate line over and over to myself with ever-increasing spectacular emphasis. This was to be *my* night. My *big* night. I wasn't going to blow it.

As the limo weaved to and fro across the road, passing through red lights and scattering pedestrians before it, I felt good inside, nervous certainly, but good. I *would* achieve great things. I *would* become a superstar. I *would* pull birds. *Lots* of birds. Lots and lots of birds. I wouldn't fail. I *couldn't* fail.

*　　*　　*

Of course, if I'd known then how things would turn out, I wouldn't have gone. I'd have stayed in the bar and talked toot.

But I *didn't* know.

I didn't know what horrors lay in store.

And.

And, well.

And, well, listen. I can't talk about this here. It demands a chapter to itself. Quite a long chapter. But a significant one. It's the next one. I can't talk any more now. I have to take another tablet and get some sleep.

But I do want to say just this, IT WASN'T *MY* FAULT.

DONER KEBABS

Hoorah for the doner kebabs
Loved by the drivers of cabs
Loved by the porters
And post office sorters
And profs in their underground labs

All hail to the doner keboobs
Admired by the men on the tubes
Food for the lift men
And cut-price-glass-gift men
The tailors and cutters of cubes

God bless the doner kebobs
Good for the gourmets and snobs
Tipsters on courses
And owners of horses
And others in dubious jobs

Shout 'Aye' for the doner kibibs
Foodstuff for me and his nibs
Toast of the Tommies
The Aussies and Pommies
The Indians, Dutch and the Gibs

Sing 'Ah' for the doner kebubs
Eaten by sailors in subs
Yearned for by waiters
Who fight alligators
And scout troops and Brownies and Cubs

They're a *very* popular dish.

9

SECRETS SECRETS SECRETS

My Uncle Brian munched upon a doner kebab and spoke to me through the lettuce. 'The journey will take precisely five minutes. Do you want to compensate for that at all? Put a bead up your nose, or stick your hat on back to front?'

I made the face that asks, Are you taking the piss?

'Not at all.' My uncle flapped his hands and spat tomato over my body stocking. 'Just trying to be helpful.'

'Well, don't be. I can manage fine. I'm learning to keep it under control now.'

'How?' he asked, and I dodged an airborne gherkin.

'If I concentrate my thoughts, really hard, on, say, a piece of poetry. If I recite that poem again and again in my head. Or if I listen very carefully to what someone is saying, really think about it, not do as most people do, just amble through a conversation, trotting out the rehearsed lines and not really listening to what points the other person is trying to make, I can stop compensating. I think it's OK.'

My uncle went, 'Hm,' which involved some tomato. Then he scrunched up his remaining kebab, wiped his hands and face on the paper and tossed the greasy item out of the window.

'Good,' he said. 'Well, we now have four minutes, thirty seconds remaining, so concentrate your thoughts on this. I'm going to tell you a little story.'

'Why?' I enquired.

'To pass the time and so you don't have to do any compensating, fair enough?'

'Fair enough.'

'All right.' Uncle Brian settled himself down into the rich tan leather of the limo's celebrity seating, composed his fingers in his lap, pursed his lips and handbagged his eyebrows. 'This is the tale of a secret,' he said, 'and how this particular secret keeps the village where I grew up very happy indeed. There's a moral in the story, of course.'

'This story isn't a parable, by any chance, is it?'

'Certainly not!'

'Go on then.'

'Right.' Uncle Brian took a deep breath, stared wistfully out of the window, let out a little sigh and then began to speak. 'There was once a teenage girl who loved a teenage boy in our village. But this girl was very shy and she didn't know how to approach the boy. And also this girl wanted to have sex with this boy, but she was a virgin and she had heard terrible tales of just how bad teenage boys are at having sex. Teenage boys generally being drunk by the time they have it.'

I sighed a little wistfully myself.

147

'Well, the shy girl didn't know what to do for the best and then she remembered the village wise woman. This venerable lady was old and blind and very wise and would answer any question asked of her. The teenage boys used to disguise their voices and ask her rude questions. And she answered them all. So the shy girl went to the old blind wise woman and told her of her problem (in a disguised voice, of course).

'The old blind wise woman smiled and said, "Many young women throughout the years have come to me with this problem and I have a secret tonic prepared for just this purpose. What you do is to pour some of this tonic into the young man's tea. He will fall asleep, but while asleep he will still be able to respond sexually. And he will awaken later remembering nothing. Thus you can enjoy completely uninhibited sex with the young man, do anything you please."

'The young woman grasped the possibilities of this immediately. With such a tonic she could have sex with any man she chose. *Any* man.'

'I thought she was just in love with the one boy,' I said.

'*She was*. I was just stressing the possibilities.'

'Fair enough, continue then.'

'All right. So the shy young girl receives a small green bottle of the secret tonic from the wise woman. Then the wise woman asks, "Young woman, are you a virgin?" and the young woman (still in the disguised voice) admits that she is. "Then it would be best if you allow me to deflower you," says the old woman.'

'*What?*' I said.

'Don't interrupt. The old blind wise woman explains that the shy young girl will have a great deal more fun with the young man if she's already got her virginity out of the way. And explains that she has a special appliance for doing this. And, in order not to be too graphic about this, the young woman bends over an armchair and the deed is gently but efficiently done. And moving swiftly along—'

'I should think so too,' I said.

'Moving swiftly along, the young woman telephones the young man and gets him round to her house on some bogus pretence or another while her parents are out. She slips some of the secret tonic into his tea. He begins to stumble about, she leads him to the bedroom. He passes out. She strips him and then she makes love to him. And she really has a great time, lives out all her fantasies. Afterwards, when he's beginning to stir, she dresses him again. And he wakes up and says, "What happened?" and she says, "You just fell asleep," and he says, "OK," and goes home.'

'And is that the end of the story?'

'Of course it isn't. The young girl confides to her best friend what happened. So the best friend goes to see the wise woman. And word passes amongst the other teenage girls and in no time at all, they're all visiting the old wise woman on a regular basis. And I have to tell you that the village where I was brought up, was *one happy village*.'

I shook my head. 'That is disgusting story,' I

said. 'I mean, those young women were just using the men as sexual playthings.'

'Isn't that what young men use young women for all the time?'

'No. I mean, well, perhaps yes, perhaps some of them.'

'And don't you think that if such a secret tonic existed that could be used on women, men would buy it?'

'Well,' I said, 'I think they possibly might.'

'Damn right they would.'

'And so that's the secret which keeps the village where you were brought up so happy?'

'Er, actually no,' said Uncle Brian.

'No?'

'No. You see the old blind village wise woman was not really old or blind at all. In fact, she wasn't really a woman. She was a man dressed up.'

'A man dressed up?'

'And that certain appliance used for the de-flowering was really his—'

'Stop!' I said. 'And what about the secret tonic?'

'No such tonic, the young men only pretended to fall asleep.'

'But what about them being sexually aroused, they couldn't *pretend* that.'

My Uncle Brian gave me the look that says, Well, they wouldn't really have to pretend, would they? What with them having a naked and totally uninhibited young woman on top of them, and everything.

'Outrageous!' I cried. And quite loudly I cried it too.

'Outrageous? Why?'

'Because the young men were using the young women as sexual playthings.'

'But surely it was the other way around. You just said it was.'

'Yes, but I didn't know the young men were only pretending to be asleep.'

'So what's the difference? The young women were using the young men and the young men were using the young women, both parties secure in the knowledge that the other didn't know. Perfect bliss all round, I'd say.'

I shook my head. 'Treachery and deception all round, *I'd* say.'

My Uncle Brian shrugged. 'That's life in a nutshell,' he said.

'And you were one of these young men, I suppose.'

'Oh no,' said my Uncle Brian, 'not me.'

'A good thing too.'

'I played the part of the wise woman. Ah look, we're here.'

And we were.

'Fangio's Bar,' I said. 'But we just left there.'

'Yes, but this time we're arriving in a limo.'

'Ah, I see.' I didn't.

'Now,' said my uncle, opening a laptop computer on his laptop, 'I've prepared your jokes. I'll give you a print-out.'

'Jokes? But I thought I was going to do a song and dance act.'

'We did discuss the jokes, didn't we?'

I nodded. We had discussed the jokes. But I

hadn't been keen. Uncle Brian had come up with what he considered to be a most original stand-up routine. I was to adopt the stage name *Carlos the Chaos Cockroach*. The routine was based, of course, on our friend the mythical mystical butterfly that flaps its wings in the Congo basin and causes a run on cut-price baked beans at Budgens in Birmingham. I would go on stage, briefly explain my persona, then launch into the gags. These would be bogus versions of the butterfly theory. I'll give you a brief example. I produce two ring-pulls and a feather from my top pocket and ask, 'What do you get if you push a feather through two ring-pulls? Answer, sandstorms in the Sahara.'

Not very funny, eh? In fact, not funny at all. In fact, a complete waste of time. But Uncle Brian had been going on and on about it being a blinder of an act and how he had worked out some really great gags on his laptop and got all the props together and everything.

'I want to do the song and dance act,' I told him. 'Especially I want to sing "Orange Claw Hammer". I've got the cherry phosphate line off just so.'

'Trust me,' said the uncle. 'You've six gigs to play tonight. If the gags don't work at the first one, then you can sing and dance your way through the rest of the evening.'

'Hang about,' I said, as one would. '*Six* gigs? Since when is it *six* gigs?'

'There's been a lot of enthusiasm. I explained about your act and the owners of the venues were dead keen.'

I shook my head. 'Ludicrous,' I said.

'Well, it can't hurt to give it a try, can it? Remember how *Sony* originally hated the idea of the *walkman*? Couldn't see how you could market a tape recorder that didn't record? Look how successful that became.'

'I was thinking more about the cigarette harness,' I said.

'Blinder of an invention.' Uncle Brian slotted a Woodbine into the one he always wore. 'Come on, give it a go.'

He pressed a button on his laptop and paper came spilling out of it. 'Here's your props,' he said, handing me a briefcase. 'Now do it, just as we practised. The crowd will love you. Trust me, I know these things.'

'And if they don't love me at the first gig—'

'You can song and dance it the rest of the evening.'

'It's a deal.' I shook my uncle's hand and he shook mine. It was a reciprocal thing.

A crowd had gathered about the limo. Crowds always gather about limos. Especially those with blacked-out windows. You always feel sure that whoever's inside a limo with blacked-out windows must be making the most of it and having sex. Oh, come on, you *do*, don't you?

The crowd peered into the limo as my uncle and I left it and those of a homophobic nature tut-tutted and shook their heads, which goes to prove something.

A number of policemen were already on the scene. These held back the crowd to either side, allowing us an unhampered stroll to Fangio's door. Have you ever noticed how there's never a policeman around when you need one, but always hundreds standing about near the pitch at F.A. Cup matches or celebrity functions? What is that all about, eh?

We entered Fangio's Bar to great applause and, as I may have mentioned before, I *do* like a warm hand on my entrance.

Fangio came up and shook me warmly by the hand. 'I've been looking forward to meeting you, Mr Carlos,' he said.

'But, Fange, it's me. I only left here five minutes ago.'

'Such a comic.' Fangio placed his hands upon his ample belly and rocked with laughter. I shook my head and sighed.

'Go on,' said Uncle Brian. 'Go up to the stage. Don't worry about me, I'll just sit here and tinker with my laptop.'

'Is that one of the new ones with digital TV?' asked Fangio the fat boy.

My uncle nodded. 'Instant access to over one hundred channels. I can call up the stocks and shares, money markets around the world, investment indexes, my own personal accounts, the lot.'

'Pornography?' asked Fangio. 'What about pornography?'

'That's what I just said.'*

'I'll just get on with it, then, shall I?' I asked.

*Satire.

'Go ahead,' said my uncle. 'Knock 'em dead.'

'Hm.'

There was a fair old crowd in, I can tell you, more than you'd usually expect for a Thursday night. But then this *was* Friday. The crowd parted to allow me the stage. I went up the step and I was pretty damn nervous.

I peered into the bright lights, took stock of the crowded bar: Fangio at the back, clapping his hands, my uncle tinkering with his laptop. I took a little bow, the crowd cheered wildly.

I explained about my persona as *Carlos the Chaos Cockroach*. The crowd cheered wildly.

I set down the briefcase and opened it up. The crowd cheered wildly.

I checked my print-out, pulled a pair of red shoe laces and a potato from the briefcase and displayed these. The crowd cheered wildly.

I launched into the first gag. 'What do you get', I asked, tying the shoelaces around the potato, 'if you do *this*?'

Hushed expectancy from the crowd.

'A tree falling silently in the New Forest, because there's no-one there to hear it.'

A moment of silence and then—

The crowd cheered wildly.

I shook my head in wonder. I knew I had charisma. But I'd never known before just *how much* I had. I peered in the direction of my uncle. He was still tinkering with his laptop and he was shaking his head. Ah well, you can't please all of the people all of the time.

155

I returned to the props in the briefcase. The next gag was, What do you get if you stick a cocktail stick in a stale British Rail cheese sandwich? The answer: heavy rainfall in Yorkshire.

The crowd cheered wildly.

Uncle shook his head *again*.

I shrugged, took a bow and went through the last two gags on the print-out; they weren't funny either.

But the crowd cheered wildly.

A woman in a straw hat bobbed up and down. A fat boy in a Motorhead T-shirt made peace signs and a teenage girl in a village peasant costume waved a small green bottle in my direction.

I took several bows, before being carried shoulder-high from the stage.

'What do you reckon, Uncle Brian?' I asked.

Uncle Brian made a so-so gesture and closed his laptop. 'OK, but you can do better.'

'But they loved me.'

'They can love you more.'

'You're right,' I said. 'I'll do the song and dance act.'

'No,' my uncle placed a hand upon my wrist. 'Always leave them wanting more. On to the next gig. I'll give you a print-out of the new gags.'

'But this crowd loved the ones I told.'

'Never tell the same gag twice.'

'Eh?'

We left in the limo and drove on to the next gig. I sang 'Orange Claw Hammer' to my uncle on the way. I think he was secretly impressed by the cherry phosphate line.

The next gig was at the Sir John Doveston Memorial Gym. The resident manager/caretaker/trainer, Mr Ernie Potts, welcomed us in. I took to the stage to wild applause and ran through the latest print-out's worth of gags, demonstrating with further props supplied by my uncle.

The gig went down an absolute storm.

But once again my uncle sat there, shaking his head and pushing the keys of his laptop.

I was shoulder-carried from the stage to very wild applause indeed.

A woman in a straw hat bobbed up and down. A fat boy in a Motorhead T-shirt made peace signs and a teenage girl in a village peasant costume kept pointing to a small green bottle and winking at me.

Back to the limo and on to the next gig.

'I'd like you to try these gags next,' said my uncle, handing me a further print-out.

'Why don't *you* laugh?' I asked him. 'Everybody else does.'

My uncle made the face that says, *I* wrote the gags. And I said no more.

The third gig was at The Flying Swan. In the upstairs room. The one usually reserved for wedding receptions or congresses of the West London Wandering Bishops.

The crowd just *loved* me.

A woman in a straw hat loved me. A young man in a Motorhead T-shirt loved me. A teenage girl waving two small green bottles loved me. Everybody loved me.

157

Everybody, that is, except Uncle Brian. Well maybe he did love me, but he just sat at his laptop unsmiling.

I was quite knackered by the sixth gig. And somewhat disorientated. I'd heard about rock stars who wake up in Holiday Inns and don't even know which city they're in, but I always put that down to the drugs. But I was certainly disorientated and *I* wasn't on any drugs.

It was the crowd. The crowd looked just the same. Same people. Perhaps that's what happens to you when you become famous, the crowd just looks the same wherever you are. Although I suppose it must look different in Japan.

But the sixth gig was notable for one thing.

My uncle.

It was just after I'd told the second gag: What do you get if you stick this safety pin into this contraceptive? Answer: A record crop of wheat in Canada, that he began to laugh. He drummed his fists on his laptop and began to go 'Yes!' very loudly.

As I finished my routine he too was cheering wildly and even joined in with the shoulder-high carrying from the stage. 'You're a star,' he kept saying. 'A *real* star.'

Outside, by the limo, I signed autographs for a woman in a straw hat and a fat boy in a Motorhead T-shirt. I'd have happily signed one for the village girl with the little green bottles but she wasn't around. Eventually the crowd drifted off towards a minibus and I was left all alone to ponder.

I was clearly on the road to stardom. What did

I think about *that*? Well, it felt pretty good. I'd have hoped for a groupie or two. But it was early days yet and I *had* been a raging success. I felt good.

I felt *really* good.

And I also felt that I needed to take a pee.

I wandered back to the venue and spotted a large box van owned by my brother. I thought I'd piddle on the back wheel, I didn't want to piddle on the limo. I quietly unzipped and stood awaiting the blessed relief. Then I heard whispered voices coming from within. I zipped up and put my ear against the van's rear door, not wishing to be nosy, but *just interested*.

'Absolute success,' came the voice of my Uncle Brian. 'The lad is worth his weight in gold.'

I smiled inwardly, and probably outwardly also.

'The sky's the limit,' came the voice of my brother. 'The world is our oyster.'

Our oyster? I ceased both smiles.

'As long as he never finds out what we're really up to,' said my uncle. 'As long as your rented crowd keeps cheering wildly and he thinks they love him.'

I scowled doubly. What was all *this*?

'Young Dog's Breath is easily led,' said my brother. 'He won't catch on that the real reason you had him doing all those things with bits of string and matchsticks and stuff was to cause fluctuations on the stock market and steer millions of pounds into your bank account. He doesn't know that *he is* the mythical mystical butterfly and

159

can make huge things happen by making tiny little actions.'

I began to grate my teeth.

'I still don't have the tiny actions down to an absolute science,' said my Uncle Brian. 'It's a bit hit and miss. Some of the things he did at the first few gigs have caused a few disasters around the world.'

'But nothing *we* give a monkey's about.'

'No,' said Uncle Brian. 'What are a few earthquakes and typhoons to us? We have the goose who can lay the golden egg.'

'The dog with the golden breath, more like.' And my brother laughed. And my uncle laughed with him.

> But *I* wasn't laughing.
> *A* few earthquakes and typhoons?
> *S* o I had been had! In order
> *T* o make money for my uncle
> *A* nd my brother. Maybe
> *R* uined the lives of thousands,
> *D* estroyed villages
> *S* o they could grow rich!

If you don't know the meaning of the word *acrostic*, you can look it up. I'm sure you know the meaning of the word BASTARDS and also REVENGE.

I went and pissed all over the limo.

NEWTS THAT I HAD WHEN A LAD

Blue-fingered mornings and bright church bazaars
Notebooks for logging the numbers of cars
Girls in their gymslips
Mouthfuls of gum
Ink on my shirtcuff
Ink on my thumb
Checking the stamps when the weather was bad
Remembering newts that I had when a lad.

Brand-new protractors from Kays in The Mall
Afternoon fag-cards in cloakroom with pal
Slipperbags dangling
Down from a string
Jamboree bags
That you felt for the ring
All of those magical times that we had
Remembering newts that I had when a lad.

Cream-coloured corridors
Green-coloured classroom doors
Chalk-squeaks and dusters
Beanos and Busters
Conkers and marbles and firestones and fights
Remembering newts that escaped in the nights.

Aaaaaah . . .

10

LITANY

When I was young and foolish and all, I had a friend called Ian. He was my best friend and he lived three doors along, in the very last house on the terrace. The one that backed on to the bit of waste ground where Martin Beacon got bitten by the dog.

Ian's father was a Russian spy. There were a lot of Russian spies about in those days, one in every street, as far as I can recall. They all had short-wave radios and they all used to 'report in' at precisely the same time each week: 6.45 Friday evenings.

My mum used to go haywire because the short-wave transmissions interfered with our wireless set and she couldn't hear *The Archers* properly. She used to bang on the kitchen wall with the business end of the sprout-masher, but Ian's dad never took any notice.

I suppose because he lived three doors along.

As my father was a carpenter we had a shed in our back garden. Not a very big one, because our garden wasn't very big. But a tall one. If you can imagine a two-storey sentry box. Then imagine it.

Our shed was not at all like that. Our shed was more like an obelisk.

Ian and I used to sit in that shed for hours at a time, playing with our pet newts, or simply ourselves.

I vividly remember one particular afternoon, early May it might have been, or another month entirely. My brother had confided a secret to me and I was eager to pass it on to Ian.

'And so,' I concluded, 'garden gnomes are, in fact, small dwarves who have been turned to stone by the glance of Medusa.'

Ian whistled through the gap in his front teeth. 'Is Medusa aquatic?' he enquired.

'Aquatic? I'm not certain. Why?'

'Well, many of the garden gnomes, the petrified dwarves as it were, are frozen in the act of fishing. Perhaps Medusa comes up out of the water.'

I nodded thoughtfully. 'I wonder where it all goes on.'

'Scandinavia,' said Ian with authority. 'We have a gnome in our garden, it has Scandinavia carved on its bottom.'

'What, on its *arse*?'

'No, underneath, at the bottom, on its base.'

'Oh.'

'But there're an awful lot of stone gnomes, and I've never ever seen a dwarf as small, walking about.'

'Perhaps they're all captives.'

'What?'

'Bred in captivity in Scandinavia. Last remnants of an ancient race. Like the fairy-folk. At a certain time each year a number of them are taken down to this lake and asked to pose for photographs. The photographer ducks his head under the black cloth and hides his face. Says "Say cheese," everyone smiles, Medusa comes up out of the lake and *wallop*, they're all turned to stone.'

'What a nightmare scenario,' said Ian. 'But as feasible an explanation as there's likely to be.'

We both sat in silence awhile and played with our newts.

'A strange thing happened in our back garden the other day,' said Ian. 'My father has sworn me to secrecy over it.'

'Tell us what it is then.'

'All right. My father was doing a bit of digging in the back garden and he came upon this brick-work. Like a wall but lying on its side, if you know what I mean.'

I nodded. 'A fallen-over wall but under the ground.'

'That's it. So my father says it's probably some old foundations of something, so he fetches his sledgehammer and starts to wallop at it. And every time he hits the brickwork there's this dull echoing sound like it's hollow underneath. Well, my father bashes away at it until he knocks a hole through. And do you know what?'

'What?'

'There's light.'

'Light?'

'Light, coming up through the hole. So we kneel down and look in and you'll never believe what we saw.'

'What did you see?'

'Well, it's like looking down into this huge cathedral, really huge, like you're looking through a hole in the dome. And there's all these sort of Gothic brick pillars that go down and down and little staircases in the distance below.'

I whistled through the gap in *my* front teeth.

'So my dad knocks a really big hole, big enough to climb through and he's talking about getting this rope and shinning down inside when this bloke comes.'

'What bloke?'

'He came along the alley and we could hear him coming, his boots made this metal clicking. He had a monk's habit on with the hood pulled low over his face and the big clicking boots and he was very tall and thin. And he came clicking up the alley, through our garden gate, pushed my father aside, climbed into the hole and was gone.'

'Blimey,' I said. 'This is incredible. Can we go round to your garden so I can have a look?'

'No,' said Ian. 'We can't do that.'

'Oh go on. I'll only take a little look and I won't tell anyone.'

Ian shook his head. 'My dad filled the hole in. He bought bricks and cement and he filled it in.'

'Why?'

'He said it was dangerous and that children might fall down it. Come on, I'll show you.'

Ian led me down the alley to his back gate. His mum wasn't around, so we crept into his garden. There were new bricks laid outside the back door.

Well, not so much bricks, more paving stones. A sort of patio, in fact.

'Put your ear there,' said Ian, pointing.

I knelt down and pressed my ear to one of the paving stones. Ian took the yard broom and banged the handle down upon the stone. There was a dull, echoey, hollow sound each time he did so.

'Blimey,' I said, straightening up.

'When I'm eighteen,' said Ian, 'I will inherit this house and when I do I am going to get a pneumatic drill and drill down to that place.'

'And go down on a rope?'

'Yes.'

'And I'll come with you. We'll go together.'

And we shook hands on the deal.

But we never went. As the years passed by we forgot all about it. And when Ian was eighteen he did *not* inherit his father's house. It was a council house, same as ours. I include the story here because it is true. Well, it's true that Ian told me and I *did* hear the echoey hollow sounds.

Oh yes and I include it because of Litany.

Let me tell you all about Litany.

I suppose I must have got drunk. Very drunk, which is why I don't remember all the details. Prior to that everything is as clear as an author's conscience.

I stole the rented limo, and with it my uncle's laptop computer and I returned to Fangio's Bar. The rented crowd was there, paid off and spending freely. Everyone went very quiet when I walked in.

I addressed them, thusly: 'I know what you were up to and you are a pack of BASTARDS.'

The crowd cheered wildly.

'No,' I said. 'You can stop all that. *I mean it!* You're a pack of BASTARDS.'

More wild cheering and someone shouted, 'Three cheers for *Carlos the Chaos Cockroach*.' I punched that someone.

A woman in a straw hat.

She went down and her companions ceased to cheer. They drank up and left. I placed the uncle's laptop on the bar and my bum upon a bar stool. 'Set 'em up, fat boy,' I told the fat boy. 'The drinks are on me.'

Fangio peered over the counter at the unconscious woman.

'What's the dame having?' he asked.

'Give her an Angel's Slingback.' I named the most popular cocktail of the day.

'Did someone say *slingback*?' A drunk at the end of the counter raised his head. His name was Lightweight Jimmy Netley, a footwear fetishist from the very first chapter.

'Go back to sleep,' Fange told him. 'I'll wake you up if anything interesting happens.'

I accepted my bottle of Bud, made payment in kind (whatever *that* means), flipped open the uncle's laptop and perused the keyboard.

'What you got there then?' asked Fangio. 'Toy typewriter, is it?'

'Portable computer.'

Fangio whistled through the gap between his eyebrows. 'What will they think of next?'

'Fuel cells. They'll make the internal combustion engine redundant by the turn of the century.'

Fangio fingered his jowls. 'Your brother told you that, I suppose.'

'No, I just know it.' And I did.

I cranked up the laptop and tapped away at the keyboard. I had to know how my uncle had cracked the code. If, as it appeared, I really did possess the power to effect great changes in the world, by the exercise of small and seemingly arbitrary actions such as rubbing two biros together, how had he discovered the formula?

The computer had printed out the 'gags', told me what I had to do (although not of course for the genuine reasons). So was there some program in the computer designed specifically toward this end? And if so, who had thought it up?'

'That guy was in again asking for you,' said Fangio.

'What guy?'

'Guy from the Ministry of Serendipity. Very nervous he seemed, very edgy.'

'You genius,' I told the fat boy. 'It's some secret government research program, that's what it is.'

'What is?'

'In this computer. Either my Uncle Brian nicked it or he's working for the Government.'

'He's not working for the Government,' said Fangio. 'Your Uncle Brian's a Russian spy. And I should know, I live next door to him. His short-

168

wave radio transmissions always bugger up *The Archers* on a Friday night.'

'Then he nicked it.' I tapped some more upon the keyboard. The word PASSWORD flashed up on the screen and a little clock that began to tick down from one minute to zero. I switched off the computer. 'Do you know any hackers?' I asked the fat boy.

'Jimmy there has a smoker's cough, you want I should wake him up?'

I made a face that says, That's a really crap joke.

Fangio made the one that says, I know.

I ordered another bottle of Bud.

And then I saw Litany entering the bar.

And I knew it was fate.

You all know Litany. By sight. You've all seen her, although you've never known her name. Until now. Litany is the beautiful blond girl in the bikini top, who is always on some fellow's shoulders down near the front at an outdoor rock concert. Yes, you see, you *have* seen her. If you've got any big stadium concerts on video, check them out. She's in all of them, and it's always her.

Recently she appeared in the audience during the Rolling Stones Voodoo Lounge tour gig at Wembley. I can personally vouch for that, because she was on *my* shoulders at the time.* But if you get a copy of the Woodstock video, she's there too, looking exactly the same.

Rumours abound, of course. The most popular being that she is some blond female version of the

---

*This is a lie, as will later be seen.

Wandering Jew. That she first appeared, no doubt cheering wildly, upon the shoulders of a Roman centurion, at the crucifixion of Christ. And that she was doomed to an eternity of such shoulder-sitting until Jesus comes again and she is finally allowed to get down and go to the toilet.

Personally I don't believe that particular rumour, plausible though it is.

But there she was, in the flesh. Her long blond hair hung over her perfect shoulders and her patterned-bikini-top-contoured breasts, exquisite enough to make a sleeper sigh.

I sighed for them and so did Fangio.

Litany stepped carefully over the woman in the straw hat, walked up to the bar and smiled at the fat boy. 'Can I use your toilet?' she asked.

Fangio dropped to his knees. 'The Second Coming,' he cried. 'We're all doomed.'

'It's in the back,' I told the beautiful blonde. 'Ignore the barman, he's from Penge.'

'Ah, I see.' And Litany went off towards the toilet. As she passed the end of the bar, Lightweight Jimmy Netley sighed in his sleep.

'Get up,' I told Fangio. 'It's not really the Second Coming.'

'Oh good.' Fangio got to his feet, rooted in the plate and thrust a piece of chewing fat into his mouth.

'I wonder what her name is,' I wondered.

'It's Litany.'

'How do you know *that*?'

'Because she's my daughter.'

'Then you—?'

170

'Yes.'

'And you didn't really—?'

'No.'

'It was all a—?'

'You got it.'

We laughed together. Such a crazy guy, that Fangio. What a shame about the way he met his end.

'Met my end?' asked the fat boy. 'What is this?'

'It's later, don't worry about it now.'

'Phew,' said Fangio. 'You had me going there.'

We both laughed again, though I can't remember why.

Litany returned from the toilet and settled herself on the bar stool next to mine. I offered her a drink and she took my bottle of Bud.

'I enjoyed your act,' she said.

'My act?' I did my best to remain calm in the presence of this goddess. 'I didn't see you in the audience.'

'The guy who's shoulders I usually sit on has a cold. I just stood at the back.'

'You were part of the rented crowd?'

'Strictly freelance. I go where the spirit takes me. What's your name?'

I told her.

'Mine's Litany.'

'So your father just said.'

Litany looked the fat boy up and down. 'He's *not* my father. I've never even seen this man before.'

Fangio shrugged. 'She's right. I remember now. I don't have a daughter.'

'Is that your computer?'

'It's my uncle's. He lent it to me, but I can't remember the password.'

'That's easy, let me have a look at it.'

I passed the computer along the bar. She took it between long slim delicious-looking fingers. 'This is government issue. An M.o.S. machine. If it's not yours, then I'd lose it fast. They can track these things.'

'I have to know how the program works.'

She tossed back her golden hair. 'This belongs to the guy who was sitting in at your gig, doesn't it?'

'Yes, but he *is* my uncle.'

'You're holding back a lot of anger, I can feel it. I don't want to get involved.'

'I only want the password. I'll give you money.'

'How much money?'

'There's the details of a bank account in there. There's a lot of money in it. You can have it all.'

'All right.' Litany's fingers trod the keyboard. I watched the seconds tick by on the clock above the bar. 3-2-1—

'There you go,' she said. 'The password is DOGBREATH, does that mean anything to you?'

I nodded dismally. 'How *did* you work it out?'

'I was looking over your uncle's shoulder.' Her eyes didn't leave the keyboard. 'There's a great deal of money in here, I don't think I should take it all.'

'Take half then, I'll have the rest.'

'All right, I'll transfer it to my account. So what

172

is it you want to see? Or is it just the money?'

'It's linked to the money. I have to know how the money got into the account, trace back the cause and effect right to its source.'

'That should be reasonably simple.' She tapped at the keyboard. 'Whoa, perhaps not.'

'What is it?'

'This is not your everyday computer system. This is bio-tech.'

'Which is?'

'Brand new. State of the art. It's organic. Artificial intelligence, if you like. Replicating DNA strands.'

'You mean something's actually alive inside the computer?'

'Yes, but not human or animal. It's vegetable. Strands of vegetable DNA bombarded by neurone particles. Very advanced and highly classified.'

'But how does it work?'

'According to theory, all plant-life on Earth is inter-dependant and inter-connected. It communicates, but not in human terms, it doesn't speak or anything. It's vibratory, on a cellular level. A marigold getting pulled up in Sumatra affects an oak tree in Windsor Great Park.'

'This all sounds very familiar.'

'It's chaos theory,' said Fangio. 'A butterfly in Dresden—'

'Shut up,' I told him.

'He's right,' said Litany. 'But then *you* know that, because you're the butterfly, aren't you?'

The explosion wasn't a large one. But it made its point. The street door was ripped from its hinges

173

and cartwheeled into the bar. Smoke and flame. Confusion and chaos.

Litany snapped shut the laptop and grabbed at my arm. 'Quick,' she shouted. 'The back door.'

I joined her at the hurry-up. My last memory of Fangio's Bar is of men in dark uniforms storming forward with guns, and Fangio shouting, 'Wake up, Jimmy, I think something interesting's about to happen.'

And then he met his end. Which *was* a shame, but these things do happen.

DROWNED SAILORS' HATS

If early some morning
You poo-poo the warning
And head for the grey mud flats
When the tide's well out
You can search about
And find drowned sailors' hats

Among the relics of the wrecks
Are plank-walked captains with hairy necks
And tattooed wrists and long frock coats
Who feed the crabs and shrimping boats

Are moth-balled clerics who went astray
Upon some long-forgotten day
Arm in arm with pirate chiefs
With rusted swords in crusted sheaths

Are pewter tankards full of sand
And diamonds big as a gypsy's hand
Are fancy pistols with silver stocks
And quill-penned parchment in a box

Barnacled bo'sun, corral shot
Rum-filled casks from the captain's cot
Charts and deeds and treasure maps
Chains and charms and braided caps

If early some morning
You poo-poo the warning
And head for the grey mud flats
You may sink in the mud
When the tide comes flood
And join those sailors' hats.

11

I LOSE MY VIRGINITY

The last thing I needed at a time like this was a poem about drowned sailors' hats.

What I really needed was a blow job.

And I'm not being facile or frivolous here. I really, truly mean it.

A friend of mine who was once in the TA told me that at that exact moment when you think you're going to die, your whole life does *not* flash before your eyes. Something quite different occurs. He'd had his experience on Salisbury Plain. He enjoyed the old weekend-soldiering, got a real buzz out of shooting real guns and throwing thunderflashes at sheep. And he'd been quite looking forward to the war games his part-time regiment was going to have against a unit of full-time regular soldiers. But things didn't go as well as they might have. He tripped in a rabbit hole and broke his ankle. Considering that the war games were over for him he gave himself up, limped to the enemy camp waving a white handkerchief. It was an ill-considered move. The regulars did not pack him off in a field ambulance, they tortured him instead. They stripped him naked but for his boots, tied him up and put him out in the rain. My friend was in such agony from the broken ankle and the freezing cold and everything that he really truly thought that he was going to die.

And did his whole life flash before his eyes?

No, as I've already said, it didn't.

What did flash before his eyes was the vision of a woman, a kind of composite of all the best-looking women he'd ever seen, and with it came this terrible revelation that making love and not war was probably a very good idea indeed and that he would have been far, far better off lying naked in bed with a woman than laying naked in mud with a broken ankle.

My friend still walks with a slight limp, he is married happily, has five children and lives in Cornwall. He is no longer in the T.A.

I ran down the alleyway after Litany, who, on long tanned legs, was leaving me behind.

'Slow down,' I called after her. 'We have to find a doorway to nip into, we have to have sex.'

This remark slowed her down. To a stop.

'What did you say?' she asked, turning and making a face I thought somewhat fierce.

'They just shot the barman, and we'll be next,' I explained, 'so we should make love now, while we still have the chance.'

'You're kidding, right?'

'At a time like *this*? I'm deadly serious, it might be the last thing we ever do.'

178

'You want me to take my clothes off in a doorway?'

It was clear that this woman had never had a friend who was once in the T.A. I'd have to explain it to her later. 'Forget about taking your clothes off,' I told her. 'I'll settle for a blow job.'

And then she kicked me. Right in the cobblers. I will never understand women as long as I live.

'If you can't run, hobble,' she shouted, and away she went once more. And out through the rear door of Fangio's Bar came the fellows in the uniforms. The ones with the big guns.

'Halt!' they shouted.

'Screw that!' And I hobbled.

At the end of the alleyway stood the limo, shiny and black, the stars reflected in its roof. The stars, white dots upon a black background, just waiting to be joined up to spell out the answer. The big answer.

Because the pattern is there, right there, in the heavens.

'Cut that crap and get in.' Litany threw open the passenger door. She was inside. At the wheel.

'It isn't crap,' I said (once inside, with the door locked and the car in motion). 'It's part of the big picture. Everything is part of a big picture. Everything links together. We are all small links in an infinite chain, all cells in the body of God.'

And then she leaned over and smacked me in the mouth. 'You're delirious,' she said, by way of explanation. 'You're in shock. Now just get your head down, there's going to be some action.'

'Oh good. You've changed your mind—'

And she hit me again!

I got my head down and sulked as she drove. And she drove very fast. My pride felt as injured as my privy parts. Well not quite so, but near as damn it. She took a right here and a left there, although I didn't know where here and there were. And once she braked very hard and my head hit the dashboard.

She may very well have braked hard again, but I don't remember if she did, because I had been knocked unconscious.

I awoke all alone in the limo
Parked upon grey mud flats
In the distance I saw
Several men, three or four,
They were searching for drowned sailors' hats.

And the sea was a ribbon of mercury
That underlined the sky
And the sky was blue
As a blue suede shoe
And sweet as apple

Smack! went a fist into the side of my face.

'Pie,' I said. 'Ouch,' I continued. 'What did you hit me for this time?'

Litany smiled in through the open car window. 'The poetry,' she replied. 'It's appalling.'

'It's a necessary evil.' I nursed my grazed cheek, felt at my fat lip and gingerly tested my testes. 'I have to keep poetry in my head. To concentrate on. Otherwise I have to compensate. Endlessly. For everything.'

'Yes, I know all about that.'

'You *do*?' She opened the car door and I scrambled out onto the mud. 'What do you know?'

'While you slept, I hacked into your uncle's computer. I know all about how you have to compensate, maintain the balance of equipoise. It's all in there, your entire case history. The Ministry of Serendipity has been monitoring you for years.'

'They never have?'

'They have too.'

'Bastards!'

'The gigs you played last night. The jokes you told from the print-outs. That was all part of a secret government experiment, to see whether you could actually affect great changes by performing small actions. Be the mystical butterfly of chaos.'

'Secret government experiment?' I shook my head, which hurt my cheek and my fat lip, but mercifully left my testicles in peace. 'So are you saying that my brother and my uncle both work for the M.o.S.?'

'It's all there in the computer files.'

'Does it say what damage I caused? They said something about typhoons, disasters.'

Litany smiled. It was a blinder of a smile. I could almost forgive her for all the hitting. Almost, but not quite. 'You didn't cause any disasters,' she smiled. 'It was a controlled experiment aimed specifically at creating fluctuations in the world's money markets.'

'But they said—'

'Forget what they said. They got it wrong.'

I shook my head once more. But carefully this time. 'They're all a pack of bastards,' I declared. 'And I'm not working for any of them.'

'So what do you intend to do?'

'Well, I'm not going home. I'll stay here. Where is here, by the way?'

'We're just outside Skelington Bay on the south coast.'

'Well, I'll stay here. I'll merge anonymously into the holiday crowd.'

'It's not a bad idea,' she said, with yet another smile, 'except for one thing.'

'And what's that?'

'If you want to merge anonymously, I think you'd better change out of your gold lamé catsuit. Come on, I'll drive you into town and buy you some new clothes.'

'*That's* not a bad idea,' *I* said. 'Except for one thing.'

'And what's that?'

'Well, if you'd care to look behind you, you'll notice that the limo has now sunk up to its roof in the mud.'

She looked and she saw and she didn't smile this time.

We walked into Skelington Bay and I must confess I did get some pretty funny looks from the passing menfolk. And some bitter ones too. But I could understand that, I mean there's nothing more annoying than seeing some jerk who's got really bad dress sense with a really beautiful woman on his arm, is there?

I didn't take to the town at all. Something felt wrong to me about the houses. If I'd known anything at all about architecture, I suppose I would have spotted it right away.

Much of the town was Neo-Georgian, but given a vernacular style because the architects had obviously vacillated between the comparatively robust forms of Palladian composition and more attenuated compositions with slightly applied ornament, as popularized by the brothers Adam, who designed in a much more virile manner.

But I knew Jack Shit about architecture, so this didn't cross my mind.

A fist crossed my mouth again. Which I found mildly annoying.

'And what did you hit me for *this* time?'

'Being pretentious.'

'Fair enough.'

We found a clothes shop (or boutique), and I let her choose me a shirt and trousers. A friend of mine, who'd actually had a girlfriend once, said that it's a really good idea to let your girlfriend choose your clothes. It shows her that you trust her judgement and she's also pleased because you look the way she wants you to look.

How vividly I recall him standing there in his pink flares and paisley-patterned shirt waving goodbye to her as she went off laughing with the bloke in the jeans and leather jacket.

Mind you, he also told me that the best present you can buy a woman is a wristwatch, because she's bound to look at it several times a day and each time she does, she'll subconsciously think of you.

I came out of the changing-room. 'Are you sure these pink flares are really me?' I asked.

Litany smiled. 'They certainly are.'

'I'd like to go on to a jeweller's next.' I examined my reflection in the wall mirror. 'I'd like to buy you a wristwatch.'

'That's all right, I already have one.' And she looked down at it and a wistful look came into her eyes.

I settled for a pair of jeans, a white T-shirt and a leather jacket. I said I'd owe her the money.

We went looking for a place to stay and as we walked along I wondered over the events of the night before and tried to draw a few conclusions.

Why was it, I asked myself, that if this Ministry of Serendipity intended using me for its own ends, they had sent storm troopers into Fangio's, blowing up the place and shooting people? I wasn't much use to them dead.

And why, I also asked myself, had Litany risked her life helping me to escape?

Well, the second one was easy. It was clear that the dame was wildly in love with me. Clearly all the hitting was her way of showing affection.

I made a mental note that as soon as I got her clothes off, I'd make a point of tying her down to the bed.

We checked into a hotel called the Skelington Bay Grande.

'Double room,' I told the desk clerk.

'Two singles,' said Litany.

'Oh yeah,' I winked at her. 'I get you. Two singles.'

She didn't wink back.

We took lunch in the Casablanca dining-suite. I had to go part vegetarian and eat only half of my lettuce to compensate for the ghastly décor. The ceiling was so high that I had to put four sugars in my coffee and take off one of my shoes.

We shared a bottle of *Châteaubriand* over the starters.

Then a carafe of *Chaudfroid* with the main course.

To accompany the cheese and biscuits we each had a glass of *Vol au Vent*.

And to bring the meal to a successful conclusion, two balloons of chilled *eau de vie*.

Well, one out of four wasn't bad for a waiter who only did basic French.

A smack in the ear informed me that I was being pretentious again.

'Just you see here,' I said, which wasn't easy, considering what I'd just drunk. 'I'm getting fed up with all this hitting. What say we dispense with all this foreplay, go upstairs and do it till we fall unconscious?'

She sipped from a schooner of *Mal de Mer* I'd failed to mention earlier and shook her beautiful head.

'Why not?' I asked, suavely. 'You're obviously gagging for it.'

'Oh I am. But not with you.'

'Why not?' I reiterated, not quite so suavely this time.

She smiled again. (I was beginning to find the habit more than just mildly annoying.) 'Look, you're a very nice guy and everything, but, well, you're—'

'What?'

'You're too old.'

'*What?*'

'I'm sorry, but there it is.'

'How old do you think I am?'

'I don't know, forty, forty-five, maybe.'

'More like fifty,' said the waiter, pouring me a pint of *vichy ssoise*.

'You keep out of this,' I told him.

'No offence, *monsieur*, but in *labial France* such practices are an everyday affair. Beautiful young woman, dirty old man. We think nothing of such things.'

'I'm so pleased to hear it. But surely you mean *la belle France*. Doesn't labial mean—'

'Trust me, *monsieur*, I know exactly what it means.'

'Do you know what bugger off means?'

'Indeed I do.' The waiter bowed by lifting his nose and departed from our table.

'Now just you listen,' I said to Litany. 'I'm not forty or forty-five or anything like that. I just look old for my age.'

'So how old are you really?'

'I'm fifteen.'

She gave me a look. It was a long look. A long long look. It was a look so long that had it been

186

a willy it would have belonged to none other than Long King Dong himself. 'Fifteen?' she said. 'Fifteen?'

'Fifteen.'

'Then you're much too young for me.'

'Now cut that out.'

'All right,' she said. 'All right. I can't go to bed with you. You might lose your powers.'

'I'm sure I'd be good for an hour or two.'

'I mean your *mystical* powers.'

'Oh *those*. I've frankly lost all interest in those as it happens. Let's go upstairs.' I didn't like to beg, begging is so undignified. 'Please,' I wailed, falling to my knees. 'Please. I'll do anything you want.'

'We mustn't,' she said. 'You are the Chosen One. I'm not worthy.'

'Pay the bill,' I told her. 'We're going upstairs.'

And she paid the bill and we went.

We went up to her room rather than mine. When we got inside I found out why. Hers was somewhat bigger and grander. I put this down, of course, to the luck of the draw. After all, what else could it be?

She went off to the en-suite bathroom to do whatever it is that women do prior to making love.

'Sit down on the bed,' she said. 'Watch TV for a few minutes, I won't be long.'

I sat down on the bed and tinkered with the controller. I don't watch a lot of TV myself. Used to, all the time, but something had happened a few months before to a friend of mine which changed all that for me.

His name was Ray Bland, but we used to call him 'Cathode' Ray. Well, we had to call him something and Ray didn't mind, because he felt that it gave him an air of individuality. Of course it did nothing of the kind, because we were only taking the piss. But Ray didn't mind that either, because he felt that we did it out of grudging respect.

This too, of course, was a fallacy, but Ray didn't mind about that either. In fact, Ray didn't mind about anything much and this was the one thing we liked him for.

'Human nature is as inexplicable in its many-sidedness as the Sunday Football League,' Ray once told Jim Pooley. And Jim felt that this was probably the case.

Ray's life was divided, far from fairly in his opinion, between working at the Blue Bird dry-cleaners (at that time still a 'wet'-cleaners), and watching television.

'In the future,' Ray declared, 'nano-technology, allied to genetic engineering, will create a classless, workless society, which will be dedicated entirely to ceaseless sensory stimulation. In the meantime, however, we must make the most of what we have, to wit, television. Whenever possible we should sate our senses at the screen.'

Sating his sense at the screen was indeed an obsession for Ray. It was indeed an addiction.

'I have seen *High Noon* twenty-three times,' he told Pooley, upon one of his rare nights out away from the screen. And then proceeded to date each separate occasion.

'That "Cathode" Ray is a dull one, to be sure,' Jim told Neville. 'Although he doesn't *mind*.'

'And lastly, 16th August 1965,' said Ray, who was not to be interrupted during the disclosure of such important information.

'Sing us some of your 1950s TV commercials, Ray,' said Old Pete, seating himself down at The Swan's elderly piano.

Pooley drank up and left, he had heard the spirited renditions of *Rael Brook Poplin, the shirts you don't iron,* and *Shippams for tea, for tea, for tea* (performed to the tune of *The Blue Danube*) all too many times.

'OK,' said Ray. 'As you're asking.'

Pooley lurched drunkenly out into a windswept Ealing Road.

From the saloon bar of The Flying Swan, the haunting strains of *Keep going well, Keep going Shell, You can be sure of Shell, Shell, Shell*, sung in a most unconvincing Bing Crosby voice, drifted after him.

'Boring little tick,' muttered Pooley.

'*The Esso sign means happy motoring,*' crooned 'Cathode' Ray Bland.

'Why doesn't he just bugger off and sate his sodding senses?' complained an old soldier, who had seen it all before and heard quite enough.

The television detector van, disguised this week as one of Lorenzo's Ice-Cream wagons (but to the trained eye an obvious fraud, as the ice-cream selections were spelt correctly), swung into Mafeking Avenue pursued by the inebriated Pooley shouting, 'Just one damn choc ice, that's all that I want.'

The driver, Aaron Lemon,★ who, in his mother's opinion, had the hands of a concert pianist, stood heavily upon the brake. 'We'll pull up here, I think,' he said.

The dull thud as Pooley's head struck the van's rear door was hardly audible within.

'Switch her on, Mickey,' said Aaron.

Mickey Vez,† who, in his mother's opinion, had the legs of an African tribal warrior, threw the switch and the dazzling rocket that masked the antennae atop the van began to rotate.

'It's a little like being at mission control,' observed the romantic Mickey.

Aaron eyed the screen, 'A little,' he replied, 'but not a lot.'

Without any warning at all, because it was quite unexpected, the little screen lit up like a piper at the gates of dawn (?). Well, very brightly, anyway!

'Great steaming bowls of sprouts,' cried Mickey, whose mother had taught him not to swear. 'What is it? A nuclear war?'

'It could be an electrical storm or something. Turn it down, it's blinding me.'

Mickey adjusted the brightness control. 'It's coming from over there,' he said, consulting his

★Great, great grandson of the infamous pirate Captain Leonard 'Legless' Lemon.
†Great, great grandson of the infamous cleric Victor 'Vaseline' Vez. (It's a small world, isn't it?)

Captain Laser wrist compass and pointing towards the east.

He checked a map and sinister government-issue directory. 'Number twenty-three Sprite Street. Name of Mr Raymond Bland.' And then his face lit up to match the screen. 'Eureka,' said Mickey. 'No TV licence.'

Below the van a prone and muddy figure with a bruised forehead mumbled, 'One bloody choc ice, is that so much to ask?'

'Cathode' Ray was back at home. He sat before, or more accurately within, his pride and joy and glory. Wall-to-wall-to-wall-to-wall television. From his swivel chair in the centre of his front parlour he could sate his senses on the screens of some four hundred televisions lining the four walls (one hundred to a wall).

'It is the dream of a lifetime realized,' said Ray, who, in his mother's opinion, had the eyes of Bette Davis.

Ray had arranged four video cameras, one high upon each wall and angled down towards his chair. The four top rows of televisions* were connected to these and by swivelling the chair, Ray could see himself continuously, whilst keeping an eye on the lower screens, each of which was tuned to an ordinary channel, controlled by a master unit strapped to the arm of his chair.

The floor was a snake-house of cables, and aerial leads ran up to the hole drilled in the centre of the

---

*That's one top row on each wall. Ten TVs to a row. It's hard to explain really.

ceiling, giving the room something of the appearance of a circus tent interior. In Ray's back garden an eighty-foot 'commandeered' electricity board pylon served as the very acme of aerials.

It was all *very* exciting.

And *very* illegal.

'Good evening and welcome to *World of the Weird*,' said the three hundred and sixty faces of Jack Black, a popular TV presenter of the day, who, in his mother's opinion, had the hair of the dog that bit him.

The ten left ears, ten right ears, ten faces and ten backs of heads of 'Cathode' Ray Bland looked on appreciatively.

'Lovely,' said the ten mouths. The other bits remained silent.

Aaron Lemon knocked upon the front door.

'Tonight,' said the faces of Jack, 'we visit a man in Norfolk who claims that he can hypnotize fruit and veg in order to increase yield. Discover just why the planet Jupiter got so very fat. Pose the question, order out of chaos, God's will or just a passing fad? And learn the terrible truth about the Scandinavian garden gnome trade.'

'Jolly good show,' said the ten mouths of Bland.

Aaron Lemon put an authorized shoulder to the front door. 'Come on, Mickey,' he said, 'this is THE BIG ONE.'

On three hundred and sixty screens a small man in a turban stood in a sprout field shouting, 'Grow, you buggers, grow,' as Aaron Lemon with the pianist's hands and Mickey Vez with the legs (of the tribesman, not the piano player), burst into

192

Ray's front parlour and came to a staggering, stumbling stop.

Mickey struggled for breath and was the first to find his voice. 'F***ing H*ll!' he went, remembering his mother.

Ten TV screens behind him showed sweat breaking out on his forehead.

'Big, big, big one,' mumbled Aaron, 'big, big . . . big . . . one,' as to right and left of him his ears looked on in batches of ten.

'What is the meaning of *this*?' roared the ten mouths of Bland. And as he struggled to his feet his waistcoat, high on the TV screens, ruffled magnificently. 'Get out of here *at once*!'

'You . . . you . . .' Aaron's jaw rattled up and down. Never in his long and celebrated career as a TV detector man had he ever seen anything to parallel this. 'You . . . you . . . I . . .'

'We'll all be in the *News of the World*,' gasped Mickey. 'I never knew I had a mole behind my left ear,' he continued, looking up at the screens.

Ray's hands began to flap about. Jack Black's three hundred and sixty faces were saying 'petrified dwarves'.

'Get out of my sanctum,' screamed 'Cathode' Ray. 'Get out of here, idolaters!'

'I want my mum,' blubbered Aaron, assuming the foetal position, thumb thrust firmly in gob.

'I could have that removed by surgery,' said Mickey, examining his on-screens mole.

And then suddenly a darkness entered the room.

And with it came the reek of Brimstone.

And with it the Angel of Death.

The Angel of Death was dark and foully be-spattered. He raised a terrible fist that clutched a terrible paling torn from the front fence outside.

'Give me a bloody choc ice or *die!*' he roared.

Now, reports vary in regard to *exactly* what happened next. The explosion was heard five miles away, registered on the seismograph at Greenwich and scored a chart position on the Richter scale.

'Cathode' Ray was out of town for a long while and when he returned he was bearded, wore the habit of a monk and referred to himself as 'Brother Raymond'.

Jim Pooley declines to talk of the incident. But I have seen him hurriedly crossing the high street before he reaches the television repair shop. And the very mention of the words 'choc ice' is sufficient to send him ducking beneath the nearest table with his hands clasped over his ears.

I lay upon Litany's bed smoking a Senior Service and sucking a Fisherman's Friend. 'That was wonderful,' I told her.

'What, the short story?'

'No, the love-making. It was my first time, I will remember it for ever.'

'Well, you didn't do too bad for a kid of fifteen, apart from when I was up on your shoulders and you—'

I put a finger on her lips, 'That's *our* secret. I think I successfully distracted the readers' attention by slipping in the short story, what do you reckon?'

Litany smiled. 'What, as a substitute for a graphic description of two hours' horny love-making? Oh yeah, I should think so.'

And then she smiled again and I didn't mind at all.

TIM DERBY'S MATCHBOX
(A foretaste of horrors to come)

The sad man called Derby walked out in the
rain
From the peak of his hat to the soles of his
feet
He was wet and he murmured again and again
It's the curse of the matchbox I found in the
street

The gay Persian matchbox I took to my flat
To add to the others I keep in my drawer
Oh who would have thought an old matchbox
like that
Could cause all this sorrow and fretful furore?

The sea smote the prom and the wind howled
with vigour
And Derby returned to his garret in gloom
And he looked at the box and he knew it was
bigger
It filled nearly half of his green living-room

So Derby took fright and he called for a cleric
To come and say things that a cleric must say
And a clergyman came with a plumber called
Derek
And made certain signs as he knelt down to
pray

Dear Lord make us free of this monstrous
matchbox

Cause it to vanish away in the night
But the spells that he spoke were as spots on a
  snatchbox
No fun at all and a terrible sight

So Tim in despair took a leap through the
  casement
Like Father Merrin had done in the flick★
And he lay very dead down below in the
  basement
The vicar just smiled and said, 'That's done
  the trick.'

EPILOGUE

The Rev and the plumber returned to the
  rectory
And guzzled away at a bottle of rum
And Del tore in half an old tel-phone
  directory
While good vicar Norman played taps on a
  drum.

Comment: It must be understood that a cleric
is under considerable mental and physical stress
when performing exorcisms upon devil-possessed
matchboxes, tea trolleys, golf carts, etc., and after a
successful exorcism it's always nice to relax with a
glass or two of rum, a telephone directory, a pair of
bongos and a consenting plumber.

★*The Exorcist*, of course.

12

LUCKY BEGGARS!

I lay upon the bed, hands behind my head, thinking.

Litany had gone off to the en-suite to do whatever it is women do there after making love.

Have a shower, probably.

As I lay there, glowing warm all over and feeling blessed that I had lost my virginity to such a beautiful woman in such elegant surroundings, a grim thought came to me.

'Now look here,' said this grim thought, 'why do you think that beautiful woman has just had sex with you?'

'Because she loves me,' I replied.

'Bullshit!'

'Why?'

'She's just after something; women are always after something. Men work on impulse but women plot and plan ahead.'

'So what's she after?'

'She's after your money.'

'I don't have any money.'

'But you could have. Once you've worked out how to do the mystical butterfly routine, you could give her the world. That's what she's after, she's planning ahead. You see if I'm not wrong.'

'Nonsense,' I said, but the grim thought got me thinking.

Now I know there's been a lot of talk that men and women are not, in fact, members of the same species, that the similarities are purely physical. And it seems to be the case that although no man has ever really been able to understand how a woman thinks, all women understand how all men think only too well.

Which gives them a natural advantage.

My Uncle Charles, whose name I can never remember, worked for a while on the railways before he went into light removals. Shifting things from one place to another always fascinated him and he told me that doing this had given him a small insight into the way women functioned.

He drew an analogy between women and trains. He said that if you consider a woman to be the locomotive and the freight, cargo, passengers she carries to be money, then much will become clear. Men, he said, were the guards and porters on the station, they directed the cargo (money) aboard, but the women (locomotives) went off with it and dictated where it ended up.

Imagine a beautiful well-dressed ambitious young woman full of fire and passion; she'd be your express-train type. Load her up with carriage loads of money and whoosh, she's off into the night.

Now an average woman, she might be your goods-train type; you put your money on board, but she comes back with a load of goods from the other end in exchange. He suggested a stable home, children and a relationship as an example of this load of goods.

And so he went on. It made some kind of sense, although not much. I understood when he said that you can't stick an express in the goods yard and expect it to function as a goods train, nor vice versa. And I think I got the general gist, which was that ultimately the distribution of money in the world (where it ultimately gets spent or goes to) is ultimately down to women (ultimately).

It's rubbish, of course. I mean, what about the blokes manning the signal boxes and the trains that break down or crash? And anyway ultimate distribution of money, where money actually goes to, is not down to women at all. Well, it is *indirectly*. But, well . . .

Allow me briefly to explain.

A short while ago I had a very strange experience. It was one of those experiences that make you re-adjust the way you think about the world. I recount it here for two reasons. The first, that it is an absolutely *true* story and the second, that it relates to what happens next in this narrative.

At the time of which I speak, I was seated in the Pizza Express, munching upon a Veniciana (10p goes to Venice in peril) and staring distractedly out of the window (watching young women go by).

As I looked on I saw this beggar* come around

---

*I know the term beggar is not considered politically correct, but please bear with me on this.

the corner. He wore the basic uniform of the new-age traveller: dreadlocks, studied-raggedness and bare feet. The bare feet marked him out as slightly different, as big boots are usually considered *de rigueur*. But it was more than this that made me notice him. It was the manner in which he carried himself. He didn't shuffle, and he wasn't sitting in a doorway with a dog on a string. This chap was begging on the move and he moved like a man with a mission who was off somewhere important, hated to have to beg on the way, but just did.

I wondered where it was he was off to and hoped that it was somewhere exciting.

Not ten minutes later, however, around the same corner he came again and then ten minutes after that, again. Each time begging and each time definitely looking as if he was off somewhere.

I was quite impressed by this technique.

I finished my meal, paid up and left the restaurant. As I did so, around the corner came the young beggar again and tried to touch *me* for my small change.

I *almost* put my hand in my pocket.

Almost.

'Now, hang about,' I said.

'I can't stop,' said he. 'I have to be off.'

'No you don't. I've been sitting in Pizza Express watching you and you've circled this block of buildings four times now.'

'So?' said he.

'Well, so, actually I'm impressed. The way you carry yourself, this impression you convey that you're off somewhere, it shows imagination, originality of thought, perseverance, all qualities that might lead a man to success. What I want to know is, why someone such as yourself, who obviously possesses these qualities, is spending his time in such a low-paid occupation as begging, when he could no doubt turn his hand to something far more profitable?'

And he looked at me as if I was quite insane.

'Low-paid occupation?' he said.

'Well, it's all small change, isn't it?'

'Small change is what pounds are made of,' and he tried to push past me.

'Just hold on,' I said. 'Surely you are wasting your talent? Surely you could find an occupation that would enable you to make big bucks rather than small change?'

He looked me up and down. 'All right,' he said. 'I'll tell you what I do. How many times did you see me from the restaurant?'

'Three times,' I said.

'And how many times did you see me beg someone for money?'

'Three times.'

'And how many times did you see them *give* me money?'

I thought about this. 'All three times,' I said.

'And during the period that I was beyond your range of vision, what do you think I was doing then?'

'You were circling the block.'

'I was begging,' he said. 'And I was being given money. If you'd sat in another restaurant anywhere on the block, or in a pub, or in a shop and watched me go by you'd have seen the very same thing. You'd have seen me beg someone for money and them give it to me.'

'They can't all have given you money,' I said.

He raised a pierced eyebrow. 'That is hardly a conclusion based on the evidence of your own observation, now, is it?'

I shook my head. 'Then you're telling me that all day long people give you money. More and more and more money?'

'More and more and more,' he said.

'That's incredible.'

He shrugged and made to push past once more.

I stopped him. 'Hold on,' I said. 'What I want to know is, what do you do with all this money? Have you got a big expensive car or something?'

'Have you ever seen me in a big expensive car?'

'No, I've only seen you begging for money and being given money.'

'Well, you can ask anyone in Brighton if they've seen me in a big expensive car, and each of them will say, no, they've only seen me begging and being given money.'

'You put it all in the bank then.'

'Have you ever seen me do that?'

'Well, no. All right. You hoard it then.'

'Seen me do that either?'

'No, but you can't carry it all on you. You'd end up having to have a Securicor truck driving along behind you.'

'That's a pretty stupid remark, isn't it?' he said.

'Yes,' I agreed. 'I'm sorry. Ah, hang about,' I

said, 'you spend it, you spend exactly the amount you earn each day. On really expensive food and wine, perhaps.'

'Have you ever seen me go into a shop?' he asked.

'No, but my experience of you is based only upon limited observation. Someone must have seen you go into a shop.'

'They haven't,' he said. 'Ask anyone, anyone at all. Ask this bloke here.' He indicated a gentleman heading out way.

'Excuse me,' I said to the gentleman, 'but have you ever seen this chap before?'

The gentleman looked at me in a most suspicious manner, put his hand into his pocket, produced a fifty-pence piece and handed it to the beggar. The beggar said 'Thanks,' grinned, and made as to move off once again.

'Hold it!' I told him. 'All right. That fifty pence, what are you going to do with it?'

'What fifty pence is that?'

'The one that gentleman just gave you.'

'I don't have no fifty pence,' he held up his hands. 'You can search me, if you want.'

'No thanks, but I just saw him give it to you.'

'And I don't have it any more.'

'So what have you done with it.'

He opened his mouth and pointed down his throat. 'It's gone.'

'You've *eaten* it?' I stepped back in amazement. 'You *eat* the money?'

'In a manner of speaking.'

'Is your surname Crombie?' I asked him.

'No. But you're holding me up from my work. Please let me pass.'

'No,' I said. 'Not until you've told me all of the truth. I don't believe you exist on a diet of small change.'

'Oh I do,' he said and then in a very dark tone, 'but you wouldn't want to know why.'

'Oh yes I would.'

A sinister gleam came into his eyes. 'Then I'll tell you,' he said. 'Why do you think it is that every country in the world except Switzerland is in debt?'

I shrugged. 'Countries owe money, they have national debts.'

'So where has all the money gone to?'

'It was borrowed and spent.'

He shook his dreadlocks. 'If it was spent then someone else must have the money, but they don't. The whole world (except for Switzerland), is in recession, more and more money vanishes away, but no-one ever knows where it really goes to.'

'And where does it go?'

'It goes to me. Me and other special ones like me. We're all over the world. We go around in circles collecting money. But the money never leaves the circle.'

'So where *does* it go?'

'In here,' he pointed down his throat again and this time as I looked I could see that it wasn't a throat at all, it was a great black endless void. 'I am one of the financial black holes of the world,' he continued, 'a monetary vortex that sucks cash in. Where to? Even I don't know that. To the past, to the future, to somewhere it is needed more?'

I was rattled, I kid you not. And I didn't really know quite what to say next. I managed 'Why not Switzerland?'

'They don't allow begging in Switzerland,' he said and then pushed right past me and made off along the street.

I never saw him again after that, although I kept an eye out. My last recollection is of him marching off around the next corner, pausing only to ask a passer-by for money, which they pressed into his hand.

Litany returned from the bathroom; she wore a colourful bikini top and a short skirt. 'Go and have a wash,' she said. 'Then let's go out for a walk.'

We strolled arm in arm along the promenade. I felt great. Although I now had nagging doubts. Such as, what class of locomotive was Litany? Was she out for what I could give her? I didn't know, but I intended to watch her closely to see what, if anything, she had in mind.

The sea was so blue that I had to part my hair on the right-hand side and pull my jeans pockets inside out.

'Stop doing that,' said Litany. 'Say a poem in your head or something.'

I said a poem in my head. It was a dark one about a devil-possessed matchbox. I was just into the last verse when this young chap in dreadlocks, studied-raggedness and bare feet came up and asked me if I had any small change.

I gave him a headbutt. 'That will teach you to suck in the world's money, you bastard,' I told him.

Litany stared at me in horror.

'Oh, I'm terribly sorry,' I said, helping the fellow to his feet. 'An awful mistake, I, er, I thought you were my brother.'

The young man stood there looking dazed.

'Give him some money,' said Litany.

'Certainly not, he'll eat it.'

'What?'

'Oh I'm sorry. Sorry.' I dug into a pocket of my leather jacket and found a pound coin. 'Sorry, friend,' I said, handing it over. He grinned, winked and made off at the trot as if bound upon some important mission.

'You shouldn't be horrid to the homeless,' said Litany.

'It was a mistake. I'm sorry.'

'Well, I think you should make amends.'

'I just did. I gave him a pound.'

'You should do more than that.'

'Well, he's gone now, so I can't.'

'*He* hasn't gone.'

'Who *he*?'

'There's a chap over there, sitting by the entrance to the pier. Chap with the dog. See him?'

'Bloke with the dreadlocks and the big boots?'

'That's the one. Give *him* something.'

'But I didn't headbutt *him*. And I don't have any more change.'

'Then this would be as good a time as any for you to use your gift.'

An alarm bell rang in my brain. 'Oh yes?' I said suspiciously. 'What do you have in mind? Do you want me to channel some more money into your bank account so you can write him a cheque?'

'Of course not, I want you to give it to him directly.'

'Oh,' I said. 'Hm, well, I don't know.'

'What harm could it do? Give it a try.'

'But I don't know *how* to do it, what actions to make.'

Litany smiled that smile again. 'I've been thinking about this,' she said, 'and I reckon you couldn't do it if you were thinking consciously about it. It wouldn't work. It has to be an unthinking, sub-conscious, almost reflex action. You'd have to set yourself the task, i.e., "give this poor man lots of money", then clear your head of all conscious thought and let things happen naturally.'

'Sounds about as unlikely as anything else.'

'But it couldn't hurt to give it a try.'

'I suppose not.'

She kissed me on the cheek. 'Go on, to make amends for your bad behaviour. Make me proud of you.'

'Proud, eh?'

'Proud.' She kissed me again, on the mouth this time, a real deep lingerer.

'Right then,' I said. 'Let's make the beggar-man a millionaire.'

And I almost believed it myself.

I set the thought in my head and then promptly forgot it, because another thought had entered, this one with blond hair and no clothes on. I mentally replayed the events of a few hours before and my hand strayed unconsciously toward my groin and twiddled near my belt buckle.

'Oh look,' said Litany. 'Something's happening.'

'I'm sorry, I can't help it.'

'What?'

'What?'

'He's getting up, the chap with the dog.'

And he was. He yawned and stretched then packed up his bed roll.

'Is he going to get rich at once, do you think?'

As if! 'It doesn't work like that,' I told her, 'if I can make it work at all. It's a chain of events, starting small then growing bigger to produce the huge event. The money wouldn't just drop from the sky.'

'Shame,' said Litany. 'So what do you think might happen next?'

'Well, perhaps he's going off now to apply for a job and he'll be given it, be successful at it and five years from now he'll be rich.'

Litany made the face that says, I don't find that very convincing.

I just shrugged.

The beggar slung his bed roll across his shoulders. Stretched again and then without any warning at all, struck down the nearest passer-by, a young man with a briefcase, snatched the briefcase and ran off, his dog at his heels.

Litany turned and smacked me right in the face. 'You bastard!' she said. '*You* did that.'

'*What?*'

'You caused him to hit an innocent passer-by and steal his briefcase.'

'I never did.'

'You did it just to spite me.'

'Spite *you*?' I shook my head, which now hurt again. I really would never understand women. 'How do you figure *that* out?'

'You wanted to make a fool of me.'

'I didn't. I didn't. I just tried to help him, like you asked me. I didn't know he'd do that. Anyway he stole a briefcase, that's not going to make him rich, is it? Perhaps he'll get arrested and serve time in prison and write a bestselling book about his experiences. I don't know. I did it with the best of intentions, to bring happiness, not to harm any innocent people.'

A crowd was already beginning to form about the young man. Litany pushed her way through it to help him up. The young man scowled at her, thrust her aside and stumbled off in pursuit of the thief.

'Didn't need any help, eh?' I said.

Litany stroked the shoulder the young man had pushed and examined her fingertips. 'He was full of rage,' she said. 'But also he was full of fear. And there was something there, something evil.'

'You really can sense these things, can't you?'

'I always have. Ever since I was little. But there was something sinister about that young man.' She shuddered. 'Something very wrong.'

And there was. Although the truth would not emerge until sometime later. I had said that I did what I did with the best of intentions, to bring happiness, not to harm any innocent people. Three weeks after the incident the young man's body was found floating in the sea. He had been cruelly tortured before having his throat cut. The police identified him as Piers Britain, notorious child pornographer and drug courier for the mob. The 'word on the street' was that he had been carrying a briefcase containing nearly one million pounds in used notes that was to be used for the purchase of crack-cocaine for sale to minors, and that the money had mysteriously 'gone astray'.

The above appeared as front page news in the *Skelington Bay Mercury*. Inside the same issue was a much smaller item which read to the effect that the local children's home had been saved from closure by a gift from an anonymous benefactor. Three-quarters of a million pounds in cash, it was. The anonymous benefactor was described as a young man with dreadlocks and a dog.

Normally you might have expected the children's home article to have merited a bit more prominence. But, as it happened, it was rather lost amongst numerous other such articles. One about a building project to house the homeless being financed by a similar gift, and one about a drug rehabilitation centre being financed by another similar gift and one about the maternity hospital and the hospice and the day-care centre and the crèche. Then there was the cats' home and the dogs' home and the donkey sanctuary and the wild-life park. Many, many millions of pounds were involved, being handed out willy-nilly to the needy.

It was as if the entire nation had woken up one morning and decided to get its priorities right.

And that was just how I intended it to be, but things didn't work out as I planned.

PLEASED AS PUNCH

I was pleased as Punch to see old Reg
The lad who sold the fruit and veg
And once gave me two tickets for the fight.
But Reg was sad, believe you me
He said he'd suffered tragedy
And he'd be glad to tell me through the night.

So I sat up with poor old Reg
Who told me that the fruit and veg
Was dropping off and trade was getting poor.
I yawned as he told tales to me
Of troubled times and poverty
And once threw up behind the kitchen door.

'It's very glum,' I said at last
And thought my watch was running fast.
'Is that the dawn that's creeping up the sill?'
But Reg was well beyond all that
He only moaned and as we sat
I swear I heard a cock crow on the hill.

When finally he took his leave
I found it quite hard to believe
That this was Reg who used to buy me lunch.
All raggedy and bad from drink
It really, really made me think
How seeing him had made me pleased as Punch.

I'm a real fair-weather friend, me.

13

GOOD INTENTIONS

It was my original intention, when first I sat down in my room at Hotel Jericho to pen this autobiography (thirty lines to the page, twenty pages to the exercise book), that I might chronicle the lives of my forebears.

I wished to write of my great grandfather, a sprout farmer and man of the cloth, who always wore weighted boots while in the pulpit, to avoid embarrassing levitations brought on during moments of extreme rapture.

And flatulence.

Of my grandfather (lay preacher, large sideburns, taste for sprouts), who spoke only in rhyming couplets to appease the spirit of his dead wife, and who owned a black pig named Belshazzar, that dined exclusively upon the aforementioned vegetables and did strange things on the back parlour wall.

And of my father (an elder in The Hermetic Order of the Golden Sprout), briefly mentioned, who practised body-modification in an attempt to win a bet with his brother Jack (a monk, not mentioned at all), that he could shin up the *inside* of a drainpipe.

But alas, time and space do not allow. And when I speak of time and space, I speak as one who knows.

Brought up, as I was, within the sacred confines of The Brentford Triangle to such worthy stock and raised upon a diet of sprouts and salvation, I was surely destined to become a God-botherer, not an iconoclast.

And such had been my intention.

When I discovered my gift and that I was the Chosen One, my only thought was to aid mankind. And to pull a few birds, but that's only fair.

Things didn't work out on either account.

So far I had pulled just the one bird and if she was typical of her sex, it was clear to me that relationships with women were a tricky old business and not to be entered into lightly.

Litany had stormed off back to the hotel, leaving me alone at the pier feeling guilty. There was no doubt in my mind that I *had* caused the beggar-man to thump the fellow with the briefcase. I do not believe in the concept of synchronicity, meaningful coincidence. Things happen *because* things happen. Each person's life consists of a chain of events interlinked with that of each other person across the globe. Imagine it as a vast Chinese puzzle which metaphysically—

'Excuse me,' said a small girl, tugging at my trouser leg.

'Yes, my dear?' I leaned down to hear what she had to say.

The small girl knotted her fist and punched me in the mouth.

'What did you do *that* for?' I asked, clutching at my face.

'A lady with blond hair and a bikini top asked me to do it. She said you'd probably be getting pretentious again. What does *pretentious* mean, by the way?'

'It's none of your business.' I cuffed the small girl lightly about the head and she burst into tears.

A large ugly-looking fellow with cropped hair, wearing nothing but tattoos, long shorts and flip-flop sandals, detached himself from the milling crowd, strode over and biffed me in the stomach. I folded double, gagging for breath.

I would have fought back, but I remembered my father's words, 'Never get into fights with ugly people, they have nothing to lose.'

'Consider yourself lucky I don't have me boots on,' said the large ugly-looking fellow, escorting his now-giggling daughter away.

I lay awhile groaning in the hope of a good Samaritan. But none happened by, so presently I upped and took my leave.

I returned to the hotel to find Litany doing likewise.

'What are you doing?' I asked her.

'I'm doing likewise.'

'You're leaving?'

'That's what it looks like.'

'Does this mean that we won't be getting engaged?'

Litany made the face that said something very rude indeed.

'Oh come on,' I told her. 'There's no need for

this, let's go back to your room and make up.' I saw the fist coming and stepped aside.

'I'm going,' she said. 'This was a bad idea. I should never have got involved with you.'

'Please stay.' I was down on my knees again, a most undignified display. 'I will make amends for the chap on the pier. In fact, I already have.'

'What did you say?'

'I've already made amends. Well, I have if it's worked. On the way back here, I made a wish and cleared my mind. I picked my nose and stuck the bogey on the end of a lollipop stick. I think it's done the trick.'

Litany's eyes had grown rather wide. 'What *have* you done?' she asked. 'What have you *wished* for?'

'I made a wish that all the poor and homeless in the area would become rich. But that it wouldn't involve anyone getting mugged. I imagined all the money that's ever got lost or has vanished away and nobody knows where it ever went to. I pictured all this money coming back from these momentary black holes' – I was *very* pleased with this bit of thinking, one in the eye for the bugger in the dreadlocks and bare feet, I thought – 'and all this money going to the needy. Pretty good, eh?'

'Pretty good.' Litany said it in almost a whisper. Then she said, 'But you didn't ask *me* about this. You should have cleared it with me first.'

'With *you*? I don't understand.'

'I'm supposed to . . .' She paused. 'Look, never mind, I'm sure, well, I *hope*, you've done the right thing.'

'I did it to please you. I thought it would make you happy.'

'Yes it does, it does. All right, look, I won't leave. Let's go up to my room.'

'And have more sex?'

'Yes, if you want to.'

'Don't *you* want to?'

'Yes, of course I do.'

But of course she didn't.

As we went up in the lift together I watched her from the corner of my eye. She was edgy, she chewed upon her hair and shifted from one foot to the other.

'Do you need the toilet?' I asked.

'No I do not!'

I recall shrugging and I also recall thinking, *I wish she wasn't so damned difficult all the time.* And then I became aware of the size and shape of the lift and had to compensate by opening my mouth very wide.

And then as the lift doors opened at her floor, Litany suddenly smiled and said, 'Look, I'm sorry I've been so difficult and everything. Let's call down for some ice-cubes and a bottle of Tabasco sauce and I'll show you something rather special.'

And she did. Oh yes indeed.

Well, no, actually she didn't.

I mean it's all rubbish that stuff, isn't it? I mean what *would* you do with some ice-cubes and a bottle of Tabasco sauce? Damned if I know.

I could make something up, of course. Or do it by implication to make you think that I know all manner of secret sexual techniques. Or I could just stick another short story in to pad it out to the end of the chapter.

But I won't.

We went to Litany's room. She called down for the ice-cubes and the Tabasco sauce. We put the ice-cubes into our drinks and the Tabasco sauce onto our roast beef sandwiches, then she showed me something rather special. It was a mint condition copy of the very first issue of *SFX* magazine, with the free gift and everything.

I was very impressed.

Then we called down for half a dozen bulldog clips, an ironing-board and a stirrup pump.

And—

No, I'm lying again.

After a game of chess, which I lost, because she 'huffed' my bishops, which I'm sure was cheating, we were interrupted by a lot of loud knocking at the door.

It was the waiter from the Casablanca dining-suite.

'One thousand pardons, *monsieur*,' he said, 'but I regret to say that you and the beautiful *young* lady must vacate the room at once.'

'Bugger off,' I told him.

'No, *monsieur*, please. We have, how do you say, the *big trouble* downstairs in the foyer. Many ragamuffins demanding rooms for the night. All with much money saying they are the eccentric millionaires. We have called for the *gendarmes* to come and hit them with sticks, but we must evacuate the hotel.'

'If they've got much money, why don't you just give them rooms for the night?'

'Ah, *monsieur* has seen through my cunning ploy. We *are* giving them rooms for the night, at inflated prices.'

'Well, that's fine then.'

'Fine for them, *monsieur*, but not for you. We're giving them your rooms, so would you and the beautiful *young* lady kindly pack your bags and bugger off?'

'No!'

'Then regrettably I must call the *gendarmes* and inform them that you have been having under-age sex with the beautiful *young* woman.'

'She's not *that* young.'

'No, *monsieur*, but *you* are.'

'That's ridiculous, it's not illegal for me to—'

Litany pushed me aside. 'Let *me* handle this,' she said.

I felt reasonably sure I could predict what might be coming and so I took an extra step aside.

Litany punched the waiter in the nose.

The waiter went down onto his bum, with a hand to a gory nostril. 'Oh thanks a lot,' he said. 'That's really sweet, that is. I'm only trying to do my job. Do you think it's any fun having to pretend you're a bloody French waiter? I'm a musician, me. I once auditioned to be the bass guitarist with Sonic Energy Authority, but I didn't get the lucky break. And now I get a punch in the nose. Thank you very much.'

I looked to Litany in the hope she might apologize. But she didn't. She just stormed off to the en-suite bathroom and slammed the door behind her. I helped the waiter to his feet.

'Look,' I said, 'I'm sorry. I know what it's like being in a crap job. If you really want to be a musician, I think I might be able to help you out.'

'Oh yeah, and how?'

'What if I could give you your lucky break? Get you the bass guitarist's job with Sonic Energy Authority?'

'But that's impossible. Panay Cloudrunner's the bass guitarist. He's never going to quit the band now they're so big.'

'Just trust me. Leave us in peace and I'll make it up to you for the bloody nose. Expect a phone call.'

'Expect a phone call? You're kidding, right?'

'I'm not, I'm certain I can do it, trust me, all right?'

He shrugged. 'All right. But if you can get me into S.E.A., then you're some kind of miracle man.'

'Expect a phone call.'

'OK.'

He stumbled off down the corridor holding his nose. I concentrated very hard and thought, *I wish that young waiter could get Panay Cloudrunner's job in Sonic Energy Authority*. And then I recited a poem in my head called 'Pleased as Punch' which I felt was appropriate, and subconsciously untucked my T-shirt and placed a five-pence piece in my navel.

Then I went and bashed upon the bathroom door.

★   ★   ★

We didn't dine that night in the Casablanca dining-suite. I didn't know *when*, or really even *if*, the waiter would get his telephone call, but anyway the restaurant was packed.

It looked like a new-age travellers' convention. I had never seen quite so many dreadlocks or small dogs on strings in one place before. Everyone looked very jolly though, and they were really tucking into the grub.

Litany didn't look best pleased, so I thought it prudent not to mention the promise I'd made to the waiter.

I suggested we take a drink at a tavern on the promenade, but it wasn't such a good idea. Conversation buzzed all around us about the strange doings of the day, how all the local homeless had suddenly struck it rich.

Some folk said that *The Big Issue* had seen fit to award its salesforce massive cash bonuses. Others spoke of wealthy American tourists heaping traveller's cheques on folk slumped in shop doorways. There was even wild talk about a mysterious scruffy chap with bare feet vomiting pound coins. We drank up and returned to the hotel.

Litany said that she wasn't feeling too well and would I mind sleeping in my own room. I agreed without a fuss. Well, I did go down on my knees and beg a bit, but she closed her door upon me and that was that.

I took the lift and then the stairs to my room. It was very small and right up in the eaves. It put me in mind of my own loft bedroom at home and my thoughts turned once more towards my evil brother. I would have my revenge upon him and my Uncle Brian, but for now I was quite exhausted. It had been a long and eventful day and although it wasn't ending in the way I might have hoped, I still felt rather warm inside.

I'd helped those homeless people, I knew that I had and I felt very good about that. I settled down upon the straw-filled mattress and went straight off to sleep.

And I slept very soundly. I remember that.

But then I would. Because, after all, from that night on, and for the next thirty years, I would never sleep again.

TRAVEL IN DISTANT LANDS

Enough of this dull existence, cried Tom, in a
    fit of gin.
I'm off to sail the ocean blue,
Walk till I wear out my shoe,
Bid the foreigner how d'you do, and grow a
    beard on me chin.

I'll drink to that, said Brother Jim, for he was
    easy going.
I'll join you, Tom, if you don't mind,
The holy grail we'll seek and find,
And Spanish gold and The Golden Hind, even
    if it's snowing.

That's not exactly what I reckoned, Tom was
    heard to say.
I thought perhaps a day at the sea,
If Aunty May comes down with me,
And we could board with Mr McGee, at his
    house in Toby Way.

You dull and dismal fellow, Tom, said Jim as
    he sought the bottle.
We'd walk in distant sunny climes,
And drink a very great deal of times,
And possibly commit strange crimes, not unlike
    Aristotle.

Though Tom tried hard he couldn't follow all
   that Jim had said.
What has this Aristotle chap
In common with this horse's crap
That you've been talking, Jim old chap, I must
   be off to bed.

14

MORE RADICAL THAN VOODOO

I awoke from a dream about travelling in distant lands, to the sound of a knocking at my chamber door. I yawned and stretched, and farted too, I must confess, and called out, 'Yes, what is it?'

'Paper, sir, and breakfast,' called back a voice I did not recognize.

I rose and stretched again and rubbed my arms, for it was pretty cold, and, opening the door, took in a tray of tea and toast and a rolled-up copy of the *Daily Sketch*.

As there was no table in my little room I set the tray down on the floor, poured lukewarm tea into the chipped enamel mug, added milk and, finding no spoon available, stirred this with a soldier of toast.

And then I unrolled the newspaper.

TRAGIC DEATH OF A ROCKSTAR

Ran the head line and beneath this—

PANAY CLOUDRUNNER DIES AGED 23

I read the news and then—

Oh boy!

He'd blown his mind out in a car. He hadn't noticed that the lights had changed.

A terrible chill ran through me as I read the time of the fatal accident. Not a half-hour after I'd spoken to the waiter with the bloody nose. Dear God, what had I done?

Well, it was all too clear just what I'd done. I'd killed him as surely as if I'd put a gun to his head and squeezed upon the trigger. I had killed a perfect stranger. This was terrible. Terrible. Beyond terrible. This was—

'Oh my God!' I wailed. Most terribly I wailed. Beyond terribly, in fact. I wailed and gnashed my teeth and beat my forehead with my fists. And then I stumbled from my room. Along the corridor, down the stairs, into the lift, out into the foyer. And into chaos.

The foyer was packed with people. News teams with cameras and boom mics like furry blimps. Others. Many others, shouting to be heard.

A woman in a Salvation Army uniform thrust a collecting tin into my face. 'Are you one of the blessed?' she asked. 'Would you care to make a contribution?'

'I don't give to paramilitary organizations,' I told her. 'Get out of my way.'

'Help save the whales,' called somebody else.

'Stuff Prince Charles,' I replied.

I fought my way through the crowd and out into the street. Here I passed more newsmen speaking into cameras.

'I'm standing here', said one, 'in what must be England's luckiest town. Yesterday nearly one hundred homeless and destitute people became the unlikely recipients of huge sums of money. Bizarre coincidence? Act of God? Who can say? I have with me a close friend of one of the lucky ones that local folk are now calling *the blessed*. Mr Colon, would you care to say a few words?'

I turned at the name and Colon flashed me a winning smile. 'Nice one, man,' he said.

I waved at him feebly, turned away, tripped on the kerb and fell directly into the path of an oncoming Blue Bird Cleaners' truck.

And black went the world about me.

I awoke with a start to a terrible shock.

'Stand clear,' said a voice and then *THWUNKQ*, which was just how it felt. My chest heaved and then I felt my eyelids being tampered with. A very bright light shone into one eye, then the other.

'I'm sorry,' said the voice and I could see its owner now, a doctor in a white coat. 'There is nothing more I can do for this man.'

Nothing more? I tried to cry out but my mouth wouldn't move. Nothing would move, not a finger not a toe.

'Time of death, two-thirty p.m. Have an orderly move him to the morgue please.'

The morgue! An awful fear ran through me. This fool thinks I'm dead, which is surely not the case.

'Are you certain?' asked a pretty nurse, gazing down at me. A voice of reason. *Yes!*

The doctor felt my pulse, put a stethoscope upon my heart, put a finger to my neck, shone his damn torch in my eyes again. 'Absolutely certain, nurse. This man is dead.'

What? The awful fear became an awful terror. Well beyond an awful terror. *Dead? I'm not dead. I'm not dead!*

'He's dead,' said the doctor.

'Dead,' said the nurse.

And 'dead', said the lady with the alligator purse (who just happened to be passing the door on her way to a nursery rhyme).

I'm not dead, you fools, I'm not dead.

And then someone pulled the sheet up over my head and I couldn't see any more. I could still hear though.

'Do we have a name for him?' asked the doctor.

'No,' said the nurse. 'There was no identification on the body. We must assume he was one of the homeless people who were accidentally allocated the grants for the secret government germ warfare project yesterday.'

'That was a right royal cock-up,' said the doctor. 'Are the police hunting those transients to recover the money?'

'No luck apparently. Word must have leaked out last night. The homeless people all left the hotel before dawn, there's no trace of them.'

'Was there any money on this chap?'

'No money, but his pockets were full of rubbish. Filter tips, lolly sticks, biro caps, bottle tops, bits of coloured wool.'

'Just another loser, eh? Well, usual procedure, morgue then the crem.'

The crem? The CREMATORIUM! I tried hard

to scream, I really did. But there was nothing. Nothing. And then I knew it. Knew it because I knew I wasn't breathing, that my heart wasn't beating, that my blood no longer flowed.

I knew that I was really dead.

Then I heard the door open, sensed others in the room. Something bumped up against my bed, hands were laid upon me and I was roughly manhandled onto, what? A trolley.

Then movement, momentum, I was being pushed out of the room, along corridors. I heard people speaking. Live people. People who weren't dead like me. People who weren't destined for *the crem*.

The morgue was very cold and dull, but at least they turned down the sheet from my face so I could see. I couldn't see much though, but for the ceiling.

I lay there. A body on the slab. A corpse.

So this was it. And the unspeakable fear that all men fear unspeakably was founded. The mind survives the body after death. The senses still function. I could feel the cold, smell the antiseptic reek, see through my dead eyes and hear through my dead ears. I would suffer it all in silent agony. An autopsy perhaps, but then *the crem*.

And then what?

I heard the morgue door open and the sounds of approaching footsteps. Two young men loomed above me.

'What happened to this bloke?' said one.

'Road accident,' said the other. 'Stepped out in front of a truck.'

'Silly bastard. Next of kin paying a visit?'

'John Doe, identity unknown.'

'So they won't be bothering with an autopsy or anything.'

'No, bung him in the freezer, we'll fire him up this evening.'

I felt a tugging at my hand. 'He won't be needing this ring then,' said one of the young men.

'Nor this leather jacket,' said the other.

And then I was lifted onto this big long filing drawer sort of thing and slammed away into freezing darkness.

I was left in absolute silence and absolute black, utterly utterly alone.

As the temperature dropped I thought of my friend and his experience at the war games on Salisbury Plain. How his past life hadn't flashed before his eyes, only a wish to make up for all the sex he'd missed out on. But I wasn't thinking of sex. All I felt was envy. Envy of the living. All I wanted was life, more life.

'And if you had it, what would you do with it?'

I groaned inwardly. That was all I needed now. A voice in my head. Not only dead, but mad with it. Perfect.

'Actually you're taking it quite well,' said the voice. 'Your average dead person is usually reduced to an incoherent mental babbler. Apart from the Christians, of course. It's all "Praise the Lord, I'm coming to glory" with those lads. You'd still be an atheist, I suppose.'

I tried to ignore the voice and set my mind to

desperate practical thinking. There had to be some way out of this.

My thoughts turned to the island of Haiti; over there voodoo priestesses were said to be able to reanimate the dead as zombies. I had all my sensory faculties about me, I could hear and see and feel. If there was some way I could send out a telepathic message to any voodoo priestess that happened to be in the area and get her to hurry on over before I went into the oven—

'That's a new one,' said the voice in my head. 'Usually it's just a futile struggle to get the personality out of the body and float off somewhere. The Buddhists have that off to a fine art. Did you know that the Dalai Lama practises dying four times a day? So he'll be prepared, you see. Whip straight off to his next incarnation.'

'I read somewhere that monks make amulets out of his poo,' I said, without moving my lips or making a single sound. 'But I'm not talking to *you*, you're just a figment of my imagination.'

'You've got spirit,' said the voice. 'I'll give you that.'

'Bugger off!'

'Now that's no way to speak to God, is it?'

'You're not God. I don't believe in God.'

'Rubbish, everyone believes in God. Some just pretend they don't.'

'Well, *I* don't.'

'Fair enough, you'll be wanting to stay in your body then. For *the crem*.'

'I'm expecting the imminent arrival of a voodoo high priestess, as it happens.'

'Well, I hope she knows which bus to catch. I think those sods who nicked your ring and jacket are coming back. They probably want to knock off early. I think they've got tickets for the Sonic Energy Authority gig at Wembley tonight. There's a new bass player, you know.'

I managed another inward silent groan. And another 'Bugger off.'

'Oh well, please yourself. I'll pop back later, after the inferno, try to catch you before they grind your bones up. That's quite an unpleasant experience I hear, even worse than the burning.'

'Hold on, wait, don't go.'

'Hah. Decided to change your mind, eh? Decided to believe in me after all?'

'I don't believe you're God.'

'Oh go on, you do really.'

'I *don't*.'

'You're one stubborn bugger for a dead bloke. But you're quite right, I'm not really God.'

'So what are you?'

'I'm your Holy Guardian.'

'My what?'

'Your Holy Guardian, assigned to watch over you throughout your life.'

'Well a shit job you've made of it. I walked under a truck.'

'Sorry about that. I wasn't concentrating. Nobody's perfect, you know. Except for God, of course.'

'Look,' I said, still without actually speaking, 'if this is the case, do you think it would be all right if I had a quick word with God? I'm sure if you were to explain what happened—'

'I thought you didn't believe in God.'

'I'm coming around to the idea. Go on, a quick word, what harm could it do?'

'It could do *me* a lot of harm. I was supposed to be on the job. Your Holy Guardian.'

'He'll forgive you, you're one of his angels, after all.'

'Well . . .'

'Well what?'

'Well, I never said anything about being an angel.'

'You said you're my Holy Guardian. That's an angel, isn't it?'

'Well, it can be. For some people. But there's an awful lot of people on Earth. More people than there are angels, in fact. Look upon me as your little gift from God's garden.'

'*What?*'

'I'm your *Holy Guardian Sprout.*'

I groaned another inward groan. A great big one this time.

'Look, don't take it so badly. Think of me as a family retainer. I've been with your lot for generations. Not that I ever get taken any notice of. What did I say to your great[3] grandaddy? "Don't go bothering the people in the field next door," I said, but did he listen? No, he didn't. And your great[2] grandaddy. What did I say to him? "Don't go on the *Titanic*," I said, "that bugger Crombie's going to be on board." Same business.'

'You've never said a word to me,' I said (silently as ever).

'I bloody have.'

'You bloody haven't.'

'I have you know, I said, "Turn on your private eye tape recorder." Back in the Gents at Fangio's Bar when you first met Colon the super-dense proto-hippy.'

'*You* made me do that?'

'I put the idea into your head. I thought you could help mankind if you knew about your gift. I thought it might earn me some big kudos with God, keep me off his Sunday dinner plate.'

'Well, it's all screwed now, I'm dead.'

'No hard feelings,' said the Holy Guardian Sprout.

'Oh, none at all. But I do hope—'

'What?'

'I hope he boils you for hours and eats you really slowly!'

'All right, I deserved that. But listen, we have to get you out of here.'

'You know any voodoo high priestesses?'

'Not as such. I don't think that voodoo stuff really works. What we need is something more radical.'

'More radical than *voodoo*?'

'There is one way we might do it, but it is *very* radical and I don't think it's ever been done before.'

'Go on.'

'OK. Well, everything so far has been seen from your point of view. You're in the first person, right? It's your autobiography.'

'It is,' I said, and it was.

'Well, what if it ceased to be? What if you moved into the third person, became part of someone else's story for a while?'

'I don't think that makes any sense.'

'Oh it does, you know. After all, you *are* dead. *You* can't write any more about yourself, can you? But someone could write *about you*.'

'Who?'

'I don't know. A biographer, perhaps.'

'This all sounds very iffy.'

'More iffy than being dead and heading for the furnace?'

'I take your point.'

'Look, just trust me on this. You have nothing to lose after all and if I can pull it off, we'll both be out of the hot water. Well, *I'll* be out of the hot water and you'll be out of—'

'All right, don't keep on about that.'

'I'm sorry.'

'So what do we do?'

'Well, the first thing we have to do is to get out of this chapter.'

'I'm very glad to hear it. But just one thing before we do.'

'What's that?'

'I don't know your name. What is it?'

'It's Bartemus,' said the Holy Guardian Sprout. 'But don't be formal, chief, call me Barry.'

COLD ROOM TILE TALK

There was more of that cold room tile talk
(Tony on the slab)
Spoke about crown folk and town folk
Travelling by cab

Saxony days by the dusty road
Bald-headed eagles on silent wings
Coffins for heroes and distant sunrises
More of that cold room tile talk

There was more of that out-and-about talk
(Tony in his towel)
Spoke of the hill folk and still folk
Monks beneath the cowl

Soft-footed beavers with ivory teeth
Wolves that bay at the hunter's moon
Coal miners' holidays hard and bleak
More of that out-and-about talk

There was more of that come-as-you-are talk
(Tony in the shower)
Spoke about shandies and mop-headed dandies
Living in the tower

Silver cadavers from moon-drowned lakes
Sad silent centaurs lost on moors
Bland leggy models on satin settees
More of that come-as-you-are talk

I have no idea what this means.
But I love the way it sounds.

15

THE EPISODE OF THE GOLDEN TABLET AS TOLD IN THE FLYING SWAN

'The last thing I expected,' said Leonard 'Legless' Lemon, as he leaned perilously upon The Flying Swan's highly polished bar top, 'the *very* last thing I expected when I opened my gaily painted front door yesterday was a bloody emissary from the planet Venus come to award me the galaxy's highest accolade.'

John Omally spluttered into his pint of Large. 'Word get out about your prize marrow then, Len?'

Leonard the legless ignored him. 'The galaxy's highest accolade,' he said once more, lingering upon each word, savouring each syllable.

'Which is?' asked Neville, who always enjoyed a good yarn.

'The Golden Tablet of Tosh m'Hoy, inscribed with the sacred formula for denecrolization.'

Omally nodded and raised his glass. 'Who would have expected otherwise?' he said.

'And what is *denecrolization*, when it's at home?' asked Neville.

'That's for me to know, and you to find out.'

'Stick another half in here please, Neville,' said John Omally, pushing his glass across the counter.

'You never believe a bloody thing I tell you, do you, Omally?' Legless Len made a brave attempt at pathos, by putting on a wounded expression, but it, like the point of owning a *file-o-fax*, was lost upon Omally.

'To be quite truthful, no,' said John. 'However, the doubting Thomas in me might speedily be put to shame, were you to produce this golden tablet for his perusal.'

'Good idea,' said Neville. 'Let's have a look.'

And others about the bar went, 'Yes.'

The legless one (and perhaps it should be explained here that this was legless as in *drunk*. Not legless as in *legless*) became momentarily flustered. 'I don't have it with me,' he said. 'I've sent it off to the British Museum to have it valued.'

'Ah,' said Omally. A meaningful 'Ah'.

And someone said, 'Yeah sure,' and someone else said, 'Cop out.'

'But I do have a photograph of it.'

'Ah,' said Omally, it was quite another 'Ah'.

'Go on,' said Neville. 'Whip it out.'

Legless Leonard felt about for his snakeskin wallet. And from this he withdrew a dog-eared photograph with somewhat tattered edges. This he held towards John.

'So what is that then, might I ask?'

John scrutinized the photograph. 'That', he announced, 'is the photograph you always show us when demanded to prove the authenticity of your

239

claims. This picture has, in the past, purported to be of you making love to Marilyn Monroe, you shaking hands with J.F.K. before he was famous, you in the SAS saving a child at an embassy siege, you parting the river Thames in the manner of Moses, you, well, need I continue?'

Legless Len made a surly face.

'For myself,' said Omally, 'and going on no more than the evidence provided by my excellent vision, I believe this to be a photograph of you on a donkey at Great Yarmouth.'

Mr Lemon swallowed Scotch and then, excusing himself with talk of 'a weak bladder brought on by all yesterday's excitement', vanished away to the Gents.

Upon his return he looked Omally up and down, declared him to be typical of his class (whatever that meant), and slouched from the bar.

Omally returned to his drinking and peace returned to The Swan, but only for a while because the phone began to ring.

'Flying Swan,' said Neville, lifting the receiver. 'Yes,' he continued after a short pause. And, 'Yes, Leonard Lemon, yes, no, he's not here at the moment. A message, hold on I'll get a pencil.' Neville got a pencil. 'Go on. Yes. British Museum, you say.'

The Swan took to one of its famous pregnant pauses.

'Golden tablet, not gold, you say. Unknown metal. Being passed on to a secret government research establishment, tell Mr Lemon to report to Mornington Crescent. Well, yes, I'll tell him—'

'Hang about, Neville.' Omally leaned over the counter and snatched the telephone. 'That horse came in at thirty to one, Len. Do you want me to collect your winnings or shall I stick the lot on Lucky Lady?'

'Collect my winnings, you bloody Irish mad man.'

Omally replaced the receiver. 'You know the terrible thing is', he said to Neville, 'that one day he'll probably turn out to be telling the truth.'

THE EPISODE OF THE GOLDEN TABLET AS LEONARD LEMON SAW IT

The previous day Len returned from his allotment. He smelt strongly of those organic substances which, though loved by rhubarb, are so detested by the traveller who steps in them.

'If my marrow does not win the coveted Silver Spade Award this year, then there is absolutely no justice left in the world,' he told his lady wife.

'Yes, dear,' she said.

'I think I might take a bit of a bath now.'

'Yes, dear.'

Legless Len ascended his vilely carpeted staircase. He had purchased the carpet whilst drunk. He was a happy man, was Len. A broad smile of the Cheshire Cat persuasion bisected his ruddy workman's face.

As he ran the bath water he whistled 'Sweet

Marrow of My Heart's Desire' (one of his own compositions).

Removing his unsavoury undergarments he tested the water with a temperature-toe. 'Oh yes,' he giggled. 'Just right.'

As he sank into the steaming scented water he heard the distinctive chimes of his musical doorbell ringing out the opening bars of 'The Harry Lime Theme'.

'Hello, hello, hello,' said Len, who had once thought of joining the police force. 'What do we have here then?'

There was some silence, then the sound of voices and then a bit more silence. Then his wife called up the stairs. 'Len,' she called. 'Len, there's two fellas here from the planet Venus. They've come to award you the galaxy's highest accolade.'

Len sank lower into his foaming bath tub. 'Tell them to come back later,' he replied.

Len's wife passed the message on.

'They say they can't wait,' she called up this time. 'They say they have to catch the twelve-o'clock tide.'

Len huffed and puffed then rose from his bath. He shrugged on his wife's quilted nylon dressing-gown and flip-flapped down the stairs leaving a dark damp footprint on each and every vilely carpeted stair.

At the door stood two enigmatic-looking bodies. Dressed in the ubiquitous one-piece cover-all uniforms so beloved of the cosmic traveller and sporting the now-traditional mirror-visored weatherdomes. They had a look which was at once familiar but, also, at twice totally alien.

'Ie-e-oo-ae-u,' said Rork, the taller of the two.

'Ao-e-uu-o-i,' replied his companion, whose name was Gork.

Legless Len, who had only done O level Venusian at Horsenden Secondary School, nodded his head.

'This is most unexpected,' he said, but so that it came out, 'Eo-i-u-o-i.'

'His enunciation of the former "i" lacked for inflection and there was far too little slant on the "o–i" modulation,' said Gork to Rork, 'but other than that it wasn't bad for O level Venusian.'

Len overheard this remark. 'Now just look here,' he said in a heated tone, 'I'm a piss-artist jobby gardener, not a bleeding professor of languages.'

The space travellers made apologetic vowel sounds.

'I should think so too,' said Len.

And then the space travellers went on to explain to Len that they had come to bestow upon him the galaxy's highest accolade.

'Did word get out about my marrow, then?' asked Len.

Sadly though, as the atmospheric conditions on Venus preclude the growing of almost any vegetable (save alone the wily and adaptive sprout), Len's question, 'Ao-e-ii-o-*marrow*-ue?' had the spacemen scratching their helmets.

Rork spoke. 'We understand that you are the inventor of the *Harris Tweed*,' was what he said in translation.

Len stroked a bath-foamed chin. 'Inventor of the Harris Tweed, eh?' Obviously the old Venusian

243

spy network was not all it might have been. Len looked the two travellers up and down: they *had* come a very long way. And it *was* the galaxy's highest accolade.

'Yep, that's me,' lied Len. 'Old Len "the tweed" Lemon, friend of the working man.'

The Venusians passed Len the Golden Tablet of Tosh m'Hoy, made a small vowel-encrusted speech, offered him a stiff salute and departed.

'Cheers,' said Len, waving. 'And thanks a lot.'

THE EPISODE OF THE GOLDEN TABLET AS ARCHROY'S WIFE OVER-THE-ROAD SAW IT

Now all who knew Archroy's wife, and many did in the biblical sense, knew her to be a woman of diverse sexual appetites. And no small sense of humour. These ranged from the 'Oh my God I hear my husband coming in the back door' routine, which had lovers shinning half-naked down the drainpipe to confront Jehovah's Witnesses on the front doorstep, to the 'Of course it won't result in any lasting injury, would I do that to *you*?', which had more permutations than Vernon's Pools.

On the day that Len received his award, and at that very moment, in fact, Archroy's wife was indulging in one of her personal pleasures, that of leaning head and shoulders out of her bedroom window, waving to passers-by, whilst being ravished from behind by a boy scout (or at least a man dressed up as one).

As the golden tablet changed hands and Len closed his front door, Archroy's wife waved down to the Venusians.

One of the Venusians waved back at her. The tall one. He waved in a friendly way, almost, one might say, in an intimate way. In fact, it was in such an intimate way that an observer who could recognize an intimate wave when he saw one might have been forgiven for thinking that here was a case of illicit interplanetary liaison.

Which was *not* the case.

Archroy's wife *had* waved because she *did* know the larger of the two aliens. And that was *know* in the biblical sense. But she knew this alien to be no alien at all.

For rather than step into some sort of telekinetic-anti-gravitational beam and levitate up to a waiting scout craft, as one might have expected of an alien, the alien removed his mirror-visored weather dome, stroked down locks of curly black hair and climbed into a Morris Minor.

'Come up and see me sometime, Omally,' called Archroy's wife, as he drove away, 'and bring the costume.'

THE EPISODE OF THE GOLDEN TABLET AS THE BRITISH MUSEUM SAW IT

The curator of *outré* antiquities and general weird shit looked up from a desk all jumbled high with jars of pickled bats' wings, plans of ancient flying

245

craft, dust-dry bones and mottled tomes, curious stones and garden gnomes, maps and caps and spats and hats and many other things.

'Ah, Sir John,' he said, adjusting his pince-nez upon the bridge of his bulbous nose, 'I had not expected you so soon.'

'I set out the moment I put down the telephone.' Sir John Rimmer, for it was he, tapped his silver-topped cane lightly upon the marble floor and removed his wide-brimmed hat. To those who had never met the world-famous psychic investigator before, his appearance had a sobering effect; to those who already had, it still did the same. As it were. Standing nearly seven feet in height, his vast red beard spread nearly to his waist. His gaunt frame, encased in lush green velvet, seemed permanently a-quiver. Steel-grey eyes glittered behind horn-rimmed specs atop his hawkish nose.

'Yes, yes,' said the curator, staring up at the phenomena that loomed above him. 'Well, the item in question turned up this very morning. It was in a shoe-box, would you believe, which had apparently fallen down the back of a radiator. Would you care to examine it now?'

'I would.'

'Then follow me.'

The curator led the long stick insect of a man down aisles of files and corridors of drawers, past cases of braces and spaces where faces of concubines and philistines stared from oils that were the spoils of war and the so much more to gaze on them was sure to quite amaze.

'If we might simply cut the poetic descriptions and get straight to the matter in hand,' said Sir John, who was not to be shilly-shallied, dilly-dallied, taken for a ride or subtly pushed aside, *'the shoe-box!'*

'It's here,' said the curator.

'Ah, so it is.'

Sir John gave the box a good looking-over. On the lid, a label bore a British Museum catalogue number and the words THE GOLDEN TABLET OF TOSH M'HOY, written on with a biro in a crude hand. Sir John blew dust from the lid and the curator, who received it full in the face, took to a fit of coughing.

'And how long has this been down behind the radiator?' asked Sir John.

The curator added a polite cough or two to his indiscriminate stream. 'About thirty years,' he said.

'Thirty years!' Sir John rose to a quite impossible height.

'Booked in in 1966.'

'1966.' Sir John's narrow head nodded. 'But of course it would have been. That was when it all happened.'

'All what?' asked the curator, who being a curator was nosy by nature. A bit like being a window cleaner really, or one of those people who views houses for sale when they've no intention of buying them, or an investigative journalist, or—

'Shut up!' shouted Sir John.

'But I only said, all what.'

'Never mind.' Sir John opened the shoe-box lid and viewed the contents. 'The Golden Tablet of

Tosh m'Hoy. And it was claimed to be of extra-terrestrial origin.'

The curator's head bobbed. 'And is it, do you think?'

'No,' said the psychic investigator. 'It *isn't*. But I'll take it with me, if I may.'

'I'm sorry, but you may not.'

'Nevertheless I will.'

'I really must protest.'

Sir John raised his cane and smote the curator on the head. The curator collapsed in an unconscious heap.

Of mounted sheep
And things that creep
And parchment scrolls
And—

'*Shut up!*' said Sir John.

THE EPISODE OF THE GOLDEN TABLET AS SIR JOHN RIMMER EXPLAINED IT

In a dungeon beneath the Hidden Tower, the manse of Sir John Rimmer, three men were gathered about a cylindrical steel coffin. Pipes ran from this to various control units, stop-cocks, temperature gauges, canisters of liquid nitrogen, electrical apparatus. It was very cold down there in the dungeon, the breath of three men steamed in air made bright by naphtha lamps.

Sir John was there with his two associates, Dr Harney, of the white nimbus hair and freckled face, and Danbury Collins, the psychic youth and masturbator.

'Gentlemen,' said Sir John, 'I have called you here, upon this dark and stormy night' (thunder crashed distantly and a flash of lightning showed beyond a stained-glass window), 'because our search is finally at an end.'

'You have found the tablet?' said the good doctor.

'At last. It has lain lost in the vaults at the B.M. for almost thirty years, handed in by a Mr Lemon who believed it to be a gift from Venusians.'

'And it's not?' asked Danbury, scratching his trousers.

'Terrestrial in origin. I have examined it at great length. It was carved in the early nineteen-sixties, then buried on the St Mary's allotment, where a Mr Omally found it and then passed it on to Mr Lemon as a prank. I believe it was intended that we come across it at the same time we acquired our chap here.' Sir John tapped lightly upon the cylindrical coffin, then examined his fingertips for frostbite. 'In 1966, however, it got knocked down behind a radiator and thirty years have been allowed to pass.'

'But it *will* do what you think it *will* do?' asked the doctor.

'The spell of denecrolization is engraved upon it.'

'What exactly *is* that?' asked Danbury.

'A spell for reanimating the dead.'

'Ooh, freaky.'

'Shut it, boy, and take your hand out of your trouser pocket.'

'Thirty years is a long time,' said Dr Harney. 'Do you think the corpse—'

'The corpse has been preserved at a temperature of two hundred and forty degrees below zero, it will be in mint condition.'

'Let us hope so. But listen, perhaps now, before you speak the spell, you might care to reacquaint us with the details of this extraordinary business.'

'I would be glad to.' Sir John took to pacing, and spoke as he walked. 'As you will recall, we rescued this chap from the hospital morgue just hours before he was due to be cremated. We brought him here and froze him up.'

'Nasty,' said Danbury.

'Not nasty, boy. He is dead, he can't feel anything, can he?'

'I suppose not.'

'I know his real name, but we will refer to him as John Doe. The story begins back in the 1950s. The Ministry of Serendipity, a secret government research department, were searching for the Alpha Man. That is a man who is number one in the process of idea-to-realization of idea. An original originator, if you like. They were not successful in their search but they later discovered someone with an extraordinary gift. John Doe here. He possessed the power of the mystical butterfly of chaos theory. He could achieve great ends by performing small feats, but he was unaware of his wild talent. The ministry nurtured him and by enlisting relatives of his, an uncle and John Doe's brother, they set up a controlled experiment: a stage act where John played Carlos the Chaos Cockroach. They worked out what actions he should perform with a specially designed computer program. The experiment was a success, but John overheard his brother and uncle in conversation and realized that he was being used. The M.o.S. put plan B into operation; they set up a phoney attack on Fangio's Bar, allowing John Doe to escape in the company of a woman called Litany. Litany was also in the pay of the M.o.S. She was one of their top agents.

'The plan was that she would be John's lover, and guide him to use his gift for the ends of the M.o.S. These ends were, naturally enough, world domination by the United Kingdom.'

Dr Harney whistled.

Danbury tinkered in his trousers.

'However,' said Sir John, 'things didn't go the way they planned. At a seaside resort called Skelington Bay, John used his talents to make all the local homeless wealthy. Call it fate or call it irony, but the money came from the coffers of the M.o.S. They were furious and tried to track down all these now wealthy homeless. But the homeless were one step ahead, they donated all their money to local charities in the town. The M.o.S. couldn't touch them.

'Now we come to the bad bit. Our John Doe here has a fatal accident. He walks into the path of a Blue Bird Cleaners truck.'

'Is that a truck for cleaning blue birds?' Danbury asked. 'As in birds in blue films?'

Dr Harney clouted Mr Collins.

'Ouch,' said Mr Collins.

'Fatal accident,' continued Sir John. 'Except it

was *no* accident. The driver of the van was an M.o.S. hitman. Mr Doe had been targeted for termination, as they say. He had become a dangerous liability. They snuffed him out.'

'That's very bad,' said Dr Harney.

'Very bad,' Sir John agreed. 'But there is a little more to the story. My investigations have uncovered that throughout the course of Mr Doe's short life there are a number of curious anomalies concerning time. For instance, this man's brother owned a disco van in 1966 in which he played the Byrds' 'Eight Miles High' on the radio. 'Eight Miles High' was not released until 1967.'

'That could just be a mistake,' said Danbury. 'Maybe it was a promo copy.'

'Possibly, but how would you explain him receiving a copy of Captain Beefheart's legendary 1969 album *Trout Mask Replica* in 1957 when he was eight years old and playing it on a 1980s stereo system?'

'I wouldn't.'

'And most recently a 1966 Lincoln Continental was trawled from the mud flats in Skelington Bay, where it had lain for thirty years. On its back seat was a 1996 laptop computer.'

Danbury now whistled.

Dr Harney didn't tinker with his trousers.

'There are many more such anomalies,' said Sir John. 'This lad's life was riddled with them.'

'Are you suggesting that *he* caused them?' the doctor asked.

'I am. Unwittingly, unconsciously, he caused things to occur. Part of some great pattern that only he knew about and yet that even he himself was not aware that he knew about. It is my belief that *he* created this Golden Tablet with the spell of denecrolization upon it so that it could be used upon him after his death.'

'That's quite incredible!' said Dr Harney.

'It's not bad, is it?' said Sir John. 'And it hasn't half tied up a few loose ends.'

'So are you going to speak the magic words?' Danbury asked.

'I am.'

'Just one thing.' Dr Harney raised a freckled hand. 'Do you think this is really a wise thing to do?'

'What do you mean?'

'I mean that perhaps it would simply be better to leave him as he is. If this man has the power to control the world, isn't he better left dead? There's no telling what he might do when he's reanimated and finds out what the M.o.S. did to him. He might take it out on us.'

'Not a bit of it.' Sir John shook his slender head. 'We will be releasing him from death. We will be his saviours. He will be for ever in our debt. Think what we might learn from him. Think what he might teach us. Think what he might *give* us by way of a reward.'

'It's iffy,' said Dr Harney, 'very iffy.'

'It is nothing of the sort.'

'But what if he *was* to find out about the M.o.S. killing him? He might take a terrible revenge.'

'But he's not going to find out, is he? Because we are not going to tell him.' Sir John tapped *very* lightly upon the steel cylinder. 'All that I have just said is *our* secret, he must never find out. And, frankly, unless he's been able to overhear our conversation, there's no way he ever will.'

Sir John laughed. And he winked as he laughed and, raising high his hands, he spoke the spell of denecrolization.

Inside the steely cylinder John Doe lay rigid. But even though suffering the agonies of being frozen two hundred and forty degrees below zero, he had heard *every single word*.

And he wasn't happy.

BLACK CAT'S RETURN

Don of The Spoon and Pusher
Said to the lads at the bar,
'Though it's closing time and the Bill be plenty,
I'll not close this pub to gentry.
Have one more, my bonny lads,
And we'll wait Black Cat's return.'

Jim the skipper quaffed his ale
And nodded with his beard.
'Though I'd best sail when the tide be turning,
I would that my boats be burning
Than leave you here, my bonny lads,
To wait Black Cat's return.'

Mick the butcher sucked his Briar
And blew out rings of smoke.
'Though I should be at slicing meat,
I'll not set one foot in the street
And leave you here, my bonny lads,
To wait Black Cat's return.'

Ben the sad librarian
Leaned back in his chair.
'Though I've fines that need collecting,
Filing drawers that need correcting
I'll stay here, my bonny lads,
To wait Black Cat's return.'

Black Cat Larson sat alone
In a pub just up the road.
'Though I've a love for The Spoon and Pusher
With its seats of padded cusher,
I'll not drink there when it's so damn crowded
I'll stay here alone.'

Ha ha.

16

BARRY

It was 1996, the sun was shining and I was marching up a high street. Marching and swearing.

'Barry, you stupid bastard!' I swore. 'That was some radical plan! Thirty years frozen at two hundred and forty degrees below zero and feeling every minute of it. You call *that* a plan? You stupid bastard!'

'Yeah, well I'm sorry, chief. It wasn't the way *I* would have written it. It was just bad luck, the shoe-box getting lost behind the radiator and everything.'

'I've lost thirty years, you ble—'

'Look on the bright side, chief. Thirty years ago when you were fifteen, you looked forty-five. Thirty years later and guess what, you *still* look forty-five. That can't be bad, can it?'

'*Can't be bad?* I have missed out on thirty years of life I could have had with Litany. That's thirty years of SEX.'

'Yeah, but, chief, Litany was a stinker, she was working for the M.o.S. She only pretended to like you.'

'You're right. And she is going to pay first!'

'*Pay first?* What about what you did back there at the Hidden Tower. That wasn't very nice, was it?'

'They deserved what they got.'

'But Sir John did speak the magic words and reanimate you; it wasn't very grateful, kicking him in the nuts like that.'

'He was going to use me, like the others did. I heard him. "Think of what he might *give* us by way of a reward," he said.'

'Maybe, chief, but headbutting poor Dr Harney like that.'

'*He* was for leaving me dead!'

'He might have had a point.'

'What did you say, Barry?'

'Nothing, chief. But what you did to Danbury Collins, that was really gross.'

'I don't want to talk about that.'

'I've never seen someone's head rammed up their own bottom before.'

'I said I don't want to talk about it.'

'Sorry, chief. Where are we going now?'

'To find Litany.'

'You won't find her, chief. This is 1996, she could be anywhere.'

'I know exactly where she'll be,' I said, and I did.

There were mammoth crowds at Wembley. Sonic Energy Authority were playing their thirtieth-anniversary concert. I pushed my way into the crowd.

'You don't have a ticket, chief.'

I headbutted a short frail-looking young man and availed myself of his wallet. 'I do now.'

'This is not a nice way to behave, chief.'

'Just shut up.'

The ex-waiter playing bass hadn't aged too well, he was going bald and had a serious paunch. The rest of the band didn't look so bad. Cardinal Cox, the lead singer, still had it. When he launched into 'Johnny B. Goode' the crowd went wild.

I stood to the side of the stage eyeing the crowd. And then I saw her, right near the front, blond hair, bikini top, up on some young fellow's shoulders. It was a right squeeze getting to her, but I managed it. I punched the young fellow right in the nose and caught Litany on the way down.

'Come with me,' I shouted.

'No I won't. Leave me alone.'

'Come with me or I'll wring your neck right here.'

'Well, if you put it that way.'

In one of the big corridors I held Litany against a wall.

'Litany,' I said, 'remember me?'

'I don't remember you and my name's not Litany.'

'Oh yes it is.'

'Oh no it isn't.'

'Is!'

'Is not, my name is Stephanie.'

'What?'

'Litany was my mother.'

'Your *mother*. So that's how it works, you lot always looking the same at all the concerts. Where is your mother? I have to talk to her.'

'She's dead.'

'*Dead!*' I stepped back in more than some surprise and not a little shock. 'Dead? When did she die?'

'Thirty years ago, as it happens.'

'Thirty years? But you don't look—'

'I'm just thirty.'

'Tell me what happened.'

'Why, what's it to you?'

'I knew your mother, she was . . . Just tell me what happened.'

'Her boyfriend was killed. My father. Nine months after he died she gave birth to me. When she left the hospital she put me into care, then she went out and bought all of Phillip Glass's records. The entire collection, she went home and played them one after the other and was—'

'Bored to death, what a terrible way to go.'

'She was quite rigid when they found her.'

'Bored stiff!'

'And completely desiccated. No bodily fluids left.'

'Bored shitless!'

'So now you know, let me go, will you?'

I released my grip, but I didn't let her go. 'You say her boyfriend died nine months before you were born?'

'Died in a road accident, yes.'

'Road accident.' I looked at Stephanie. Deep into her eyes. And then I knew. This was *my* daughter. Litany had died for love of me. I took the girl in my arms.

'Get your frigging hands off me!' she screamed.

'No, you don't understand. About your father. He didn't die. He just went away.'

'He died,' she said.

'No he didn't. He just went away.'

'He died!'

'He didn't. Listen, I know who your father is.'

'*Was*.'

'Is.'

'*Was*, he's dead.'

'He's *not* dead. Your father's name is—' And I named myself.

'Crap,' said Stephanie. 'My father's name *was* Panay Cloudrunner.'

I marched out of Wembley Stadium and along another high street. Wembley High Street. I pushed through the Saturday shoppers. 'That does it, Barry,' I shouted. 'That *really* does it!'

'Now don't do anything hasty, chief.'

'Oh I won't be hasty. I've thought about all this. For thirty years I've thought about all this. I am going to change this rotten world from the ground up. I am going to build a brave new world, without liars and cheats and exploiters. A real world. A decent world. A world of love and, and, little fluffy animals.'

'Sounds pretty gross, chief.'

'Oh you'll love it, Barry. You and the Big Figure.'

'God, chief?'

'Chief God! He's going to love it too. And although having spent thirty years at -240, the idea of +240 up your arse in the cooking pot does have a certain appeal, I'm actually going to let you share the glory.'

'That's very nice of you, chief.'

'Yes, isn't it? God will probably make you chief breeding sprout. Do sprouts have sex, by the way?'

'SPROUTS DO IT IN THEIR BEDS. I read that once on the back of a tractor. I never exactly knew what it meant, though.'

'Well never mind. I've had a dream. A thirty-year dream, squeezed in amongst the nightmare. And I will make it come true, because, after all, I *am* the Chosen One. Didn't I rise from the dead?'

'Well, you did, chief, but it took you thirty years. It only took the other bloke three days. And you know who I'm talking about.'

'He had help.'

'Chief, I really don't think it's right.'

'But you suggested it, Barry. You said that if you'd been able to pull it off, you would have earned big kudos with God and got to stay off his dinner plate.'

'Yeah, chief, but I'm just worried about—'

'What?' I tore the head from a doll clutched in the arms of a passing child and bit its eye out.

'Your *attitude problem*, chief.'

'I don't have an attitude problem! It's this lot!' I gestured at the passing folk, who were regarding me with cold-fish eyes, as folk will when confronted by someone ranting to himself. 'It's this lot that have the attitude problem. People. All crooks and cheats and swindlers, the lot of them.'

'Now hang about, young man,' said a lady with a straw hat.

'Hear that, chief, *young man*, you still carry your age well.'

'Shut up, Barry!'

'Don't tell me to shut up, young man. And my name's not Barry. And *I'm* not a crook and a cheat.'

'Yeah, well, I didn't mean *you* specifically.'

'All right, so I may be a swindler, but swindling's different. That's not a real crime. Not, say, like rape.'

'There's no such crime as rape,' said an old bloke who had been shuffling by. 'Confucius he say, rape impossible, woman with skirt up run faster than man with trousers down.'

'Rape is a serious issue,' said a stumpy woman with short hair and badges on her anorak, as a crowd began to gather. 'Rape is a heinous crime.'

'Rape's not *that* heinous,' said a young-fellow-me-lad, slinging in his two-ha'penny worth. 'Murder's more heinous than rape.'

'Not as heinous as rape *and* murder,' said another young-fellow-me-lad, the first young fellow's chum. 'Or murder, *then* rape. That would be *really* serious.'

'You're being facetious,' said stumpy of the anorak. 'You're taking the piss, like this old bloke.'

'Don't call me *old*,' said the old bloke. 'I'm only forty-five.'

'Hear that, chief? Makes *you* look good.'

'Shut up, Barry.'

'Don't call *me* Barry,' said the old bloke, shaking his fist. 'I suppose that's some acronym, is it? Like Bloody Auld Rotten Reprobate Yobbo. You can't bandy words with me, I once won *Mastermind*.'

'You never did,' said the lady with the straw hat. 'There was only one bloke who ever won *Mastermind* and he was a taxi driver called Fred. Everyone remembers him.'

'Fred Trueman,' said a cricket fan who was on his way to the sports shop.

'Freddie Mercury,' said the stumpy woman.

'Freddy Kruger,' said one of the fellow-me-lads.

'Fred Flintstone,' said another.

'Yeah, well I *was* on it,' said the old bloke. 'And I did win. And *my* name's Fred. And I'm not having this bastard calling me a BARRY.'

'I wasn't calling you a Barry,' I told him, as the crowd began jostling and pushing. 'I was talking to another Barry.'

'Well, don't look at me,' said the first young-fellow-me-lad. 'I ain't no stinking Barry.'

'Nor me,' agreed his mates in unison. There were three of them.

'So what's a BARRY, then?' asked stumpy the anorak wearer. 'Is a BARRY a challenge to your manhood, or something?'

'Nothing challenges *my* manhood, darling,' said the first young fellow.

'Well I do, *darling*!' said stumpy.

'I'm not the *darling*, darling, I'm straight.'

'Implying that I'm not, I suppose?'

'Maybe. So what are you anyway?'

'I happen to be a radical feminist.'

'You mean lesbian.'

'No I don't.'

'Of course you do, all feminists are closet lesbians.'

'And all heterosexual men are closet bumbandits.'

'Are you asking for a smack in the mouth?'

'Hit a lady, would you?'

'No, but I'd hit you.'

'Hey. Cool it, cool it,' said the young fellow's fellow young fellow, young fellow number two. 'Let's all be friends. Respect each other's sexual preferences.'

'Yeah, well . . .' said the radical feminist.

'Everybody has a right to be what they want to be,' continued young fellow number two. 'Now let's all smile and make up. Listen, I'll tell you a joke. Why did the lesbian cross the road? Answer. To suck my coc—'

The radical feminist lesbian swung her shoulder-bag. It evidently contained an Aga.

And she caught me right in the face with it.

I went down as the fists began to fly and I mouthed words to the effect of 'why do bloody women always hit *me*?' It was the lady in the straw hat who helped me up again. I put up my hands. 'Stop fighting,' I shouted, 'or someone's bound to get hurt. Behave yourselves, all of you.'

Now why did I say *that*?

'You bloody started this, moosh,' said the old bloke, who had a young fellow by the throat. 'Calling perfect strangers BARRYS. What you

265

need is a dose of the army with a sergeant major up your back passage.'

'Up my *what*?'

'Did I say back passage? I meant, rear guard action, no, that sounds as bad, doesn't it?'

'There you go,' said the radical feminist lesbian. 'All closet bum-boys. What did I tell you?'

'Well, you didn't tell *me* anything,' said the lady in the straw hat. 'And *I'm* your mother. And here you are "outing" yourself in the High Street with everyone looking on. What will the neighbours say?'

'They'll say', said the radical feminist lesbian daughter, 'what they always say: "Don't be late on Thursday, it's wife-swapping night." '

'They never do, do they?' asked the fellow-me-lad whose throat was being held.

'They bloody do,' said the old bloke, releasing his grip. 'I'm always round there on Thursdays with *my* missus. Swapped her for a lawn mower once.'

'You hetero-fascist,' shouted you-know-who, bringing her shoulder-bag once more into play and hitting *me* once more in the face. And then the fight got well and truly started.

'Just break it up!' I shouted, staggering about in the mayhem. 'Break it up, everyone, please!'

'Calm down, chief, it's not your business.'

'SHUT UP, BARRY!'

It must either have been twenty-past-something, or twenty-to-something, because as I shouted that out there was this one brief moment of absolute silence.

And then, in total unison, the entire crowd shouted, 'DON'T CALL ME A—' and fell upon me.

I couldn't pick out what the last word was, they kicked me to unconsciousness. I think it might have been BARRY.

17

THE LITTLE HOSPITAL CHAPTER

'Look on the bright side,' said my Holy Guardian Sprout. 'The swellings will soon go down. The fractures will mend. Your hip joints will be reset and they've almost finished the reconstruction of your rib cage. Once the heart-lung implants go in on Friday you'll be as right as rain.'

I groaned. Inwardly.

'You'll come up smiling like the trooper you are, chief. Listen, have you thought about what kind of job you might apply for once you leave hospital? Perhaps something in the entertainment industry. You liked being on the stage, didn't you? Chief, are you listening to me?'

'No I'm bloody not. Leave me alone.'

'Now you *thought* that, chief, didn't you? You didn't actually say it.'

'Well, I can't bloody say it, can I? Not with my jaws wired together. Oh shit, I need the bedpan again.'

'I wish I could help you out, chief, I really do.'

'Well that's nice of you, at least.'

'Oh I wasn't trying to be nice, it's just that we share the same nose.'

'Will you *please* leave me alone!'

'Sorry, chief, sorry. Oh look, here come the doctors again.'

'And so how are we feeling today?' asked one of the doctors, taking up the regulation clipboard from the bottom of the bed and giving it that once-over look that pretends to be a *real* once-over look. 'Everything hunky-dory?'

If I'd had any teeth left I would have ground them.

'We'll soon have you up and about, old fellow.'

'You hear that, Barry? He thinks I'm old.'

'It's just a figure of speech, chief. You look like a million bucks.'

'I do?'

'Yeah, green and wrinkly.'

'What was that, Barry?'

'Nothing, chief.'

'Well, just keep your pecker up,' said the doctor. 'What you have left of it anyway. Nurse, are we thinking of sewing his nose back on?'

'Sorry, doctor, there's been so many other bits to do.'

'Quite so, nurse.'

'Here, chief, that reminds me of a joke.'

'I don't want to hear it.'

'Of course you do, chief, it will cheer you up.'

'I don't want to be cheered up.'

'Of course you do. Now just listen. There was this bloke, see, and he was in hospital, just like you, all bandaged up from head to foot, and the

269

doctor comes in, and the doctor says, "Ah, I see you've regained consciousness. Now you probably won't remember but you were in this pile-up on the motorway. Now you're going to be OK, you'll walk again, everything, but something happened. I'm trying to break this gently, but your penis was chopped off in the wreck and we were unable to find it." '

'Turn it in, Barry.'

'No, listen, chief, so the bloke groans, a bit like you just did, but the doctor says, "But it's going to be all right, we have the technology now to build you a new one that will work as well as your old one did, better in fact. But the thing is, it doesn't come cheap. It's a thousand pounds an inch." And the bloke perks up a bit at this, even though it's a thousand pounds an inch. "So the thing is," the doctor says, "it's for you to decide how many inches you want. But it's something you'd probably better discuss with your wife. I mean if you had a five-inch one before and you decide to go for a nine-incher, she might be a bit put out. But if you had a nine-inch one before and decide to only invest in a five-incher this time, she might be disappointed. So it's important that she plays a vital role in helping you make the decision."

'So the bloke agrees to talk with his wife and the doctor comes back the next day. "So," says the doctor, "have you spoken with your wife?"

' "I have," says the fellow.

' "And has she helped you in making the decision?"

' "She has," says the bloke.

' "And what is it?" asks the doctor.

'The bloke looks up and says, "We're having a new kitchen." '

'That is a very sick joke, Barry.'

'Yeah, and an old one too, but a classic, chief, a classic. Very, very funny.'

'But not too funny if you were the bloke.'

'Oh no, chief, not too funny at all. Hey look, the doctor's leaving, good riddance, eh?'

The doctor turned as he reached the door, 'Nurse,' he said, 'about the other bits you still have to sew on. Did you come across his penis?'

The nurse shook her head. 'They never found it,' she said. 'And you know what a new one costs. I hope this chap has an understanding wife.'

18

SIX MONTHS AND TEN
THOUSAND POUNDS LATER

'I feel like a million bucks,' I told Barry, as I stood outside the hospital, the sunlight dancing upon my new cheek-bones and twinkling in my glass eye. My prosthetic limbs were all a-quiver and I felt mighty fine. 'I feel mighty fine,' I said. 'And have you noticed something else, Barry?'

'What's that, chief?'

'The poetry's gone from the beginning of the chapters.'

'Don't knock it, chief.'

'No, I wasn't. But I know why. Since my "accident", I don't have to compensate for anything any more. I don't need the poetry in my head. I'm totally recharged and I'm totally charged up.'

'That's nice, chief, that's really nice. So what are you going to do now, hit the job centre?'

'No, Barry, I think I'll do something else instead.'

'Hit the beach then, a bit of a holiday?'

'No, something else.'

'Go to the café for a cup of tea?'

'No.'

'Care to give me a clue, chief, it wouldn't be—'

'Change the world, Barry. Rebuild it from the ground up.'

'Ah, it would be *that*. I thought it might just be that. Look, chief, we've been through all this.'

'You've been through it, Barry. I haven't started yet.'

'But your – dare I say it? – *attitude problem*.'

'All sorted, I'm a new man.'

'Well, a lot of you is. Especially the—'

'I am going to do the right thing this time, use my gift for the good of all mankind.'

'But you tried that last time, chief, and it wasn't a raging success. I don't like to mention it, but you must recall the matter of the bass-playing rock star.'

'I have paid my debt to him, Barry. Thirty years' cold turkey.'

'I'm not going to be able to talk you out of this, chief, am I?'

'No, Barry, you're not. We are now going to a hotel where I am going to set up shop. I have formulated a plan for world-wide renewal. I will assemble all the foolish bits and bobs I require and then I will begin. I will build a glorious world. A utopia where all men will be free and happy. And honest. A world in which mankind will reach its true potential. A fine world. A happy world. A world of love.'

'I don't mean to rain on your parade, chief, but a speech like that is generally preceded by the words "They thought me mad, the fools, I who have created life" and generally ends with the line,

"We belong dead." That one spoken by Boris Karloff, of course, before he pulls the big switch.'

'Quite finished?'

'Well, there's the villagers with the flaming torches.'

'There will be no villagers with flaming torches, only people with bright smiling faces.'

'Don't trust those, chief. I've seen those at Phillip Glass concerts.'

'What's with all the Phillip Glass references?' I asked. 'What have we got against Phillip Glass?'

'Perhaps it's a running gag, chief. We've been quite short of those.'

'Well it's not very funny.'

'Perhaps the humour lay in you drawing attention to it. But let's not improvise here. Smiling faces, you say?'

'A veritable carpet of smiling faces.'

'Carpets are made to be walked on, chief.'

'A host, then. An exuberance.'

'Oh dear, oh dear.'

'Perk up, Barry. Today we check into a hotel. Tomorrow we make the whole world smile.'

'I'm really not keen, chief.'

'Listen, Barry, I'm going to make everything right this time. Every decision I make is going to be the right one. And my first right decision is that we're going to check into that hotel over there.'

'Which one is that, chief?'

'That one. Hotel Jericho.'

19

SUSPICIONS REGARDING
WHAM, POW AND ZAP

And so you came here. That *YOU* then, that is the
ME now. The me who sits alone in this room at
Hotel Jericho. Recording the events as they happened. Writing in my red exercise books, thirty
lines to the page, twenty pages to the book. Alone
here, the walls and windows painted black, water
dripping from the tap, the smell of old stale
cabbage always in the air.

But don't let me spoil the mood, your mood.
Your mood was optimistic then. You really *knew*
you couldn't fail.

And perhaps you didn't. Really.

'All right, chief, I give up. How did you do it?'

'Do what, Barry?'

'Arrange all this. We turn up at a hotel, picked
seemingly at random, to discover a suite already
booked in your name. And what do we find when
we come up to it? Your favourite beer in the
fridge, a full computer set-up on the desk, a row
of televisions and a young woman of negotiable
affections waiting to try out your ten-inch todger.'

'There's nothing magic about it, Barry. It's all *very* straightforward.'

'But none the less, I'd like to know.'

'Fair enough. I'm sure you recall that during my convalescence at the hospital, there was a certain bed-pan over-spill incident, which led to a sheet-besmirchment and nose-hold situation.'

'Recall it all too well, chief. I popped out of your head for half an hour to have a little drift about outside.'

'That's right. And while you were gone I made a telephone call. Called in a favour or two.'

'Go on.'

'I called the present bass guitarist of Sonic Energy Authority. The ex-waiter. He covered all my hospital expenses and agreed to fund my set up here. It's as simple as that.'

'Well, it's always nice when something so simple can tie up such ENORMOUS loose ends, chief.'

'Hm.'

'So, you've had a beer and a woman and a bit of a kip, what say we hit the beach?'

'No.' I took up the remote controller and switched on a TV.

'I have to catch up on thirty years of world news, find out what's gone on in my absence, decide exactly where I should start with the from-the-ground-up reconstruction.'

'Start tomorrow, chief. It's a lovely day outside.'

'I'm starting *now*.'

'I really don't think you should, chief. It might upset you.'

'I can no longer be upset, Barry. Nothing can

faze me any more. I know this world is a rotten place, I know it is my destiny to change it. Nothing can get to me any more, I am immune to all upset.'

'That's very nice to know, chief.'

'Who's that?'

'Who, chief?'

'That man on the screen.'

'Him? Just a man, chief. I think he's the, er, I think he's the present Prime Minister. Yes, that's who he is.'

'There's something very familiar about him.'

'They all look the same, don't they, chief? Winston Churchill, Margaret Thatcher, hard to tell one from the other. Switch the TV off, let's hit the beach.'

'No, Barry. Oh my God!'

'Oh my God?'

'It's him! It's him!'

'God, chief?'

'Not God. You know exactly who it is, don't you?'

'It's just a man, chief, it's—'

'*My brother! It's my bloody brother!*'

Actually, I think I took it *very* well, considering. All right, so I trashed the room. All right, so I threw a television set out of the window. All right, so I got into a fight with the policemen who were called to deal with the disturbance. And, all right, so they did give me a kicking down in the cell. But considering the circumstances, I still think I took it very well.

Apart from the kicking, of course. I didn't take

that too well. And as I lay there on the cell floor, all bruised and battered, I must confess that I didn't take the next bit too well either.

'I'm sorry, chief. What can I tell you? I'm sorry.'

'It's not your fault, Barry.'

'Well it is, chief, that's why I'm saying sorry.'

'Forget it. You didn't want me to watch the television, because you didn't want me to find out that my brother is now the Prime Minister. You didn't want to upset me. That's OK.'

'That's not what I'm apologizing for, chief.'

'Well, you don't have anything else to apologize for, do you? It's not as if *you* made him Prime Minister, is it?'

'Well, chief . . .'

'What do you mean, *well, chief*? You *didn't*, did you?'

'Well, chief . . .'

'*WHAT?*'

'I was only trying to help, chief. I mean I *am* the family retainer. For *all* your family. I'm your brother's Holy Guardian Sprout too. And what with you banged up in the freezer for thirty years and your mum and dad thinking you were dead and everything—'

'My mum and dad. I hadn't even thought about them, are they still alive?'

'They're fine, chief. But what with them thinking you were dead, I thought that if your brother became really successful, it would ease their grief. And it did, you know. I don't think you've crossed their minds in the last twenty-five years.'

'You stupid—'

'Steady on, chief. He's not a bad Prime Minister. Obviously he's not a *good* one, none of them are. But he's no worse than any other. And he's a real crowd-pleaser. Brought back conscription and hanging and—'

'Don't tell me any more. I don't want to hear it.'

'The ducking stool.'

'He brought back the ducking stool?'

'I told you he wasn't too bad, chief.'

'Well, good, bad or whatever, he's going to be out of office tomorrow.'

'Don't be hasty, chief, please.'

'We've been through all this, Barry, and there is no hastiness at all involved. I've made my telephone call and as soon as the bass player bails me out, it's back to the hotel and on with the show.'

'Oh dear, oh dear, oh dear.'

'I suppose there's no other little skeletons in the family cupboard you'd care to mention, Barry? I mean you haven't made my Uncle Brian President of the USA or anything, have you?'

'Well, chief, now that you mention it.'

'*WHAT?*'

The bass player did bail me out, but he made a right fuss. He said I'd behaved irresponsibly and that throwing a TV out of a hotel window was a disgraceful thing to do. I, in reply, asked just what kind of a rock'n'roller he thought he was, with an attitude like *that*? And then he told me that he had recently been elevated to the status of Cardinal by the new Prime Minister.

There was some unpleasantness then, and I ran off.

'Is it heresy to headbutt a Cardinal?' Barry asked, once we were safely back at Hotel Jericho.

'No,' I said, looking dismally around the trashed-up room, 'but it does mean that we'll have to go this one alone from now on.'

'So what are you going to do now?'

'I'm going to start at once, Barry. And you are *not* going to stop me this time.'

'As if I'd try, chief, as if I'd try.'

'As if you would. But just listen to me for a moment. Thirty years ago I became aware of my special gift, I used it to bring wealth to some homeless people, then *WHAM!* I'm run over and killed. I spend the next thirty years in frozen pain. I get defrosted and I tell you that I intend to go on with my mission. Then *POW!* I'm involved in a fight in Wembley High Street that puts me in intensive care for six months. I survive and we come here. I tell you that I am *still* determined to continue with my mission, and what happens, I see my brother has become Prime Minister and *ZAP!* I'm banged up in a police station. Now call me paranoid if you will, but I have the definite suspicion that someone, or some*thing* is trying to stop me from changing the world.'

'I hope you're not implying that I have something to do with it, chief.'

'What you, who made my rotten brother the Prime Minister, and my uncle, *Pope*? Perish the thought. So now, if you don't mind, I intend to begin. The door is locked, the blinds are drawn and there is nobody here for me to get into a fight with. There is nothing, absolutely nothing that is going to stand in my way this time.'

'Did you hear *that*, chief?'

'What, Barry?'

'It sounded like a car crash outside, do you think you should go down and see if anyone's hurt?'

'You're lying, Barry, aren't you?'

'I can't lie, chief, I'm a Holy Guardian Sprout.'

'So *was* there a car crash outside?'

'No, chief. But there might have been. You never know. Best go and check, eh?'

'No, Barry, I am going to remove my brother from office. This is the new phase one in my from-the-ground-up reconstruction.'

'It's not a good idea, chief. Please don't.'

'Silence, Barry.' I took a deep breath and concentrated all my thoughts. *Remove my brother from office*. And then I snapped my fingers, tugged upon the lobe of my right ear and stamped upon my own left foot.

There came a great pounding at my door. 'Fire, fire!' someone shouted. 'Evacuate the building!'

'Nice try, Barry,' I said, 'but too late.'

20

AHA!

'You *again*!' said the doctor, staring down upon me. 'what happened to you this time?'

'He can't speak,' said the nurse. 'He has forty per cent burns. Refused to leave his room when they were evacuating the hotel.'

'Was this *the* hotel? Hotel Jericho?'

'That's right, doctor.'

'Well indeed, I suppose it makes this chap a little part of history, doesn't it?'

'How do you mean?'

'Well if there hadn't been one guest left in the blazing hotel, then the fire crews would never have gone in. And if they hadn't gone in, they would never have burst into the secret room by mistake and found all the documents that proved the Prime Minister was selling nukes to the Iraqis. I just heard on the news that he's resigned from office. And apparently the Pope was in on it too. And he's had to resign as well.'

If I could have managed a smile, I would have.

But I couldn't, so I did not.

So, Barry, I thought, What do you have to say for yourself?

'About what, chief?'

About the nukes, perhaps?

'Oh those.'

Yes, *those*.

'It was all quite innocent really. He was doing it for the good of all mankind.'

Bunging nukes to Iraq? For the good of mankind?

'Certainly. Your brother reasoned that a country *with* nukes dare only nuke a country *without* nukes. Because if another country *has* nukes, it will nuke back, right?'

Right.

'So if every single country in the world has nukes, then no country would ever dare to nuke any other country because it would fear the inevitable retaliation. It was what he called a world peace initiative.'

'It would never have worked.'

'Why, chief?'

'Well . . .' I tried to think of a why, but . . . 'just *because*, that's all.'

'Fair enough, chief. We'll never find out now, will we? Not now he's resigned from office.'

'Hmph,' I said, and it didn't half hurt.

Actually I didn't look too bad once the plastic surgeons had finished with me. I could have passed for forty, as long as I wore a hat. They told me my hair would eventually grow back and that the no-eyebrow look was the current chic. They were also very apologetic when they handed me the bill, saying that before the old government got ousted over the nuke scandal, all the work could have been done on the NHS. But the new government had privatized all hospitals, so I'd just have to pay up.

I told them that this created no problem, that I would just telephone my friend who was a cardinal, and then I slipped out of a back door and ran.

I returned to my room at Hotel Jericho. There wasn't much of it left and the bed was down to bare springs. But I wasn't beaten yet.

'Have you ever heard the expression, *sucker for punishment*, chief?' Barry asked.

'Just shut it, you.'

'But, chief, come on. Surely you're getting the message. Every time you do something small that causes something big to happen, it bounces right back upon you and you end up in the ka-ka.'

'All right, you don't have to rub it in.'

'I'm just trying to look after you, chief, provide a bit of Holy Guardianship. If you get snuffed out a second time, I don't know whether I'll be able to rescue you. I mean, let's face it, it was a pretty far-fetched do the last time, Golden Tablet of Tosh m'Plonker, or whatever.'

'Aha!' I said. 'Aha!'

'What are you "aha-ing" about, chief?'

'You've just given me a *very* good idea.'

'Was it the one about hitting the beach, by any chance?'

'No, it's a reworking of the more-radical-than-voodoo one. I am going to withdraw from the plot and let other people do all the doing.'

'But, chief, I won't be able, I mean *you* won't be able to have any influence over them.'

'Wanna bet?'

'No, stop, chief, this chapter's too short, you can't end it like—'

21

THE BIG ANSWER

'The greatest darts player I ever met was George Bernard Shaw.' This extravagant claim emerged from the not-particularly-extravagant lips of John Vincent Omally, The Flying Swan's Liar in Residence.

'Old George and I once fought for the love of a good woman,' said Gimlet Martin from The Shrunken Head. 'I won, he came second.'

'I only met him on a single occasion.' The voice belonged to Derby Phil Wainscot of The New Inn. 'And that was in a former incarnation.'

And that earned Derby Phil the point and he took that round clear. The scores now stood at ten apiece, but Omally was warming up nicely.

'George Bernard, or Podger, as he liked me to call him, was a great man for the hang-gliding. Not a lot of people know that.'

'I knew it,' said Gimlet Martin.

'Me too,' said Derby Phil. 'Went gliding with Podger many a time.'

'So,' continued John, unabashed, 'we were up one day at about two thousand feet and Podger said to me, well he sort of *called* to me. "John," he called, "John, you and I have a lot in common. We both enjoy a game of darts, the company of rough-looking women and the study of inter-planetary communications." '

'I hope Omally knows what he's doing,' said Neville the part-time barman. 'We could really do with a win this year.'

For this was The Flying Swan's fifth annual *All Brentford Open Lying Competition* and out of the original one hundred and fifty contestants for the much coveted Silver Tongue Trophy and the even more coveted fifty-pound prize, three alone had survived to the final.

The crowd that remained to witness this event was of that discerning variety one observes mostly at darts matches and road traffic accidents. Little was spoken, but for the occasional appreciative gasp, depreciating exhalation or whispered order for drinks. There was fifteen minutes left on the clock and all was even on the scoreboard.

Gimlet Martin took up Omally's challenge. 'The study of interplanetary communications has for me always been an interest second only to that of viewing women's legs on escalators. But as I have an uncle who is married to a Venusian woman with very long legs, I am able to combine my interests.'

'What's your uncle's name?' enquired Derby Phil. 'Perhaps my Cousin Stubby, the Martian ambassador knows him.'

'If it's his Uncle Barry,' said Omally. 'Then we all know that old deviant well enough and if he's married a Venusian, then I will eat the hat Orson

Welles once gave me. The one he wore in *The Third Man*.'

'Get your knife and fork out then, Omally,' said Gimlet Martin.

'Did your uncle marry a south Venusian or a north Venusian?' asked Derby Phil, as if it *really* mattered.

'South, from the D-Zm lake region.'

'I know the place well,' said Derby Phil. 'I was there last week with my Cousin Stubby. We went to a movie, *Roswell Alien Autopsy: The Director's Cut*.'*

'The place has gone down since the tourists have moved in,' said Gimlet Martin. 'But the beer's good.'

'Oh yeah,' Phil agreed. 'Good beer.'

And this turn in the conversation found the three finalists studying their now empty glasses.

'Your round, Phil,' said Omally. 'A pint of Large, please.'

'Certainly,' said Phil and rising purposely, began to pat his pockets. 'Oh no,' he said, 'you'll never guess what.'

But by the rarest of coincidences both John Omally and Gimlet Martin *did* guess. Correctly.

'Surely,' said Gimlet, 'I am right in assuming that you're next up in line for getting them in, Omally.'

John Omally grinned. 'If only such *were* the case, I would gladly oblige. But I know for a fact that the lot falls to you, and I have no wish to insult us both by muscling in.'

*A special thank-you to SPROUT LORE for that one.

'Your nicety is a thing to inspire us all,' said Gimlet. 'But you see Phil here was carrying *my* money also. Why not then lend him the cash and he will get the round in.'

Omally turned up his hands. 'If only I could, but on the way here I was accosted by two Jehovah's Muggers.'

Neville called for a time-out and the three finalists repaired to separate tables for refreshment, and some scholarly advice from their trainers.

Jim Pooley spoke close at Omally's ear. 'Don't keep changing the subject,' was what he had to say. 'You started well on George Bernard Shaw but within a couple of minutes the talk had turned to beer on Venus. I hope you know what you're doing.'

Omally sucked upon his orange. 'I know *exactly* what I'm doing,' said he, 'and I'm moving in for the kill.'

The battered Guinness clock above the bar struck nine silent strokes, which meant it was ten o'clock. Something to do with British Summer Time ending and nobody getting around to climbing up and altering it. Or possibly, as has been mooted, it was a tradition, or an old charter, or something.

The finalists returned to the competition table.

'I was having a word with God the other night,' said Gimlet Martin.

'Which one?' asked John Omally.

'How many are there?' came the rhetorical reply.

'Six to my knowledge,' said John. 'Although I'm

only on first-name terms with three of them, myself.'

'Which three do you mean?' enquired Derby Phil. 'Only another of my uncles happens to be the Dalai Lama and he's not just on first-name terms with the gods, he has them round to tea on Thursdays.'

Omally shook his head. 'These gods are strictly pagan,' said he. 'Your Lamaic uncle wouldn't know these lads.'

Derby Phil nodded sagely.

Gimlet Martin wondered what he'd got himself into. 'Which gods are you talking about, *exactly*?' he asked.

Omally raised his eyebrows. 'The six tertiary gods, of course: Goth, Mebob, Kalil, Narfax, Bah-Reah and little Wilf. The three to which I reverently refer, and before whose images I prostrate myself three times every day, are Goth, Mebob and Bah-Reah, born of the dreamtime world BLISH, apprentices to the big jobber Zematod, who plumbed in the universe after the great flood.'

'I have an uncle who chats with a dead Red Indian via the medium of a golden megaphone,' said Phil, 'although the communications seem strangely one-sided to me.'

'An uncle of mine died once,' said Gimlet Martin. 'My aunty says he's gone to see God.'

'As I was saying,' Omally continued, 'Goth, Mebob and Bah-Reah, apprentices to the celestial plumber who guards the big stop-cock, which if turned would see the entire universe vanish down a great plug hole.'

290

'Black hole,' said Gimlet Martin.

'Plug hole,' said John. 'And I don't just speak to them, they speak to me also.'

'Perhaps you might ask them to say something to you now,' said Phil.

There was a long pause.

'We are all blessed,' said Omally. 'Fancy them saying that.'

'I didn't quite catch it,' said Phil.

'I did,' said Gimlet Martin. 'It was something about you having the price of a round hidden in your boot, wasn't it, Omally?'

'Not even close,' said John. 'It was, in fact, the Big Answer.'

'The Big Answer,' said Phil. 'I've had that from the wife. It's "no" mostly.'

'It's bigger than that,' said Omally. 'This is the *Big Answer*.'

'It's "yes" then,' said Gimlet Martin. 'No answer could be bigger than "yes". Although some could be a lot more complicated.'

'This one is very straightforward,' said Omally, 'although it may take a little time to interpret correctly.'

'Oh, one of those, is it?' said Phil. 'Then it will probably turn out to be the instructions for the erection of flat-pack kitchen units. An uncle of mine had a go at those once, he ended up eating his own foot. I don't think that was in the instructions. I think he just went—'

'To Margate?' asked Gimlet Martin. 'I was told that Margate was good for arthritis, so I went there and I got it.'

'*The Big Answer*,' went Omally in a big voice, 'from he who speaks behind the eyes, between the ears, beneath the tongue—'

'Under the clock?' Phil suggested.

'All around my hat?' said Gimlet.

Omally raised a glass which had been refilled during time-out. 'To Goth and Mebob, and to Bah-Reah,' he toasted, 'and to the Big Answer.'

'And to Arsenal Football Club,' said Phil.

'And Ruby Keeler,' said Gimlet, 'whose legs went all the way up to her bum.'

The three drank.

'I feel that the gods will be favouring me shortly,' said Omally.

'Crocks of gold, or a touch of immortality?' Phil asked.

'Or possibly three wishes of the Aladdin persuasion,' said Gimlet. 'An Irish uncle of mine was offered three wishes by a Genie he freed from a Persian matchbox. He asked for a bottle of Guinness which would never run dry, much after the manner of the now legendary cornucopia. After taking a couple of swigs and seeing that the Guinness had not gone down at all, he used up his two other wishes. "Give us two more of these wonderful bottles," he said.'

'Very droll,' said Omally. 'I am stating that my gods will be favouring me with the interpretation of the Big Answer. It is the Big Answer to all the world's problems. It will bring peace and love and happiness to every man, woman and child on the planet.'

'Will they be favouring you before closing time?'

292

asked Gimlet Martin. 'As you may care to get a round in to celebrate.'

Omally shook his head. 'Not nearly so soon, I'm afraid. We are now in the year 1966. I suspect that it will take at least thirty years for me to correctly interpret the Big Answer.'

'Well that is a *Big* surprise,' said Gimlet Martin.

'Talking of *Big*,' said Derby Phil, 'I had an uncle who lived in India. He used to circumcise elephants for a living. The pay wasn't too good, but the tips were enormous.'

Omally rose from his chair. 'Enough,' he cried. 'Enough of such trivial talk.' And his eyes flashed fire and his face shone like burnished bronze. 'Something is occurring. Something phenomenal. A great change will come over the earth. There will be signs and wonders in the heavens, there will be peace and joy and love.'

His two fellow finalists looked up at John in some awe.

'I am pulling out of this contest,' said Omally. 'I have no use for a trophy and a fifty-pound prize. I must dedicate myself instead to the Big Answer.'

And that was the particular lie that won John Omally the much coveted Silver Tongue Trophy and the even more coveted fifty-pound prize.

But what if he *wasn't* lying?

22

NEXT MORNING

'Oh no!' cried Barry, loudly in my head. 'Oh no, chief. Look at them all.'

And I *was* looking, down from the window of my room at Hotel Jericho, the smoke-stained window, cracked and pitted. Looking down upon the folk who thronged the street below. Very happy they looked. Very very happy. They were smiling, each and every one.

'*You* caused this to happen, chief.'

'What, caused all these people to smile like this? Are you sure, Barry? I mean if I'd done it, surely a tree would have fallen on me by now, or a rogue satellite crashed through the ceiling.'

'You made it happen, chief. You put the idea of the Big Answer into that Omally's head and then gave him thirty years to figure out how to work it.'

'Am I really *that* clever, Barry?'

'That *bloody devious*, yes.'

'But I don't see what you're complaining about. Look at all the smiling faces. The street is carpeted with them.'

And it was '*carpeted*', well that's what it looked like from where I was standing.

'Bad, bad, bad,' went Barry. 'Very bad indeed.'

'Sounds like sour grapes to me,' I said. 'Just because I managed to pull it off without your help, or *your hindrance*.'

'You call *that*, pulling it off? Look at them, chief, look at them, what have you done to them?'

'Given them their freedom, Barry. *The Big Answer* in my opinion is to give people their freedom. Unshackle them from everyday tedium, allow them to blossom into their true selves. Offer them love and peace and happiness. Pretty damn cosmic, eh, Barry?'

'Oh dear, oh dear, oh dear.'

'Come on, let's go down and mingle, I could do with some breakfast. Let's see how the Brave New World is shaping up.'

It was a jolly nice day for a brave new world. A big smiley sun in the sky. Dear little clouds scudding by. And no doubt Blue Birds of Happiness nestling on the telegraph wire, if not on the dry-cleaner's roof. The kind of day that might inspire poets to verse, in fact.

I shinned down the scaffolding
Supporting the hotel,
I stretched and joined the smilers
Who were looking very well.

'How goes it?' I asked a passer-by.
'Splendid,' came the firm reply.
'Happy then?' I asked another.
'Sure am friend, each man's my brother.'

'Sheer poetry,' I said to Barry.

'It doesn't scan, chief, it's all over the place.'

'Hush, you cynic. Let's do breakfast.'

I didn't really know the eating houses in this town. Come to think of it, I didn't even know the name of this town. It was just a town with a hotel, Hotel Jericho, and I had been drawn here by the magnet of my dream. Or the fishing-line of fate. Or the dog lead of destiny. Or even the silk scarf of serendipity. The last two of which can be a lot of fun, so I'm told, if you know what to do with them. I tried a café called The Plume, but it wasn't open. One a little further up the street was, it was called the *Tengo Na Minchia Tanta*. I pushed upon the door and went inside. I was feeling great. Really great. I felt my old self again, the old self that had wanted to be a private eye. I'd almost forgotten about that old self. I was glad to have him back. The thought of having him back made me smile.

I parked my butt on a chromium stool before the counter and smiled at the guy behind it. A tall guy with sandy hair. The tall guy's name was Sandy, but how was I to know?

'A cup of coffee, please,' I smiled. 'And a buttered bap.'

The tall guy smiled in ready response. 'You're welcome to the coffee, friend, but I have no baps today.'

'A crusty roll then please.'

'No rolls.'

'Then I'll just have a slice of Hovis.'

296

'Sadly no.'

'Croissant?'

'No croissants.'

'Wheatbread? Flapjack? Waffle? Muffin? Crumpet?'

The tall guy shook his head.

'Bath bun? Patty? Pasty? Oat cake? Scone? Shortbread? Gingerbread? Doughnut? Profiterole?'

He shook his head once more. 'You sure know your pastries, fella,' he said.

'Listen,' I told him, 'in my business, knowing your pastries can mean the difference between being as fat as a butcher's dog or thin as a wino's whippet, if you know what I mean, and I'm sure that you do.'

'I haven't the foggiest,' said Sandy. 'But as long as you're happy.'

'Any hot-cross buns?' I enquired.

'None. I'm afraid the bakers haven't delivered today. They phoned to say that as the sun was shining, they'd decided to hit the beach instead.'

'Nice day for it,' I said. 'Just the coffee then.'

'You'll have to take it black I'm afraid. The lads from the dairy went with them. They're having a volley ball tournament, I think.'

I smiled at the tall guy and he smiled back, we introduced ourselves and he poured me a black coffee.

I sipped at it. 'It's rather cold,' I said.

'It's last night's,' said Sandy, with a smile. 'My waitress always makes the fresh coffee, but she phoned in today to say—'

'That she thought she'd hit the beach?'

297

'I'd go myseif, but I prefer it here. I get a real pleasure from giving my customers just what they want.'

'Nice sentiment. Do you have any sugar at all?'

'I did have, but I threw it all away this morning. Call it a whim if you will, but too much sugar is bad for your health and I wouldn't want to feel that I had in any way contributed to another soul's ill health by supplying them with sugar.'

'I've heard the same said of coffee,' I suggested.

'Yes, you're quite right.' Sandy snatched the cup from my hand and poured its cold contents into the sink. 'How thoughtless of me, sir, allow me to apologize.'

'That's quite all right. Do you have anything else on the premises that I might eat or drink?'

'Well I do, but I can't be sure now whether any of it's OK. I mean the fried stuff, that can give you heart disease, and too many carbohydrates, that's tantamount to administering poison. I'm going to have to review all my stock, sir. Thank you for drawing my attention to the dangers.'

'Could I have one of those bars of chocolate you have behind the counter then?'

'Oh my Lord no, sir! You might come out in a rash. I'd never forgive myself.'

'Fair enough.' I smiled at Sandy. 'Then I suppose I'd better be off.'

'And take care crossing the road, sir. Perhaps I'll see you later, down at the beach.'

'Perhaps. Goodbye.'

*   *   *

I stood outside the *Tengo Na Minchia Tanta*, stretching and smiling.

'What are you smiling about, chief?' asked Barry. 'That clod just talked you out of your breakfast.'

'He was doing the right thing, Barry. He was caring for his customers.'

'He'll care them all to death at that rate.'

'No he won't. He will see to their dietary needs. People do eat things that are far too unhealthy. All that's going to change now. Change from the ground up.'

'You had that written into your BIG ANSWER, did you, chief?'

'Caring, Love, Peace, Honesty and above all Freedom.'

'No mention of breakfast in there, I suppose?'

I smiled and patted my belly. It felt a bit hollow. 'We eat far too much,' I told Barry. 'In future I shall scrub around breakfast. Just take a five-mile jog instead.'

'A five-mile jog? Chief, you've never jogged in your life. You get a nose-bleed running for a bus.'

'Time to shape up then. Look after your body and it will look after you.'

'Oh dear, oh dear.'

'I think I might become a vegetarian.'

'Please, chief, you are talking to a sprout here.'

'No offence meant, Barry.'

'None taken, chief.'

'Isn't it just great to be alive?'

'Oh dear, oh dear, oh dear.'

★　　★　　★

I took a stroll about the town. Most of the shops had 'closed for the day' signs up and I noticed that the roads were very crowded with cars. I also noticed that most of the occupants wore shorts and Hawaiian shirts, and the children in the backs carried beach balls and body boards.

A perfect day to hit the beach.

I wondered if I should join them.

'Bar snacks,' said Barry.

'Pardon me?'

'Pub grub, as in breakfast.'

'Well, I am a tad peckish as it happens.'

'Here's a pub, chief. What's it called? Ah, Fangio's Bar. Now how about that?'

'How about that indeed.' And I entered Fangio's Bar with a smile.

And the first thing that caught my laughing eyes was the décor. It hadn't changed a bit. It was still the same old clapped-out, run-down, knackered-up, wretched—

'Can I help you, sir?' asked the barman.

And it was him. Fangio. Standing there and smiling.

'Am I glad to see you,' I said.

'I don't know, sir, are you?'

'Fangio, it's *me*. And it's *you*.' And he hadn't aged by a single day. By thirty years yes, by a single day, no. He was the same old clapped-out, run-down, knackered-up, wretched—

'Can it really be you?' Fangio looked me up and down like a thirteenth-floor elevator and tipped me the kind of wink that accidentally buys you contraceptives in a chemist, when you're asking for a packet of aspirins.

'My old brown dog,' said Fangio. 'It *is* you. The same old clapped-out, run-down, knackered-up, wretched—'

'Any chance,' I asked him as I parked my behind upon a stool that hadn't known such joy for more than thirty years, 'any chance of a drink?'

'Certainly, sir, what would you care for?'

'What *exactly* do you have?'

Fangio made a thoughtful (though still smiling) face. He stroked at his chins, ran his tongue about his lips, then across his nose and all around his eyebrows. 'What *exactly* would you like?' he asked.

'How about a bottle of Bud?'

'Right out of Bud, I'm afraid.'

'Lager?'

'No.'

'Bitter?'

'No.'

'Stop me if I get to one,' I said. 'Draught beer? Bottled beer? Stout? Brown ale? Cider? Scrumpy? Porter? Punch? Bourbon? Scotch? Irish? Highball? Brandy?'

'What was the last one?'

'Brandy.'

'No, the one before that.'

'Highball.'

'Oh, I thought you said something else. Carry on.'

'I'm not getting close yet, eh?'

'Go on to wines,' said Fangio. 'Do wines.'

'OK. Red wine? White wine? Rosé? Fortified

301

wine? Sparkling wine? Spumante? Madeira? Port? Claret? Hock? Champagne?'

'Champagne,' said Fangio.

'You have champagne?'

'No, but I love champagne, don't you?'

'Oh yeah, champagne's wonderful. Now where was I? Sherry? Burgundy? Chianti? Rezina?'

'You sure know your potables, sir.'

'Listen,' I said, 'in my business, knowing your potables can mean the difference between humming a tune to that old devil moon and shouting "spam" at a spaniel, if you know what I mean and I'm sure that you do.'

'My lips are sealed,' said Fangio. 'Do you want to go on to cocktails now?'

'Listen,' I said once more, 'I'll take whatever you have.'

'Would you care for a Horse's Neck?'

'Is that a cocktail?'

'No, it's a horse's neck. It's not proving as popular as the chewing fat used to.'

'Bring me a large slice and a glass of water.'

Fangio placed a meat cleaver upon the counter. 'Would you mind helping yourself?' he asked. 'The horse is out the back in the paddock.'

We both laughed at this. What a wag that Fangio, what a shame the way he met his end.

'Now don't start that again,' he said. And we laughed again.

I'd forgotten just how much I enjoyed being a private eye, standing about in bars, drinking and talking a lot of old toot.

'I hate to keep harping on,' I told Fangio, 'but

would there be any chance of a drink, do you think?'

'Certainly, sir, what would you like?'

'I'd *like* a bottle of Bud.'

'Coming right up.'

'But you said—'

'Don't take any notice of anything I say, sir. I've never been the same since I was shot in the brain at the Somme.'

'You were never at the Somme, were you?'

'Did I say the Somme, sir? I meant of course that I once had my head shut in a fridge door. Student's rag week I think it was, or National Trust demonstrators.'

Fangio served the beer and I drank it back with relish.

'Are you sure you wouldn't like a bit of horse's neck to go with that relish?' asked the fat boy. 'Or perhaps a buttered-bap.'

'Yes please.'

'That's a shame, because—'

'Never mind, I'll stick with the beer.' I smiled at Fangio and he smiled right back. 'I see you've got a TV behind the bar,' I said. 'Would it be all right if we had it on?'

'With the greatest of pleasure, sir. My heart's desire is to please my customers, mind you—'

'What?'

'Well, I had it on earlier and there was only a test card with the words THE STATION REGRETS THAT ALL ITS PRESENTERS HAVE GONE TO THE BEACH. NORMAL SERVICE WILL BE RESUMED AS SOON AS POSSIBLE.'

'Then let's see if it has.'

'Let's do that, sir.' Fangio switched on the TV then came around the bar and sat down beside me. The screen cleared to display the smiling face of a male presenter, with a crowded beach in the background. And then pulled back.

'Isn't that Jack Black?' I said. 'Used to present *World of the Weird*?'

'Still does,' said Fangio.

'So why is he wearing a dress?'

Fangio shrugged. 'I suppose he just felt like it today. I know I did.'

'I see.'

'And here I am at the beach,' smiled Jack. 'And what a wonderful day for it. The sun is shining, the sky is blue and the water is warm, warm, warm. And what a crowd we have here. Reports say that London is virtually empty, only one per cent of the working population actually having turned in at their places of employment today, and most of those folk who run their own businesses. As for the rest, they're in for a swim.

'And on the world front. It's the same game. Folk taking to the beach and smiling. I've never seen so many happy people before. It's just as if the whole world woke up today and said, "Let's do it." This is Jack Black, cross-dressed and proud of it, returning you to the studio.'

And then the test card came up on the screen.

'What a very nice dress,' said Fangio. 'I wonder where he bought it. And what a wonderful day. Would you care for another beer, on the house?'

304

'I certainly would,' I said, and I smiled as I said it.

Fangio went around the bar to pop another bottle.

'Come on, chief,' said Barry, 'you can't sit around all day drinking. You've got to put all this right. The whole world's taken the day off and it's all your fault.'

'The whole world is happy and smiling,' I said. 'And I'm proud of it.'

'Me too,' said Fangio.

'I'm sorry, I wasn't talking to you.'

'Oh no problem. You were talking to your sprout, I suppose.'

'My *what*?'

'Your Holy Guardian Sprout. I've got a radish, you know. Never even knew I did until this morning when it started talking to me. Robbie, his name is.'

'Robbie the radish?'

'Wotcha, Robbie,' said Barry.

'Hi, Barry,' said Robbie.

'Hang about,' I said. 'What is all this?'

'The merciful arrival of the cavalry I hope, chief. As you've brought the world out on strike, let's pray the Holy Guardians can persuade everyone to go back to work tomorrow.'

'But that's cheating. That isn't free will. That's not the freedom I wanted everyone to have.'

'It's all for the best, chief, really.'

'Why, you sneaky little sod. You've been trying to persuade me to change everything back and while I'm saying no, your mates are trying to persuade everyone else. This is sabotage.'

'Not really, chief. It's just that you neglected to mention it in the small print of your BIG ANSWER.'

'Well I won't forget it next time.'

'Next time, chief? What do you mean, next time?'

'You wait and see.' I began wishing very hard and doing strange things with my fingers.

'No, chief, you can't, you can't, chief—'

'Wanna bet?'

HUGE BLACK BULLET

Farmers in gaiters looked up from their
  digging
Sailors in bell-bottoms watched from the
   rigging
Dons in their dinner suits choked on their egg
When the huge black bullet landed

Fey window dressers fumbled their frocks
Men from the Ministry registered shocks
Tall executioners leant on their blocks
When the huge black bullet landed

Cavalry officers out on fatigues
The elves who make boots that can walk seven
  leagues
The lovers of Dresden turned off Arthur Negus
When the huge black bullet landed

The glass-blower's clerk laid down his
  crucibles . . .
Don't be silly!

The carpenter's lackey put down his new plane
  (that's more like it)
The toffs watched from seats on the Paddington
  train
The chef dropped his pudding and cried out in
  pain

When the great big
Coal black

Horrible
Beastly
Huge black bullet landed.

And that's why I'm late for my first day at work—
The huge black bullet landed.

HUGE BLACK BULLET II
BLACK CAPSULE (SON OF BULLET)
To be intoned in a deep dark voice.

Oh black capsule
Son of bullet
Relative of Dick
Brother to
Lord Vindaloo
(The stuff that makes me sick)

Oh black capsule
Friend of Jimmy
Lover of Van Gogh
Mucker to
Lord Vindaloo
(That makes me choke and cough)

Oh black capsule
Chum of Derek
Pal to Simon Dee
Buddy to
Lord Vindaloo
(I had some for my tea)

Oh black capsule
Loved by Lemmy
And George Bernard Shaw
Cousin to
Lord Vindaloo
(I don't want any more)

But blood *is* thicker than water.
But I'm in trouble deep.

23

SSSH NOW, I'M WAGGLING

The sound made by the explosion of an atomic bomb has been likened to that of a great door slamming in the depths of Hell. The sound I now heard wasn't quite like that, but it wasn't far off. The blast that tore the door of Fangio's Bar from its hinges this time was one of quite considerable force. I was lifted off my feet, carried backwards across the bar and straight out through the exit. I would surely have met with certain death against the wall of the building next door had I not had the good fortune to strike a woman in a straw hat who was dragging a deckchair. We went down amongst plastic rubbish sacks, Styrofoam food cartons and rotting fruit and veg.

I shook a dazed head and glanced all around. A shrill wind howled down the alleyway. Overhead the sky was—

'Green. The sky's turned green.'

'Call them back, chief,' cried Barry in my head.

'Do what?'

'The Holy Guardians, chief, call them back, as quickly as you can.'

'I bloody won't.'

'You must, chief, you must. Things have turned *really* bad. You've done a really bad thing. *Two* poems at the start of the chapter. That's *really* bad. Call them back, chief, the Holy Guardians, call them back.'

'I will *not*.'

'Chief, we don't have a lot of time. In fact, if you don't call them back, there isn't going to be any more time, period.'

'What are you talking about?' I ducked as a dustbin whistled past my head. It was whistling the famous tune, 'When Your Grey Hairs Turn to Silver Won't You Change Me Half a Quid?'

'Did you hear that dustbin?' I shouted.

'Stuff the dustbin, chief, call back the Guardians. Twiddle your thumbs about quick, while you've still got thumbs to twiddle.'

'What are you going on about? And why has the sky turned green?' I took to cowering in a doorway, all manner of stuff was blowing by. Bicycles and barnacles, cigarette packets and blue book jackets, parsnips and pomegranates, old grey wigs and suckling pigs.

'It's chaos, chief.'

'You're damned right. What *is* going on?'

'Call back the Holy Guardians, chief, I'll tell you then.'

'Tell me *now*.'

The bricks of the building next door started to separate, they weren't bricks any more, they were small living things that began to jostle in an agitated fashion.

'That Fangio must have slipped a tab of acid into

my beer,' I shouted. 'I'm having a really bad trip here, Barry.'

'It's no trip, chief, call back the Holy Guardians. Do it now, chief, or the entire planet will go down the plug-hole.'

'It's only another trick, Barry, to stop me putting the world to rights.' I struggled out of the doorway, bracing myself against the driving wind and blundered into the street.

Folk were running madly about. And not just folk. There were other things, vague, indistinct, dark forms, low and scuttling.

'Call them back, chief, please call them back.'

'I did this, didn't I?'

'Just call them back, please.'

'All right.' I twiddled my fingers.

A great jagged crack tore across the sky.

'It didn't work, Barry, my fingers – *God, my fingers!*'

But they weren't fingers any more, they were tubes of toothpaste. All with the tops unscrewed and these streams of different-coloured toothpaste oozing out and twisting all about.

'Do something else, chief. Wink your eyes, waggle your ears, anything. Anything.'

I winked and waggled for all I was worth.

A black limousine drew up beside me. A black window swished down and the face of Small Dave grinned out. 'Time to be off to the gig,' he giggled.

'That's not right.'

'Waggle some more. Do something, anything.'

'I've got your brother in the back,' called Small

Dave. 'He's all ready for you. All trussed up. If you butcher him now, we can eat him together.'

'Barry, get me out of this.'

'Only you can, chief, only you.'

The ground began to sink beneath me and I jumped aside. Something rose from the earth, something huge and hairy. Parts groaned open to expose green things within. Emeralds surely, large as tennis balls.

'Run, chief, and waggle while you run.'

The street tipped alarmingly and I ran in the downhill direction.

'That's him,' cried a woman in a straw hat. She sat astride a great white horse, at the head of a legion of Cossacks. 'He's to blame for it all. Deviant, he's destroyed the entire programme. Trample down the deviant.'

'Run and waggle, chief, run and waggle.'

I ran and I waggled as I ran.

'Tell me what's happening, Barry,' I howled.

And then I was in amongst the crowd, the cheering crowd.

The cheering, singing, stamping crowd. And it wasn't thousands, it was millions. Millions and millions.

I was near the front. Near the stage. I could see the band. Sonic Energy Authority. They seemed to be playing in slow motion, but the sound was accelerated. Too fast to catch, a high-pitched scream. And then I saw the bass player, Panay Cloudrunner and he looked down at me and he pointed and the music stopped and the crowd stilled and they all looked at me and they stared and they pointed. And Litany was there, sitting on my brother's shoulders and she stared and pointed too and so did he.

'*He* never killed me,' said Panay Cloudrunner, pointing at me. 'I killed myself. I was speeding out of my brain, I'd run down seven people before I hit the road block. They never put that in the paper. They wanted him to feel guilty, they wanted him dead.'

'Is that true, Barry?'

'Don't take any notice,' said my Uncle Brian, putting his hand upon my shoulder. 'They're just trying to confuse you. It's the iron, you see. The iron in the guitar strings. If you can free yourself from the influence of iron, you can do anything, absolutely anything.'

'Don't listen to your uncle, dear,' said my mum. 'He's quite mad. The whole family's quite mad. Always has been, always will be. Of course you were adopted, the fairies left you on the doorstep.'

'They were *my* fairies,' said Uncle Brian. 'The lad had a mission. He was the Chosen One, sent up from below to balance things out. If he hadn't run off I would have explained everything to him.'

'Everything about *what*? Barry, what is he talking about?'

'This isn't real, chief, you're imagining it all. Please try to concentrate, waggle your fingers, bring back the Holy Guardians.'

'I don't understand. What's happening?'

'It's very straightforward,' said my Uncle Brian. 'The world is dissolving. Reality is dissolving. Everything is returning to chaos.'

314

'I didn't mean that to happen. I wanted people to be free.'

'Well, they're going to be free now. Free of all existence. That's the ultimate in freedom, I suppose. Well done.'

'That's not what I intended.'

'Waggle your fingers, chief. Stop it now.'

'I want to know the truth. Won't anyone tell me the truth?'

'I'll tell you.'

I turned at the voice. What a voice that was. Charismatic. A real blinder of a voice. The kind of voice that could talk a Tesco's frozen turkey into a tug-o-war team.

'Colon,' I said, 'the super-dense proto-hippy.'

'You'd better call the Holy Guardians back,' said Colon, sweet as you please.

'I must know the truth.'

'There is no ultimate truth,' said my Uncle Brian.

'You keep out of this.'

'I'll tell you the truth.' said Colon. 'But first call back the Holy Guardians.'

'No I won't,' I said, surprising even myself. 'Not until I know the truth.'

'One part of knowledge', said Colon, 'consists of being ignorant of such things as must never be known.'

And then the green sky cracked completely and night was upon us. Colon and I stood alone upon an endless expanse of absolutely nothing. Black earth below, black sky above, but a sky made beautiful by stars.

Colon stared up at them. 'Have you managed to

315

join up those dots yet?' he asked. 'Have you divined the Big Answer?'

'No, I haven't.'

'That's a pity. I felt sure that you would.'

'Have *you*?'

'Oh yes,' said Colon.

'You lying git.'

'I have too.'

'You never have.'

'Have too.'

'So what is it then?'

'It's the future,' said Colon. 'The light from the stars comes to us from the past, it spells out the future.'

'What a load of old rubbish. Where are we, by the way? It's getting very nippy.'

'Allow me to explain', said Colon, 'about your gift, about everything.'

'Will any of this be the truth?' I asked. 'Because so far everyone has lied to me about pretty much everything.'

'People mostly lie because they don't know what the truth is.'

'You're never caught short for a New Age platitude, are you?'

'Will you bloody shut up and listen?'

'Well, excuse *me*.'

'Your gift,' said Colon, in rather a stern voice I thought. 'The mythical mystical butterfly of chaos theory—'

'I know, the one that flutters its wings up the Orinoco and causes the price of condoms to go up in Tierra del Fuego.'

'The same. It's the butterfly of *chaos theory*. Not the butterfly of *Order Theory*. When it flutters its wings it does not bring order out of chaos, it does exactly the reverse. When you used your "gift" you did exactly the same.'

'I only tried to help people. To help mankind, and I would have succeeded, but I kept getting exploited and sabotaged.'

'But you could have expected nothing more. You couldn't change the world for the better, no matter how good your intentions were. You could only make things worse by your interference.'

'My heart was in the right place,' I said. 'There's nothing wrong with trying to change mankind for the better. They all got a day at the seaside. Well, most of them did. Listen, all right, I'll have another go. I won't screw up this time.'

'You can only screw up. You don't understand how things work.'

'Because no-one will tell me the truth. Will *you* tell me the truth? Now, before I waggle the fingers that I see have returned to me.'

'The Holy Guardians,' said Colon.

'Oh, not them again.'

'Yes, them again. What do you think Guardians do?'

'Well, they guard things, obviously.'

'And what do the *Holy* Guardians do?'

'Guard people, I suppose.'

'From what?'

'From other people, from themselves—'

'Wrong,' said Colon.

'Oh well, I don't know, you tell me.'

'Chaos,' said Colon.

'That again, eh?'

'That again, yes. The order that is life on earth is a very fragile affair, difficult to maintain and easily tipped back into chaos. The universe isn't still and peaceful, it's whirling chaos. Chaos is its natural order. The Holy Guardians are there to protect mankind from this chaos, and also to be the conscience of man, the inner voice. What raises man above the animals, what will one day allow him to join up the dots and read the Big Answer.'

'And Captain Kirk told you this, right?'

Colon made an exasperated face. 'Trust me,' he said. 'The universe is a very chaotic place.'

'It doesn't seem too chaotic to me, the moon goes round the Earth, the Earth goes round the sun.'

'And in a couple of billion years the sun will go super nova and explode, which will be pretty chaotic.'

'Yeah, well that's a long way off in the future.'

'That's diddly-squat in universal time, that's half a second.'

'Well, I don't think that concerns us here.'

'Well it concerns me. I'm responsible.'

'You're *what*?'

'Well, I am God,' said Colon.

'You're *who*?'

'God,' said Colon. 'I think you've heard of me. You've dispatched all my Holy Guardians and reduced my planet to chaos. I should be very angry with you.'

'You're never God,' I said. 'If you're God, then

318

tell me something, why did you invent the blue-bottle?'

'I don't believe I'm hearing this. I have just told you I'm God and you're asking me about blue-bottles. You don't feel that perhaps you should be prostrating yourself and begging forgiveness?'

'Frankly no,' I said. 'Because I don't believe any of this. I think I'm probably lying unconscious in a gutter somewhere, dreaming the whole damn lot.'

'OK,' said Colon. 'If that's the way you want it, don't believe in me. See if I care.'

'Fair enough, I won't.'

'Just waggle your fingers and return all my Holy Guardians.'

'No.'

'What do you mean, no? You can't say no to God.'

'Oh yes I can. If you're God, then *you* waggle *your* fingers. You bring back your stupid Holy Guardians.'

'I can't.'

'Why not?'

'Because I'm not allowed to interfere in human affairs.'

'Why not?'

'Because it's written into my contract. I only have the franchise for this particular planet and it's a real struggle to hold it all together I can tell you, but I can't act directly. I can't interfere.'

'You're interfering now. You're trying to persuade me to do something.'

'It's a vision. Visions are allowed.'

'This is all absolute nonsense. I'm getting out of here. But I'll tell you one thing.'

'What's that?'

'You've just given me a great idea. I *will* bring back the Holy Guardians, if it's the only way to restore some kind of order, but I think you're on to something with this God business. I think I'll give that a go.'

'You'll *what*?'

'Sssh now, I'm waggling.'

MORE ABOUT PIRATES AND CANNIBALS

The longboats of the sorry wreck
Brought pirate men ashore.
Cloony, hiding on the deck
Was not too keen on desert isles
And cannibals with pointed smiles
And so he thought he'd stick it out and wait
    for dawn to come.

The longboats landed on the beach
The pirates disembarked.
Cloony sat and ate a peach,
And looked around the captain's bed,
And wondered what the captain read,
And downed another glass of rum and ran himself
    a bath.

The longboats lay on golden sand
The pirates all were gone.
They really were a dismal band,
And filled the guts of native folk
Who have no time to sing and joke
But have enormous appetites for men and fish
    and fowl.

At dawn the ship broke free again
And Cloony floated off,
And soon was in Dundee again,

With captain's robes and piles of gold,
But luck is hard and luck is cold
For Cloony was arrested as a pirate and was
hanged.

24

THE CHURCH OF THE
CHOSEN ONE

The way I saw it was this. if God puts an idea into your head, you'd be a fool not to take advantage of it. I didn't know for certain whether I'd actually met God, or merely hallucinated the entire event. After I gave my fingers a waggle and brought back the Holy Guardians, things got back to normal in a big way. And fast too.

People stopped hitting the beach and they all went back to work the next day. Within a week the whole business had been forgotten. It was just as if it had never happened.

And perhaps it hadn't.

But I still wasn't giving up. Even in the face of all the setbacks and chaos, I was still absolutely determined to make this world a better place. But a bit at a time, this time. Not over-extend myself. Do the job properly. From the ground up, but upon firm foundations.

And it was so simple, I was surprised I hadn't thought of it before.

The first thing I had to do was to 'acquire' about a hundred acres of prime beach-front property in

California. Because, let's face it, if you're thinking of setting yourself up as the New Messiah, where better to do it than California?

I had no problems whatsoever in 'acquiring' the land. I simply made a little wish and moved two of my Asprey's fountain pens from the left top pocket of my Savile Row suit to the right, during the voyage over on the *QE2*. I had become very much into the science of acquisition. I was careful, of course, nothing flashy, nothing too big at the one time. Just a little twitch of a nostril to make someone drop their wallet, a flick of the wrist to make a shopkeeper misread my bus ticket and take it for an American Express gold card. No lasting harm done to anyone. Not strictly honest perhaps, but all in a good cause.

The lawyers were waiting for me as the ship docked. And the media. Who was this unknown fellow from England to whom a hundred acres of valuable land had been donated by a Wall Street consortium? they wanted to know.

Only me.

But did I say *only*?

I don't know who the big limousine (much bigger than the one my Uncle Brian had once hired) was *really* waiting for. I diddled with one of the mother-of-pearl buttons on my handmade silk shirt and the chauffeur was sure it was *me*. We drove west.

We picked people up along the way. I talked to them in diners and donut houses, Mcdonald's and Jack in the Boxes, gin joints and go-go bars, lounges and Taco Bells.

I sized them up on a simple criteria. Marks out of ten for beauty. Anyone found scoring less than nine was not in the running. I would smile and stare into their eyes and shuffle two beer tops in my trouser pocket and make a little wish. It worked every time. They followed me. By the time we swept across the state line into good old Cal-if-orn-eye-ah, we had us a mighty convoy.

We had some problems with the police. But each time I just gave them the smile and the stare and shuffled the beer tops.

I was getting it down to a fine art.

I soon found that it was second nature to me. I didn't have to think about it at all. I recall an occasion in one of those lap-dancing clubs some-where in the mid-west. I spied out a particularly worthy-looking disciple. A young blond woman of quite outstanding beauty and gymnastic capa-bilities. I was just walking out of the door with her, when this bruiser, evidently her boyfriend, laid most unfriendly hands upon me. I only gave him the look. If I did anything else I was not aware of it. Just the look it was. He stuck his hand down his throat, and, well, it wasn't too pretty. My police escorts laughed though. One of them called Joe Bob did it in a really high voice.

I got to quite like Joe Bob. It was a shame the way he met his end.

Now, the sun really knows how to shine in California. It's not the same kind of sun we have in England. Ours is a small-scale kind of sun, California's is really panoramic. Big time. The sea was very blue also. I suggested (without saying anything, of course, just by winding my watch a couple of times) that everyone take off all their clothes and go in for a swim. They readily obliged.

The water was really warm. I made love to three women in that water. And that made me so happy and contented that I plucked a hair from my right nipple and everyone else made love too.

This did cause a bit of trouble, what with all the media types who had followed us down with the cameras and all. I had to get out of the water and flex my toes in the sand.

The media types came and joined us in the sea.

Food and drink came in by truck and helicopter. I found that if I simply wished for it before I turned in for the night with whichever disciple I'd chosen to honour with my body, things would occur. Manifests became confused at depots, delivery notes were misread, whatever I desired was delivered straight to the door the next morning.

And I did not have to wait too long for new disciples to appear. Word soon got around. They arrived in campers and Volkswagens, bronzed young men and women, eager to see what was on the go. And I told them what it was. 'You can join me and be happy,' I said, 'or you can go away and be miserable.'

Simple choice, and I meant every word. Everyone who turned away was *very* miserable later. I saw to that.

My people were happy people. They smiled *all* the time. I imposed certain penalties for not smiling, because not smiling has a tendency to spread, it's infectious. So not smiling was a punishable offence. People smiled a lot.

And they went out of their way to please me, to do little things to make me happy. Keep my white robes well ironed. Put out their hands to catch my cigarette ash. Wipe my bum and pull the chain. As you would, for the Chosen One.

My, but we all lived well.

Once in a while some representative from the IRS or some state committee would appear on the scene. But they were easy meat. I'd dispensed with the beer tops, I only shuffled Krugerrands now.

And once in a while Barry would cut up really rough in my head, shouting that I was taking advantage and being corrupt. But as I said to Barry, 'Shut the F**k* up!'

When the chaps came over from Hollywood to discuss the making of my life story as a motion picture I entertained them royally. I had one hell of a party. Dwarves with lines of cocaine on their shaven heads moving amongst the crowd, live performances by specially favoured acolytes, the whole caboodle.

I decided I would direct the picture myself.

And after a shuffle of the old Krugerrands they readily agreed.

It was a very short step from there to politics. Of course, I knew that the picture would be a success. I really wished hard that it would. And America is never happier than when it has an ex-film star for a president.

*I have a mother too.

My campaign was as basic as could be. 'Vote for me and be happy,' I told the people. 'Don't and then don't.'

They did.

I enjoyed the campaign trail. I enjoyed all the motor cavalcades. I enjoyed the speeches and the interviews, I promoted certain soft drinks and razors. Well, I owned the company. And when finally I sat down in the oval office there was a big smile on my face.

'Right then, lads,' I said. 'So what needs sorting?'

'Well,' said senator someone or other – they all looked the same, just suits and bright faces – 'here's the list,' and he handed me a tome, big as a church Bible and thicker than two short planks.

'That's a *very* big list,' I told him.

'There's never any shortage in the supply of world crises,' he replied.

'And that's just what I'm here to deal with,' I said. 'So where should we start?'

'Well,' he said, 'there's welfare.'

'What's that, exactly?'

'The budget for the poor and needy.'

'Give the poor and needy everything they want.'

'But we'd have to cut down on other things then.'

'So do it.'

'What things, Mr President?'

'What things do you have?'

'There's arms.'

'Cut down on those. In fact, do away with those.'

'But we can't do away with those.'

'Look,' I said, 'I'm not going to declare war on anybody, dump the arms.'

'But you don't understand, Mr President. One in twenty people in America work directly or indirectly for the arms industry. After the illicit and illegal sales of drugs, armaments are the biggest import/export industry in the world.'

'Is that right?'

'Yes, it's right.'

'Well, we'd better not cut down on them, then. What else do you have?'

And he told me what else he had. And every time I tried to take money from this and put it into that, I kept being told that the books would not balance, that people would be put out of work, that some dire consequence would arise. Eventually, when it came right down to it and I was getting very fed up indeed, I asked, 'Well, what *can* I do?'

And he said, 'Nothing, Mr President. You can do absolutely nothing.'

'Then what exactly is the point of me being the President?'

And the senator shrugged and all the other senators or whatever they were shrugged and one of them said, 'Well, the buck stops with you, sir.'

'*What?*' I said.

'Well,' said the senator, 'if you look at it this way, huge events occur all around the world. No-one exactly knows why they occur. They build up, from little things. Like the First World War being started by an assassination. And in order to balance these huge events, certain people are chosen to compensate for them. These people are Prime Ministers and Presidents, people like that. They don't actually cause anything to happen, they can't, their hands are tied by the sheer complexity of Government. But the world events reflect upon these leaders of nations and they make speeches about how they have all the answers and such like, but what they're really there for is to act as scapegoats for the public.

'They're there to blame. It's a little like the mythical mystical butterfly of chaos theory. But in reverse. And that's your job, Mr President, and we're really pleased to have you on the team.'

25

FACING THE FINAL CURTAIN

And that was almost it for me. Almost, but not quite. I quit the White House. I made my excuses and left. It seems strange to me now, when I watch some Prime Minister on the TV that I should never have seen them before for what they really are.

I should have recognized the slightly out-of-kilter clothes, the curious haircuts, the odd turns of phrase, the mispronunciations of simple words, the flapping hands, the whole body language thing. Recognized them for what they really are: compensators, just like I used to be.

As I sit here now in my room at Hotel Jericho, writing in my red exercise books, thirty lines to the page, twenty pages to the book, I look at it all and I don't feel bad.

Certainly I failed to change the world for the better, I can hardly deny that. My every attempt, no matter how well intentioned, was doomed to ultimate failure. But it wasn't my fault. I tried my best. Of course there are those who might consider some of my motives questionable – all right, so I *did* enjoy all that free love in California – but I *did* have good intentions. I was a *good* person.

And so before I sing 'I Did It My Way', take another tablet and slide off to my sorry bed, I would just like to relate to you one final episode.

It is an episode not without interest, and it does at least provide an explanation to all that has gone before, while at the same time being an absolute joy to read.

Which can't be bad.

Can it?

SPROUT MASK REPLICA
(At last the truth.)

The black and unmarked helicopter swept in low, searchlights dicing the night sky. With clattering blades stirring dust clouds about, it settled into the compound. An electrified perimeter fence had been raised around the area of devastation to discourage the curious, and within armed guards stood at twelve-yard intervals, guns held at the ready to reinforce this discouragement.

The date was 17 August 1977. The place was Brentford. The time, eleven o'clock of the evening. Clear night, full moon.

The hatch slid open in the helicopter's belly and disgorged three men wearing silver one-piece coverall suits. A tall slim one with a prodigious red beard, a middle-sized one with a nimbus of white hair and a short young one who was scratching his groin. They were greeted by more men in uniform.

'I am Captain Vez,' said one of these, offering a stiff salute. 'And you are Sir John Rimmer?'

The tall slim figure with the beard flashed an official ID. 'On secondment to the Ministry of Serendipity,' he said, 'above-top-secret classification. Are all the perimeter fences manned and secured?'

'Yes, sir.'

'And the drilling rig is fully operational?'

'Yes, sir, ready to go.'

'And you are absolutely certain that the area has not been compromised, that nothing has been tampered with?'

'A few locals were poking about earlier in the day, sir. But nothing was disturbed. The entire area is now fully secure.'

'Good.'

'But, sir—'

'Yes, soldier?'

'What is it all about, sir? What have we got here?'

Sir John exchanged glances with his middle-sized companion. 'What do you think, Dr Harney?' he asked.

'These men have all signed the Official Secrets Act,' said the good doctor, 'and we will need their assistance with the excavation and the containment. We have no choice but to tell them.'

'So be it.' Sir John stared down upon the captain, a man of no small size himself. 'We have an alien abduction situation,' he said. 'Seismic scans suggest that the craft is still in the area, in a disabled condition.'

Captain V turned about in circles, dragging his gun from its holster. 'Flying saucer?' he went.

'Where is it? Have we fenced off the wrong bit? It isn't round here.'

'You're standing on it,' said Sir John.

The captain took a jump backwards and angled his pistol towards the ground. 'It's buried?' he asked.

'More like dug in,' said Sir John.

'I don't understand.'

Sir John pulled out a map of the area and tapped at it with a finger shaped not unlike a haricot bean. 'The building that stood here', he said, 'was the Sir John Doveston Memorial Gymnasium, known locally as the Johnny Gym. The abductee's name was Nigel Bennet, brother of the boxer Billy 'The Whirlwind' Bennet who won last night at Wembley.'

'And a bloody good fight it was,' said Captain V. 'I was there myself, local boy making good and all that.'

'Quite so. However, while Billy was scoring great points in the annals of boxing, his brother packed dynamite into the foundations of this gym and blew the bugger to kingdom come.'

'But why?' asked the captain, which was reasonable enough.

'He was compelled to do it. Compelled by something alien.' Sir John tapped at his temple. 'Something made him do it.'

'And then he got abducted?'

'You have it.'

'But you say the craft is still here. Why didn't it fly off into space?'

'The craft didn't come from space, Captain. It

came from right here.' Sir John redirected his haricot bean. It pointed this time down towards the ground. 'The aliens we seek do not come from above, they come from below.'

'Saints preserve us,' said the captain, whose mother didn't like him swearing. 'But surely if it came from below and it's returned below, we've lost it.'

Sir John shook his long slim head. Search light twinkled in the lenses of his horn-rimmed specs, and he smoothed down his beard as he spoke. 'The Ministry of Serendipity has been monitoring this area for years. Brentford is what is known as a *window area* for *outré* occurrences and weird shit generally. Ministry sensors are buried in the ground all over this borough. The explosion last night set the needles rocking at Mornington Crescent HQ. The sensors picked up the craft making its escape, they also picked up its collision with a vast metallic object one hundred feet beneath the surface.'

'Fascinating,' said Captain V. 'So what is this vast metallic object, do you think?'

'It could be anything. Victorian debris from the ill-fated Brentford Thames tunnel, Second World War unexploded bomb.'

'*What?*' went the captain, taking another back-aways jump.

'We shall have to drill rather carefully,' said Sir John.

The captain took off his cap and scratched at his military head. 'One thing puzzles me though, sir, and that's the size of this alien craft. We've

335

located what we were asked to look for, "a point of entry", but it's not much bigger than a rabbit hole.'

'Sounds about right,' said Sir John. 'Dr Harney, show the captain the photograph. And, Danbury.'

'Yep?' asked the lad.

'Leave your groin alone.'

Dr Harney brought out a dog-eared photograph and held it up before the captain. 'Scout craft,' he said.

The captain stared at the picture, replaced his cap upon his head, then removed it again. 'Surely,' he said, 'that is a picture of you on a donkey at Great Yarmouth.'

'No, look, there.' Dr Harney went point point point.

'That's a Scotsman in a kilt,' said the captain.

'Yes, of course it is. But what's that *on* his kilt?'

'It's a sporran.'

'It's a subterranean scout craft,' said Sir John. 'Manned by sprouts.'

'*What?*' Now there are many kinds of *What?* expressing various forms of surprise, horror or amazement. The captain's *What?* expressed, shall we say, a certain element of doubt. 'You are suggesting', he said, carefully, 'that Nigel Bennet was abducted by a sporran full of sprouts?'

'Not just any old sprouts,' said Sir John. 'These are very special sprouts, sentient sprouts. A different order of sprout. A different order of being. Some genetic mutation, or possibly something originally not of this world.'

The captain took off his cap once more, then

realizing that he already had it off, he put it back on again. 'Now just you listen here,' he said. 'I know I'm a soldier and therefore not very bright. But I'll have you know—'

'Sir,' a soldier came ambling up.

'What is it, Sergeant Lemon?'

'We have RUPERT fired up and ready to go, sir,' Sergeant Lemon replied, saluting as he did so.

'What's RUPERT?' asked Sir John.

'The robot digger and retrieval unit,' said Captain V. 'Stands for Remotely Operated Bio-Electronic Recovery Tractor.'

'Ah,' said Sir John. 'I see what you mean about you not being very bright. Shall we set RUPERT off down the rabbit hole then?'

Captain Vez scratched at his cap. 'At the double, sir,' he said. 'But carefully. And before we do, is there anything else of an above-top-secret nature you'd care to share with me? Just in case,' he paused, 'in case we don't come out of this thing alive.'

Sir John nodded his slender head. 'We are dealing with a particularly cunning adversary. Back in the 1950s the Ministry of Serendipity set up the Alpha Man project, an attempt to discover society's original thinkers, those who begin the process of original idea to realization of original idea. They found *one*. A chap called Larry, we have no record of his surname. In the cause of science, doctors at the Ministry removed Larry's brain and floated it in a nutrient solution. Larry, unfortunately, did not survive this experiment. An autopsy of his brain, however, revealed something startling. An implant.

Larry had been abducted at some earlier time in his life and implanted.'

'What was this implant?' asked the captain.

'A sprout,' said Sir John. 'Of course. The sprout was still alive and it was removed to Area 51 in Nevada USA for interrogation. It revealed, after some initial encouragement which involved showing it a saucepan of hot water, that such abductions have gone on throughout the course of human history. The vegetable kingdom has *us* under surveillance, captain. They are a race far older than man and with the growing trend towards vegetarianism we pose a threat to them. Every time they locate an individual whom they consider represents a particularly large threat, they abduct and implant him. Control him, in fact. They are attempting to slow mankind's progress. Not destroy him, not yet, not until their hybridization scheme is perfected.'

'Their *what*?' asked the captain (a slightly different *What?*, that time).

'Hybridization,' said Sir John. 'A cross-breeding of the two races. A new order of mankind. Half-man, half-vegetable. But mostly vegetable.'

'Like Phillip Glass,' said Danbury Collins.

'I quite like Phillip Glass,' said Captain Vez. 'Catchy tunes.'

'Quite so,' Sir John inclined his head. 'And, with all that said, I suggest we put RUPERT into operation and see what we can winkle out.'

The soldiers saluted and marched off towards the drilling rig. Sir John and his colleagues followed, Danbury bringing up the rear.

'What do you reckon to this load of old toot?' whispered Danbury to the doctor.

'I reckon it ties up pretty much *all* the loose ends,' the doc whispered back. 'So unless you can think up something better, don't knock it. And, Danbury—'

'Yep?'

'Do leave your groin alone.'

'Sorry,' said the lad. 'But talk of "tying up loose ends" always gets me going.'

'Danbury, the sight of me dipping my sausage in a boiled egg at breakfast had you going.'

'It certainly did,' said the lad, grinning like a good'n.

'Hurry up, chaps,' called Sir John. 'And Danbury—'

'I know,' said the lad. 'The groin, leave the groin.'

'Good boy.'

RUPERT was positioned at the opening to the burrow.

'I don't see how a grown man could have been sucked into such a tight opening,' said Captain Vez.

Danbury Collins made sniggering sounds. Dr Harney biffed him in the ear.

'How exactly does this contraption work?' Sir John asked.

The captain did lapel preenings to imply a great knowledge of the subject. 'It's a robot,' he said. 'With tracked wheels, a light on the front with a little video camera and a pair of extendible arms with moveable grippers on the end. We control it here, by means of this hand-held controller, seeing what it sees with its camera on this video monitor, here.'

'Very impressive, Captain. So how do you switch it on?'

The captain made a baffled face. 'How *do* you switch it on, Sergeant?' he asked.

'Search me,' said the sergeant. 'I've got the instructions, but I don't know if they're the right ones. They look more like something for the erection of a flat-pack kitchen. An uncle of mine tried that once, he ended up eating his own foot, I don't know whether—'

'Give *me* the controller,' said Sir John. 'Let *me* do it.'

'I can't allow *that*,' said the captain. 'This is a piece of military hardware.'

'Well, get someone military to operate it.'

The captain sighed and turned to his men, who were standing around with their hands in their pockets. 'Ten-shun,' he shouted. The men stood to attention. 'Now,' said the captain, pacing before them, 'does any man here know how to operate RUPERT?'

'I do, sir,' said a private, stepping forward, with a smart salute.

'And your name, Private?'

'126765-zero Robert McGeddon, *sir.*'

'All right, McGeddon, operate RUPERT.'

'I can't do that, sir, I don't have the rank.'

'*What?*' (Another variation on *What?* but a subtle one.)

'No combatant on active duty below the rank of captain is permitted to operate a RUPERT, sir. Section 14, paragraph 12, Army Field Command Orders.'

'You certainly know your orders, soldier.'

'Certainly do, sir. In my business, knowing your orders can mean the difference between coming home smothered in glory and coming back home in a body bag. If you know what I mean, and I'm sure that you do, sir.'

'Could we get a move on with this please?' asked Sir John.

'Don't interfere in military procedures, sir. Soldier, I am ordering you to operate RUPERT.'

'I regret to disobey a direct order, sir,' said Private McGeddon. 'But I must reiterate, section 14, paragraph 12. No combatant on active duty below the rank of captain.'

'Aha,' said the captain.

'Aha, sir?'

'I hereby make a field commission, I hereby raise you to the rank of captain.'

'You can't do that, sir. I'd have to become a corporal, then a sergeant, then a—'

'Don't you want to be a captain?'

'Well I'd like to, sir, like to very much.'

'Then you *are* a captain, OK?'

'Well, OK, yes, thanks very much.'

'And so, *Captain*, will you now operate RUPERT?'

'As soon as I receive orders so to do. Yes.'

'I have just issued you orders so to do.'

'But I now hold the same rank as you, Captain. You can't order me to do anything.'

'Sergeant Lemon, arrest this man,' ordered Captain Vez.

'Ignore that order, Sergeant,' said Captain McGeddon.

'Stop all this *at once!*' shouted Sir John Rimmer. 'I'm not fooled by these delaying tactics. One of you's an enemy agent. One of you has a sprout in the head. Which one is it?'

'This man is clearly a fruit cake,' said Captain McGeddon. 'Sergeant, have him removed to beyond the perimeter fence.'

'It's *you!*' screamed Sir John.

Captain Vez drew out his pistol. 'Leave Sir John alone,' he ordered, 'and *you, Captain* McGeddon, stand out of the way.'

'Drawing a weapon on a fellow officer is a court martial offence,' said the new captain. 'Paragraph 23, subsection 18. No officer shall—'

'Shut up. And you're now stripped of your rank, you're a private again.'

'You can't do that. Only a senior officer can strip me of my rank. Article 15, Clause 28.'

'I thought Clause 28 was something to do with homosexuals,' said Danbury Collins.

'We don't have homosexuals in the armed forces,' said Captain McGeddon.

'Perhaps you're not asking nicely enough,' said Danbury. 'Perhaps if you put up some posters in gay bars you—'

'Shut up!' shouted Captain Vez.

'Touchy,' said Danbury.

'All closet bum boys,' called a stumpy woman through the perimeter fence.

'Oh come on, *please*,' implored Sir John. 'This is of the utmost importance. We must capture the alien craft.'

'Capture an alien craft?' called an old bloke, joining the stumpy woman. 'Bloody Army couldn't capture a dose of the clap nowadays. It's all virtual reality and battle simulations. Not like in my time when we were sticking it up Jerry.'

'Another one of them,' said Stumpy.

Danbury tittered.

'Remove those civilians,' ordered Captain Vez.

'Stuff you,' called some young-fellow-me-lads. 'We're on our side of the wire.'

'Give me that controller,' said Sir John, making a snatch for it.

'Certainly not,' said Captain Vez, stepping backwards and falling over RUPERT.

'Drunk on duty,' said Captain McGeddon. 'I am hereby assuming command.'

'No you're bloody *not!*' Captain V fired his pistol (he still had it in his hand, the hand that wasn't holding the remote control unit – in case you were wondering). He shot Danbury Collins in the foot.

'Aaaagh! I'm shot!' howled Danbury, collapsing into the line of soldiers and knocking several down.

Outside the wire, members of the Brentford populace howled also. The shooting of civilians by military personnel was something deeply frowned upon in this neck of the suburban woods.

'Give me that gun,' shouted Captain McGeddon, leaping onto Captain Vez and wrestling at his wrist.

As the crowd outside the wire began to grow and to shout abuse, Sir John snatched the controller from Captain Vez's other hand.

'Give that back, and let go of me, McGeddon. Shoot this officer, someone, there's a commission in it for the first man who does.'

Those soldiers who hadn't fallen under Danbury hastened to load their weapons. But not all were on the side of Captain V. Some, as if driven by an inner compulsion, an inner-head compulsion, turned their guns not upon Captain McGeddon, but upon Captain Vez himself. 'Not me, *him*!' shouted the good captain.

'Break this up,' shouted Sergeant Lemon, drawing a weapon of his own and firing it into the air. It was an unlucky shot, ricocheting as it did from one of the helicopter blades and blowing the straw hat off a woman in the growing crowd.

'Storm troopers and Cossacks!' bawled the old bloke, beating on the wire with his fist and receiving an electrical discharge that set his wig ablaze.

A bit of a mêlée then ensued.

Soldiers within the wire began to fight amongst themselves, as soldiers will when the opportunity arises. The pro-Captain V contingent fell upon the pro-Captain M contingent and likeways about. Those undecided fell upon each other. Some fell upon Danbury who was struggling up.

'You're all bloody mad,' cried Dr Harney, striking down Sergeant Lemon.

Sir John Rimmer crept under the helicopter, dragging the video monitor with him and began to twiddle at the controls. RUPERT rumbled off into the hole in the ground.

'Storm the wire!' cried the old bloke, beating out his wig. 'Overthrow the military dictatorship.'

Certain young fellow-me-lads who had arrived upon the scene as the pubs were turning out took to hot-wiring a nearby car, in preparation for a ram raid.

The stumpy woman consoled the lady without the straw hat. 'All men are bastards, Mum,' was what she had to say.

'Call me an ambulance,' cried Danbury.

'You're an ambulance,' replied the crowd, eager to respond to such a classic.

More soldiers fell on Danbury and he said nothing more. RUPERT had his headlights on now and Sir John steered him along the tunnel, seeing what he saw on the video monitor.

Soldiers biffed and bopped and banged at each other. Dr Harney rolled by with Sergeant Lemon clinging to his throat.

Brrm, Brrm, went a nearby car, now thoroughly hot-wired.

'I'll deal with these soldier boys,' said the straw-hatless woman, whipping out a Saturday-night special.

'I'll join you,' said daughter Stumpy, drawing an Uzi from her shoulder-bag.

Brrm, Brrrm and Rush-Forward, went the hot-wired car.

'Fire at will!' shouted the still struggling Captain Vez, as the car passed through the wire fence in a burst of electrical sparkings. 'Fire at will!'

There was a sudden silence, which either meant that it was twenty-to-something or twenty-past-something, or simply meant that no-one present really had the nerve to reply 'Which one's Will?' Well, not after the ambulance gag, anyway.

Bang! Bang! went the soldiers' guns, firing every which way.

Bang! Bang! also went the hatless woman's Saturday-night special.

Rat-at-at-at-at-at-at went Stumpy's Uzi. (Now there's a proper gun for you.)

'Urban guerrillas!' cried a military fellow, labouring to pull the pin from a hand grenade.

Brrm, Brrm, went the hot-wired car, running over the top of him.

Sir John Rimmer stared at the monitor screen. He could see it, the sporran-shaped scout craft. Its opening parts part open, the glimmer of green within.

'Gotcha!' said Sir John, twiddling at the controller and extending the arms with the gripping end-pieces. 'Out you come, you little—'

Rumble, went something. Something *big*. It was a rumble to be heard and felt above the shouting voices, the firing guns, the scream of a hot-wired engine, this was a rumble that said, I AM A RUMBLE.

Much in the way that an earthquake does.

As Sir John's eyes widened behind the lenses of his horn-rimmed specs he saw on the screen a pin-point of light appear through the scout craft's opening parts and grow to a blinding flash that blew out the tube of the monitor. The rumble became a shudder, became a fierce vibration. A dazzling laser-like beam of energy shot up from the burrow and soared into the sky, mini-lightning flashed about it. The rumble grew and grew.

'It's going to blow,' cried Sir John, leaping to his feet and striking his head on the underside of the helicopter. 'It's going to self-destruct. Run everyone, run as fast as you can.' He looked all around. 'Oh, I see that you have.'

And they *had*. Well you don't catch the folk of Brentford napping. They've seen all this stuff too many times before.

Sir John snatched up Danbury by the collar of his one-piece coverall and took to his not-inconsiderable heels.

Within the wired-off, though now holed-by-a-car, compound the ground cleaved open and a massive space craft, easily the size of, well, let's see, oh it was huge, I don't know, how about St Paul's Cathedral, that's pretty big, rose slowly into the sky. It was round and it was green, in short (or in spherical), it was sprout-like. Lights twinkled on its shimmering sides, or side (because a sphere has only the one), and through lighted portholes small green spheroids could be seen bouncing up and down.

Up and up it went into the star-strung sky until with a sudden mind-jarring acceleration and a trailing stream of bright green sparks it was gone into the heavens.

Sir John Rimmer raised his head from behind a garden wall and stared up at the night sky. All silent

347

now. Just white dots on a black background. And as Sir John looked he fancied that he could see numbers upon those dots, as if one could join them up and spell out a message. And as he traced dot to dot with a finger not unlike a haricot bean, he also fancied that there was a message there.

And the message was.

WE'LL BE BACK.

THE CURES
(Dedicated to Spike Milligan)

The scales of the fish
Help to ward off the plague
When worn in a sack round the neck
The wings of the gull
Stop pains in the skull
And convulsions that leave you a wreck

The froth from your beer
Is good for diarrhoea
And sand is the thing for the pox
A helping of stew
When poured in your shoe
Fills up the holes in your socks

Frogs, say the sage,
Will starve of old age
Jelly's the thing for the gout
A spoonful of soot
Stops athlete's foot
And soon has you up and about

Eight pints of oil
Soothe the spot and the boil
Some speak of cider and cheese
But the stuff for the flu
Is a tube-full of glue
And cabbages strapped to the knees

Or so my gran says.
But what about my ringworm then, Gran?

26

THE END

And so it ends as it began, with a simple poem.

And as I sit here all alone in Hotel Jericho, drawing the final line beneath the final paragraph on the final page of my final red exercise book, I feel a sense of satisfaction, if not a little of finality.

For sure I never changed the world for the better, but who really could? As Colon might have said, life is not about what happens to you, it's about how you deal with it.

I rarely venture far from the hotel and when I do it is only at night. I have to be conscious of my every movement. I became too adept at causing change to occur during my stay in America. Now I have to take great care over everything I do. From the way I clip my toenails to the side I part my hair.

A millimetre too short on the right big toe and Germany might win the cup again. Too many hairs to the left-hand side and flares will be back in fashion. I abused my gift and so must pay the price of solitude.

I have some pleasures left. Small pleasures, trivial things. I watch a lot of television. I like to see all the politicians compensating away, never causing anything to happen, just balancing what does with a hand-tuck into a tailored suit or an adjustment of the spectacles.

I have few callers now. The occasional Jehovah's Witness, a lady with a straw hat who sharpens my biros. But I am contented.

Given my time over again, I might have done things differently. I don't think I'd have walked out into the path of that dry-cleaning truck for a start and I really would have dedicated my time to having a lot more sex.

But what is done cannot be changed.

Except of course, for plumbing.

'Is that it, chief?'

'I think so, Barry, I can't think of anything else to write.'

'Not too morbid this last bit, not a feel-bad ending?'

'I don't think so. Just a bit of repentance and introspection to show that I'm really a caring sort of fellow.'

'That's nice, chief. So what shall we do now?'

I rose from my desk, went over to the window and drew aside the greasy curtain. Sunlight fell upon my ghostly features.

Golden sunlight falling from a sky of the deepest blue.

'Stuff it in here,' I said. 'Let's hit the beach.'

THE END

A SELECTED LIST OF FANTASY TITLES AVAILABLE FROM CORGI BOOKS

THE PRICES SHOWN BELOW WERE CORRECT AT THE TIME OF GOING TO PRESS. HOWEVER TRANSWORLD PUBLISHERS RESERVE THE RIGHT TO SHOW NEW RETAIL PRICES ON COVERS WHICH MAY DIFFER FROM THOSE PREVIOUSLY ADVERTISED IN THE TEXT OR ELSEWHERE.

All Transworld titles are available by post from:
Book Services By Post, P.O. Box 29, Douglas, Isle of Man IM99 1BQ.
Credit cards accepted. Please telephone 01624 675137, fax 01624 670923 or Internet http:/www.bookpost.co.uk or e-mail: bookshop@enterprise.net for details.
Free postage and packing in the UK. Overseas customers allow £1 per book (paperbacks) and £3 per book (hardbacks).